THE NINJA LIBRARIANS
THE ACCIDENTAL KEYHAND

JEN SWANN DOWNEY

sourcebooks
jabberwocky

Published by Sourcebooks Jabberwocky, an imprint of Sourcebooks, Inc.
P.O. Box 4410, Naperville, Illinois 60567-4410
(630) 961-3900
Fax: (630) 961-2168
www.jabberwockykids.com

Library of Congress Cataloging-in-Publication Data is on file with the publisher.

Source of Production: Worzalla, Stevens Point, Wisconsin, USA
Date of Production: February 2014
Run Number: 5000584

Printed and bound in the United States of America.
WOZ 10 9 8 7 6 5 4 3 2 1

For my mother, Christine Swann, who believed in books.

In searching for the truth, be ready for the unexpected. Change alone is unchanging. The same road goes both up and down. The beginning of a circle is also its end. Not I, but the world says it: all is one. And yet everything comes in season.

—Heraklietos of Ephesos

CHAPTER 1
BOOKS AND SWORDS

TWELVE-YEAR-OLD DOROTHEA BARNES WAS thoroughly un-chosen, not particularly deserving, bore no marks of destiny, lacked any sort of criminal genius, and could claim no supernatural relations. Furthermore, she'd never been orphaned, kidnapped, left for dead in the wilderness, or bitten by anything more bloodthirsty than her little sister.

Don't even begin to entertain consoling thoughts of long flaxen curls or shiny tresses black as ravens' wings. Dorrie's plain brown hair could only be considered marvelous in its ability to twist itself into hopeless tangles. She was neither particularly tall or small, thick or thin, pale or dark. She had parents who loved her, friends enough, and never wanted for a meal. So why, you may wonder, tell a story about a girl like this at all?

Because Dorrie counted a sword among her most precious

belongings. Yes, it was only a fake one that couldn't be relied upon to cut all the way through a stick of butter, but Dorrie truly and deeply desired to use it. Not just to fend off another staged pirate attack at Mr. Louis P. Kornberger's Passaic Academy of Swordplay and Stage Combat (which met Tuesdays behind the library after Mr. Kornberger finished work there) but, when the right circumstances arose, to vanquish some measure of evil from the world.

Dorrie regarded every opportunity to prepare for that moment as a crucial one, and the Passaic Public Library's annual Pen and Sword Festival—always bursting with costumed scribblers and swashbucklers—afforded, in her strongly-held opinion, one of the best. On its appointed day, she pounded down the wide battered staircase of her home long before the rising sun finished gilding the rusty dryer that sat, for lost reasons, on top of it. She did so in the one tall purple boot she could find, dragging her duffel bag behind her.

At the bottom, in the vast chamber that had once served as a ballroom, Dorrie caught a glimpse of herself in the mirror that hung over a bureau by the back door, and hiked up her wide leather belt. She had buckled it over a hideous, electric-blue-and-black-striped suit jacket with ripped-out sleeves that Dorrie's father swore he had worn proudly out in public in a bygone era. Underneath it, a shirt with great puffy sleeves and dangling cuffs screamed "pirate" loudly and well. After taking a moment to tug on the hem of the moth-eaten velvet skirt that was meant to hang to her knees but had got caught in the waistband of her underwear, she glowered into the mirror, her sword aloft. Despite the missing boot, the overall effect pleased her.

"Yo ho, Calico Jack," called her father. "Put this back in Great-Aunt Alice's sitting room, will you?" Dorrie looked away from the mirror to see her father, holding a tiny carved owl. He wore a ruffled, candy-striped apron that read, "You Breaka My Eggs, I Breaka Your Fast". With his free hand he was stirring a pot of glopping oatmeal in the part of the old ballroom the Barnes called "The Kitchen". Other parts of the once grand chamber served as "The Living Room", "The Office", "The Rehearsal Hall" for Dorrie's fourteen-year-old drum-pounding brother, Marcus, and "The Playroom" for Miranda, Dorrie's four-year-old sister.

Dorrie made her way to her father across one of the dozen rugs bought cheap from thrift stores currently living out their end days beneath the daily burden of ill-conceived art projects, the occasional mislaid plate of scrambled eggs, and books. Heaps and hills and hoards of books. Books left open on the back of the sway-backed sofa and under the piano, on the top of the toaster and hanging from the towel rack.

"Miranda borrowed it," he said, dropping the carved owl into Dorrie's outstretched hand. Dorrie gave her father "a look." Her sister had a deeply ingrained habit of "borrowing" things. Dorrie set off for Great-Aunt Alice's sitting room, which lay on the other side of the deteriorating mansion.

Great-Aunt Alice had invited Dorrie's family to live with her two years ago when her sprawling home had become too much to care for by herself.

Besides the ballroom and a few bedrooms, the rest of the mansion was her territory. Just as shabby, she kept it spare and clean and orderly. Great-Aunt Alice claimed the Barnes side of the house gave her fits of dizziness.

After Dorrie set the owl back on its shelf in Great-Aunt Alice's empty sitting room, the thick hush tempted her to tuck her sword beneath an arm and open a little stone box that stood beside the owl. Inside lay an old pocket watch and a silver bracelet set with a cloudy black stone.

The doorbell rang, and Great-Aunt Alice's voice in the marble-floored hallway made Dorrie's hand jerk so that the box's lid fell closed with a small clack.

Hurriedly, Dorrie pushed the box back onto the shelf. Then, in a silly horror at the thought of Great-Aunt Alice— who often seemed as remote and unfathomable as a distant planet—catching her snooping, she wrenched open the lid of a cavernous wicker trunk that stood against the wall and scrambled inside, sword and all. She pulled the heavy lid down on top of her. It bounced on her fingers, trapping them, just as

Great-Aunt Alice hobbled into the room. Dorrie sucked in her breath, the pain making her eyes water. She heard the sitting-room door close.

"Well, did he see you go in?" asked Great-Aunt Alice.

"Oh, he doesn't have the imagination to suspect," said a young woman breathlessly.

Dorrie pressed her eyes to the gap made by her swiftly swelling fingers. Amanda, Dorrie's favorite librarian at the Passaic Public Library after Mr. Kornberger, stood now, inexplicably, just inside Great-Aunt Alice's sitting-room door. Everything about Amanda Ness was long. Her skirts, her hundred braids which hung down below her shoulders, and her nose—which had been given the usual infant inch and had taken a mile. If a long temper was the opposite of a short one, well, she had that too.

"You should be more careful," said Great-Aunt Alice, stopping at her writing desk. She smoothed a few white hairs back toward the tight bun at the back of her head. "Has anything changed?"

"Not yet," said Amanda, sitting down on the edge of a little pale-blue sofa.

"No. Of course not," said Great-Aunt Alice, easing herself down into a straight-backed chair. "It's patently absurd that we're even discussing the possibility."

Amanda looked vaguely hurt.

"I don't know what I've been thinking," said Great-Aunt Alice. "Sneaking around in there like a thief these past weeks."

Amanda clasped her hands together. "You were thinking that the stories might be true!"

Dorrie listened so hard that she could almost feel her ears trying to creep away from her head.

Great-Aunt Alice picked lint from a sweater hung on the back of the chair. "Well, I'm a foolish old woman." She caught Amanda staring at her. "Oh now, don't look so disappointed."

"Give it more time!" pleaded Amanda. "He said he wasn't sure how long it might take."

Great-Aunt Alice absently toyed with a little jar of pens on her desk. "I'm ashamed that I believed even for a moment in the possibility."

In her wonder at the thought that Great-Aunt Alice could believe in anything fantastical for even the briefest of moments, Dorrie barely felt the wicker strands of the trunk embedding themselves in her knees. After all, Great-Aunt Alice had frowned disapprovingly when Miranda asked her to clap her hands so that Tinkerbell wouldn't die.

Amanda leaned toward Great-Aunt Alice. "But it's obvious that something special is supposed to happen there." Dorrie held her breath so as not to miss a single word. The conversation positively bulged with mysterious possibilities.

"It's obvious my father *wanted* something special to happen,"

Great-Aunt Alice corrected. "My believing that it will happen is as ridiculous as Dorothea believing that she's going to corner modern evil with a sword."

At the mention of her name, Dorrie nearly lost her grip on the sword in question and had to scrabble to keep it from falling noisily to the floor of the trunk. There was a moment of silence during which Dorrie felt certain that Amanda and Great-Aunt Alice could hear the small cave-in taking place in the general vicinity of her heart, but her great-aunt only sniffed and began to talk about Mr. Scuggans, the new director of the Passaic Public Library, calling him insufferable.

Dorrie began to breath again in shallow little huffs. Ridiculous! She turned the stinging word over in her mind. Dorrie had never stopped to think about whether her desire to wield a sword against the villains of the world was sensible or ridiculous. It just was. She squeezed the hilt of her sword, drawing strength from it until the crumbling hollow feeling in her chest faded a little.

The conversation outside the basket had turned to the difficulty of cleaning the library's gutters, and stuck there for what seemed like an excruciating eternity until, at last, Great-Aunt Alice showed Amanda out. Dorrie, her heart pounding, slipped from her wicker prison, and back through the double doors that led into her family's side of the house.

She stood still for a moment, her thoughts whirring

madly. *Insults aside, what had Great-Aunt Alice and Amanda been talking about? Something important. "Special," Amanda had said.*

Her gaze fell upon the clock hanging slightly askew on the wall above the back door. Shocked at how much time had passed in the trunk, Dorrie sprinted halfway up the staircase. "Come on, Marcus!" she bellowed. "Hurry up! The Festival! We're gonna be late!"

With relief, she heard Marcus let down his drawbridge, the chains rattling as they lowered the doubled-up piece of plywood that he had attached to the outside of his bedroom window. It landed with a muffled thud on the roof of an old garage that served as their chicken shed. Somehow, being able to do his chicken-feeding chore without having to technically leave his room counted as a great victory in her older brother's battle to do less—a battle he waged with a fanatic's energy.

After a hurried circuit of the ballroom in search of her still-missing boot, Dorrie threw herself down on the rug in front of the Barnes' threadbare barge of a couch and began to grope beneath it. A splash and a cry of "Oh, Miranda!" came from the bathroom below the stairs. Dorrie's mother emerged, a wet cell phone held up gingerly between two fingers.

Behind her, Miranda clanked along, a velvet ribbon around her neck hung with two spatulas, a ring of old keys, and a plastic funnel. Her bushy red hair was inexplicably full of paper clips. Miranda stopped to rearrange her dangling collection. Dorrie noticed a porcelain kitten in a tiny basket hanging between the two spatulas.

"Hey, you little magpie," said Dorrie. "That's my kitten!"

"It likes me better," Miranda said, just as Marcus landed at the bottom of the stairs with a furniture-shaking thud.

"You're not even dressed yet!" Dorrie howled at him.

Marcus yawned. "Shirt," he said pointing to the black T-shirt he'd worn to bed. White letters across the chest read, "Apathy is Hard Work." He pointed to the reindeer-print flannel pajama bottoms that covered his giraffe-like legs. "Pants."

"That's what you're wearing?"

"Not every pirate was a fashion icon."

"You're not taking this one bit seriously!"

Marcus yawned luxuriously. "Who would?"

Dorrie felt her face warm as Marcus sauntered away toward the refrigerator. *I do*, she said to herself, swallowing hard.

"I can't find my boot!" she shouted at the top of her lungs.

"And I can't find any of my duct tape," her father said calmly, stooping to pick up the mail that had just come cascading through the letter slot in the back door.

Dorrie's father built prototypes for people who thought up interesting inventions but had no idea how to use a screwdriver. He used a lot of duct tape.

"Ask little Lady Lightfingers about it," said Marcus, looking back darkly at Miranda. "She took my drum key right out of my pocket."

Dorrie swept her arm under the couch again. It landed on a half-sucked lollipop. Trying to shake it off, she upset a tottering stack of books that had grown to the height of an end table beside the couch. Dorrie only had time to cover her head with her hands before they came bouncing and tumbling down upon her. She sat up with a jerk, and *The Princess Bride: S. Morgenstern's Classic Tale of True Love and High Adventure* slithered to a stop beside her knee. It held within its pages her favorite sword fighting scene of all time.

Dorrie slowly picked the book up, the echo of Great-Aunt Alice's words in her ears. Staring at the cover, it suddenly dawned cold and hard on her that though she might want to wield a sword against modern villains, modern villains probably had not intention of making themselves available to her for a spearing. Not the spectacularly vile wicked ones who really knew how to brew up trouble. Not the ones who surely lurked behind the radio news stories about bombs and starving kids and poisoned rivers. Not in the cooperative way they used to once upon a time, at least according to the books she liked to read.

Her father's voice interrupted the terrible thought. "Dorrie," he called in a singsong voice.

She tossed the book aside and stood, full of hot confusion. Modern villains probably wouldn't make themselves helpfully obvious with swirling black cloaks, scars in all the right places, or fiendish laughs, either.

"Please find *The Three Musketeers*, will you? " asked her father, sifting through a fresh pile of violently yellow envelopes, every square inch of them stamped "Urgent" and "Overdue" in blood-red ink." Before Mr. Scuggans buzzes the house in a helicopter."

"I've been looking!" said Dorrie, tossing *The Princess Bride* aside, and getting to her feet. And she had. For the last three weeks, Dorrie had suffered for the missing book, not daring to set foot in the Passaic Public Library. Whenever Mr. Scuggans caught sight of a delinquent borrower, he liked to publicly announce the size of any fines owed with a bullhorn. Amanda and Mr. Kornberger always took care to lower their voices when delivering any bad news about fines or the blocking of borrowing privileges. It was rumored that Mr. Scuggans wore a toupee.

Dorrie's mother's phone rang. "Well, praise Neptune, it still works," her mother said, looking pleased as she threw a handful of spoons on the table and placed the phone gingerly alongside her ear, if not exactly touching it. "Hello?" Dorrie's mother listened for a moment and then fixed Dorrie with an exasperated grimace. "Oh hello, Mr. Scuggans."

"I don't think she's so pro-Neptune anymore," said Marcus, jamming his hand into a box of cereal.

"Yes, she...yes, I...yes, she's...uh...actively looking for it."

Dorrie's mother flailed one arm at Dorrie as though she were a chicken who needed shooing.

For the third time that week, Dorrie hurriedly lifted the sofa cushions. *The Three Musketeers* wasn't there. But her missing purple boot was. She held it up to her mother triumphantly. Her mother did not look impressed.

"Yes, we have the title," Dorrie's mother continued into the phone, as Dorrie hopped on one foot, tugging on the boot. "Hmm? No, I don't think I need the bar code numbers. Well, of course I'm taking this seriously." The doorbell clanged again in the front hall. Dorrie's mother put her hand over the phone. "Go get it," she hissed.

Dorrie jabbed her finger at the clock. Her mother jabbed her finger toward Great-Aunt Alice's territory. After giving her mother what she hoped was a suitably put-upon look, Dorrie stomped through the separating doors, Miranda skipping along behind her.

In the black-and-white marble-tiled front hall, Dorrie heaved open the door. Her eyes traveled upward. An immense man in a dark overcoat, crisp white shirt, and shining tasseled loafers stood on the doorstep. His silvery hair seemed to absorb the sunlight. At the curb behind him idled a long, black car with tinted windows.

Dorrie blinked at the man, struck by the thought that the red bow-tie he wore did not look the least bit merry on him.

"We don't want any!" said Miranda, pushing her head out from beneath Dorrie's arm.

"Charming," the man said in a velvety voice, as though the word didn't taste very good. At his side, the fingers of one gloved hand began to move up and down like piano hammers as he rolled two walnuts around and around each other in his palm.

Dorrie's face reddened. Now, strangers ringing Great-Aunt Alice's doorbell were hardly unusual. Great-Aunt Alice was an anthropologist who wrote long books filled with very small type about humans and the things they believed in. For as long as the Barneses had lived with Great-Aunt Alice, a steady stream of peculiar guests had come to be interviewed by her.

Dorrie felt these visitors came in two varieties: ones who would rather give up a kidney than talk to Dorrie, and those who, if allowed, would ensnare Dorrie in long, bewildering conversations about the mystical symbols buried in dollar bills or their identities as kings or queens of lost civilizations. The men tended to sport long walrus-y moustaches, and the women, fringed shawls and carpetbags. This man had none of these things. A hair-raising sort of wet growling was coming from inside his car.

Dorrie thought back to the conversation she'd overheard. The morning was getting stranger by the minute.

Miranda made her own gurgling, growling sound and,

with bear claw arms, began to run in tight circles around the stranger.

The stranger stared straight ahead, his gaze not so much resting on Dorrie as burning through her. In his hand, one of the walnuts cracked smartly, and bits of nuts and shells fell in a thin, dusty shower onto the doorstep.

"Sorry about her," Dorrie said, hastily grabbing the back of Miranda's shirt as she passed and hauling her back inside. "Can I help you?"

"I'm Aldous Biggs. I've come to see Alice Laszlo. Is she in?"

"I'm Alice Laszlo," said Great-Aunt Alice from her sitting-room doorway, where she leaned on her cane. Dorrie found it hard to meet her eyes. "How can I help you, Mr. Biggs?"

"I've come in response to your advertisement. About the book."

"Ah," said Great-Aunt Alice. "I haven't run one in some time."

"Just the same."

Great-Aunt Alice studied Mr. Biggs. "Please come in." She opened her sitting-room door wide for him. Relieved to escape Great-Aunt Alice's gaze, Dorrie began to drag her sister back across the hall. Once firmly back in Barnes territory, Dorrie pretended not to notice when Miranda stepped with a splash into her imaginary dog's bowl full of very real water.

Dorrie's mother dropped her phone on the counter, looking exhausted. "Dorrie, you've *got* to find that book."

"I will," Glancing at the clock again, Dorrie slid into her seat, seized her spoon and began to shove oatmeal into her mouth double-time.

"I already did," said Miranda primly, as her mother lifted her out of the bowl of water and set her on a stool next to Dorrie.

Dorrie and Marcus and their mother and father all stopped what they were doing and stared at Miranda.

Miranda dug her spoon into the sugar bowl. "I put it in her bag."

"Oh, praise Nataero!" said her mother, grabbing the spoon back before Miranda could close her lips around it.

"Thank you?" said Dorrie, looking suspiciously at Miranda and not at all sure the Roman god of lost things deserved much praise in this case.

"New burning question," said her father loudly, as he passed around a bowl of hard-boiled eggs. "Who was fooling around with my helium tank?"

"Could have been me," said Marcus, his voice unnaturally high.

"Well, don't do it again. You left the valve open," said her dad. "You could knock someone out leaving that on."

"So are you ready for today's performance?" said Dorrie's mother, peeling an egg for Miranda. "Marcus says yesterday's rehearsal went pretty well."

Marcus began to gesture furiously, his mouthful of

oatmeal traveling from cheek to cheek. He finally choked it down. "I believe my exact words were, 'It wasn't an unmitigated disaster.'"

"I wish I could watch the performance," said Dorrie's father, "but—"

"The helium-suit field-test," everyone else at the table intoned together.

"Assuming I can find the duct tape," said Dorrie's father, wiping his mouth and getting up. He grabbed his goggles, distributed kisses, and disappeared through the back door.

"I wish I could see the show, but I won't be back from the conference until late tonight," said Dorrie's mother, fishing Miranda's ribbon of treasures out of her oatmeal. Dorrie's mother taught Latin and Italian at Passaic Community College. Her classes were never full. "Miranda will be at the babysitter's, and you two are on your own for dinner."

Dorrie threw her bowl and spoon in the dishwasher with extra force. As she slung her duffel bag over one shoulder, she turned to see Marcus making a sandwich at the counter. "We just ate!"

"Be riiiiiight with you," said Marcus, busy interspersing slices of meat and cheese to create a teetering tower of sustenance.

Dorrie's mother pointed to Dorrie's glass of orange juice which still sat on the table. "Finish that before you go."

"I don't have time," said Dorrie, picking up her sword.

Miranda held the glass out to Dorrie, her small face looking its most angelic. "It's good for you," she said. "It's got medicines."

"Okay, okay!" said Dorrie, grabbing the juice and downing it in one long gulp. Miranda beamed at her. Dorrie lowered her glass. "Why is she looking at me like that?"

Marcus slapped a piece of bread atop a massive avalanche of mayonnaise and looked up. "I think she just poured water from the imaginary dog's bowl into your juice."

Dorrie spat into her glass and looked at Miranda. Her little sister clutched a squat, silver bottle in her fist, its stopper dangling from a short, thin chain. "Miranda!"

"Go," said her mother, pushing Dorrie toward the door. "Marcus will catch up." She tucked a hank of hair behind Dorrie's ear, dug some money out of her pocket and handed it to Dorrie. "Go get 'em, tiger. Come tomorrow, things will be back to normal around here."

Just then, Miranda, who had picked up an abandoned hard-boiled egg, shot the yolk into the pot of oatmeal, sending a warm spatter flying over the table. "Normal!" she squawked happily.

CHAPTER 2
A FRIENDLY WAGER

A T THE PARK ACROSS the street from the library, colorful pennants flew from a scattering of tents. Above the park's entrance fluttered the familiar "Pen and Sword Festival" banner. Dorrie hurried in. A crowd had already gathered around a blacksmith's fire for a demonstration of sword forging. Nearby, a woman in checkered breeches and a rough jerkin lifted and lowered the top of an old-fashioned printing press. Fire-eaters wandered through the crowd, unnerving small children.

Mr. Kornberger's Academy students would be gathering on the other side of the park behind the big "Ye Olde Village Inne" tent. Dorrie took the path that curved around the circle of straw bales where, later in the afternoon, packs of adults dressed in medieval clothing would wield heavy Styrofoam-covered swords against each other in the barely controlled chaos known as the Melee. She couldn't wait to watch. In front of the meat-pie tent, Dorrie came to a sudden halt.

Nearby, a flock of photographers clicked and flashed as the Mayor of Passaic shook hands with a group of festival visitors gathered in a little clump around him. Every time he wrung another hand, his doughy jowls shook slightly. Dorrie felt her mouth go dry. Not because she had any particular fear of shaking jowls, but because slightly behind the Mayor, looking as mean-eyed and black-hearted as ever, stood his daughter Tiffany Tolliver, her blond ponytail rooted darkly to her scalp. The Mayor smiled a big, hammy smile for the photographers and put an arm around Tiffany, which made her face go from sullen to mutinous.

For a short time, Tiffany had been part of the Passaic Academy of Swordplay and Stage Combat, long enough to demonstrate to Dorrie and the other students that the slightly older girl either didn't understand or didn't care that they weren't actually supposed to hurt each other during staged sword fights. Dorrie rubbed her arm, remembering when Tiffany had nearly broken it.

Now, Dorrie noticed, Tiffany wore a yellow T-shirt that read "The White Hand Fencing Club." She also had a long bag slung over her shoulder. For the sport fencing tournament, no doubt. This year, in what the Academy students viewed as the most total of noncoincidences, the Mayor had insisted that

Mr. Kornberger invite modern sport-fencing teams, with their sleek new-fangled electrified outfits, to participate in the Pen and Sword Festival.

As Tiffany looked her way, Dorrie ducked her head and hurried off through the crowd. Before she'd gotten halfway to Ye Olde Village Inne, a gravelly voice called to her. Dorrie looked up to see a stooped man as white-haired as Great-Aunt Alice heading her way.

"Elder!" She threw her arms around his waist and squeezed him hard.

"Strong as a plains-hardened Mongol," he said, giving her back a pat.

Elder had started out as one of Great-Aunt Alice's visitors months ago. Unlike her other guests, he'd stayed on in Passaic, moving into a tiny room at the Rutland Arms Hotel. Mr. Scuggans had reluctantly hired the elderly Elder to shelve books at the library. That was after the fourth person to hold the job under Mr. Scuggans was discovered having a nervous breakdown in the self-help section. So far, Elder seemed to have suffered no ill effects from having Mr. Scuggans for a boss.

Sometimes Elder ate meals with the Barnes family and Great-Aunt Alice, or sat by the fire with them to tell stories about his lifetime of travels. Elder was one of those grown-ups who never made Dorrie feel ignored or trapped.

"You looking forward to your performance?" asked Elder as

a round of clapping broke out, making Dorrie and Elder look back at where the Mayor had just finished saying something. Tiffany was slipping away toward a boy and girl who stood nearby wearing the same T-shirts.

Dorrie bounced the tip of her sword against her shoe. "I guess."

Elder leaned back and cocked his head to one side as if to get a better look at her. "You told me once that the Academy was the best part of your life."

"It was," said Dorrie. "I mean, it is. It's just... I thought..." She gave Elder a sidelong look. "I've been planning to use what I've been learning. You know, to...sort of stop people from doing bad stuff." She checked to make sure he wasn't laughing. He wasn't. Watching her steadily, he was listening in the way Dorrie appreciated, with his whole self it seemed. A powerful wave of horrified disappointment washed through her. "But what use is a sword going to be against guns and stuff?"

"Not so much, these days, I suppose," said Elder.

"So all my practicing has been a waste of time! She kicked mightily at pebble and missed.

Elder rolled the pebble up onto the toe of his shoe and jerked his foot so that it flew upward. He snatched it out of the air. "Nothing you choose to practice long and hard is ever a waste of time."

Dorrie stared at the pebble in Elder's hand and sighed. She

supposed she might still be able to use a sword to stop a very minor villain like the man she'd once seen throw a rock at a stray dog.

Elder lifted the lime-green golf hat that perched on his thin carpet of hair and settled it down again more snugly. "I, for one, am looking forward to your performance."

"The performance!" cried Dorrie. "I'd better go!"

"How about I try to get your Aunt Alice to come see it?"

"She can't," said Dorrie, hitching her bag more securely on her shoulders. "She's entertaining."

"Mustache or carpetbag?"

"Neither. Some fancy-looking man. He said he wanted to see her about an advertisement."

Elder stiffened. "I think I will stop in on her."

"But what about the performance?"

Dorrie's disappointment must have shown on her face because Elder gave her a quick smile and chucked her under the chin. "I won't be long." He walked off as quickly as his rickety body would allow. Dorrie ran.

Marcus caught up with her not far from Ye Olde Village Inne. Cardboard painted to look like timbers and plaster rose up on either side of the tent's entrance. A sandwich board set outside read: "The Memorable Defense of Ye Olde Village Inne, 11 a.m." Her brother still wore his pajamas, but he had tied a scarf around his head. He held a meat pie in each hand.

"Are you trying to embarrass Mr. Kornberger?" Dorrie asked.

Marcus shoved almost one whole meat pie into his mouth. "Mr. Kornberger spends half his life at Renaissance fairs, and the other half dressed as though he's on his way to one."

"So what?" said Dorrie hotly, as they hurried along.

"So nothing. I like him. I'm just saying he's a hard man to embarrass."

Dorrie had to admit, not out loud of course, that Marcus had a point. Someone tugged on the end of one of her sleeves. She glanced away from Marcus to find Rosa, the youngest of Mr. Kornberger's students, gazing up at her admiringly with her one eye not covered by a pirate's eye patch.

Rosa couldn't speak at the moment because she was busy sucking like mad on the business end of an inhaler. Her other hand was wrapped around the handle of a flimsy-looking fold-up luggage cart that held a wire cage. In it sat her constant, beloved companion, a cantankerous mongoose that had been abandoned at the animal shelter where Rosa's grandmother volunteered. Dorrie stopped walking while Marcus, having seen a friend, jogged on.

She squatted beside the cage. "Hey, you little monster." Moe's brown eyes gleamed. He bared his teeth in his usual way and made a little chittering sound.

Rosa released her breath. "I had to bring him. Granny's trying to vacuum today, and he always tries to fight the hose. He thinks it's a snake."

Moe's nose twitched with bad temper.

Rosa tucked away her inhaler. "He'll be good. No one will even know he's here."

Dorrie raised a doubtful eyebrow at Rosa. "Come on," she said, standing up.

They edged into the circle of students clustered around Mr. Kornberger in time to see Marcus happily smack his friend Justin on the head, and Justin punch Marcus hard in the arm. They both looked satisfied.

Mr. Kornberger wore a tricornered hat, a billowy white shirt, and knee-high black boots over red-and-black striped pants. Like Miranda, things dangled from him: an economy-sized pewter mug, a leather canteen emblazoned with a grinning skull, about five pounds, worth of treasure chest keys, and a sword so long it dragged on the ground. A thick, messy line of black encircled each of his eyes, making him look, despite the truly hideous earrings dangling from his earlobes, more like a linebacker than a pirate.

"Ah, good, you're here" said Mr. Kornberger, catching sight of Dorrie and Rosa. "Erica Burnbridge won't be. She's come down with dropsy. Well, not really. She has a cold, but dropsy sounds so much more historically fitting. I was afraid we'd lost you too."

He took sudden and committed hold of the hilt of his sword, pulled it out of its scabbard in a flashy, dramatic arc, and held it aloft. "Today," he bellowed, "some of you will be heroic defenders of a village beset by evil pirates, and some of you will be those vicious reprobates!"

Heads turned in the direction of their huddle.

Mr. Kornberger half lowered the sword and his voice slightly. "I thought a little preperformance dramatic role-play might get us into the right spirit."

He lifted his sword again and went on with his monologue, but Dorrie had stopped listening. Nearby, Tiffany Tolliver had puffed up her cheeks and stood holding a long, skinny sword aloft in a near-perfect imitation of Mr. Kornberger. Dorrie stared, unable to look away. Tiffany's friends doubled over with nasty laughter. Dorrie swallowed hard and forced herself to focus on Mr. Kornberger.

"So places in five for 'The Memorable Defense of Ye Olde Village Inne,'" said Mr. Kornberger, bringing down his sword in a sweeping cut.

Her heart pounding with indignant anger on Mr. Kornberger's behalf, Dorrie ran to take her opening position. A large crowd had gathered for the performance. The first scene went well, despite Rosa's sword breaking in half and Justin's breeches falling down, and ended in a smattering of applause. Now Dorrie, Lavinia, and Rosa stood offstage breathing hard and watching Scene Two unfold. Dorrie watched Justin and Marcus circle each other warily, their blades up.

"When we first met," shouted Marcus, taking an enormous leap forward, "I was the pupil. Now I am the master!"

Lavinia's eyes narrowed angrily in her wide pink face. "That's not what he's supposed to say!"

"It's a line from *Star Wars*," sighed Dorrie, glancing guiltily at Mr. Kornberger as he flipped through the script looking confused. "Marcus likes to slip them in whenever possible."

Onstage, Justin's blade knocked dully against Marcus's. Dorrie watched Justin stagger and fall to the ground, his cloak billowing nicely. That was Dorrie's cue. She flew toward Marcus, yelling "Unhand him, varlet!" at the top of her lungs. She took on one, two, and three of the villainous pirates single-handedly.

The whooping and hollering in the crowd seemed to grow to a feverish pitch. It made Dorrie's heart swell and sent fresh energy to her sword-wielding arm. She reached farther, slashed harder, jumped higher. And then in a sickening moment, she realized that in the middle of the sea of sound was laughter. Not appreciative laughter, but the stinging, ridiculing sort. On cue, the pirates she had vanquished fled around one corner of the tent and Dorrie ran around the other.

There, Dorrie heard the laughter again. Nearby, Tiffany stood bent slightly over while one of her friends wrote something on the back of her T-shirt. Noticing Dorrie staring, Tiffany unbent and began to stagger toward Dorrie with the long sword she'd held up earlier. Her friends followed close behind.

"Oooo, are we pretending?" Tiffany said, eyes wide in an exaggerated expression of goggle-eyed idiotic delight. She stabbed clumsily at a garbage can, which caused her friends to dissolve into another gale of gasping laughter. "Unhand him, varlet!"

Tiffany abruptly ended her imitation and stared at Dorrie with malevolent glee. "You so wanted it to be real out there. I mean, you should have seen your face. Pathetic."

Dorrie felt a roaring in her ears. She wanted to fly at Tiffany and pummel her with her fists. She wanted to knock her to the ground and shout, "*Take it back!*" into her face, to squeeze her around the neck until she *had* to take her words back. Until they disappeared back down her throat like dirty water down a drain. Instead she croaked, "So what?"

"So what?" Tiffany mocked. "You looked like an idiot out there. Totally Kornberger. And as we all know…" She did a little runway model half-spin so that Dorrie could see the back of her T-shirt, while flashing Dorrie a wide artificial smile. Crooked letters spelled out: "Mr. Kornberger is a big, fat fool." Tiffany fluttered her eyes at Dorrie. "I'm going to wear it in the sport fencing tournament."

"You can't!" cried Dorrie.

"Watch me," said Tiffany making her sword blade whistle smartly through the air.

Dorrie found herself lifting her own stage-combat sword without thinking about it, and staring from Tiffany to the boy who'd written on the T-shirt, and back to Tiffany. "Make him cross the words out!"

Tiffany snorted. "Or what? You're going to use your toy sword on me? You Academy geeks wouldn't know what to do with real swords."

"We know more than you think," choked out Dorrie, hating the quaver in her voice.

"Oh, really?" Tiffany thrust her chin toward where the other Academy students had taken the stage again. It was an unfortunate moment. Marcus seemed to be imitating a Wookie. "Then I challenge you to a real sport-fencing bout. Three o'clock behind the bathrooms. Three touches wins."

"What about the shirt?" demanded Dorrie through gritted teeth.

Tiffany smiled like a cat who'd figured out just which part of a tasty mouse to bite into first. "We'll make it a bet. If you win, I won't wear the shirt." She seemed to almost shiver with pleasure. "But if I win, then you have to wear the shirt. At the festival. In front of everyone. For the rest of the day."

Wariness flared feebly in the sensible part of Dorrie's brain.

At Tiffany's next words, it died a quick death. "If you dare."

Here at least was something useful that Dorrie could do with a sword. "Yeah, I dare!"

Tiffany tossed her sword onto the ground at Dorrie's feet. "I've got others. Feel free to practice."

Cackling and staggering around with laughter, Tiffany and her friends disappeared into the crowd.

After the Academy students had finished taking their bows, they gathered around Mr. Kornberger for his thoughts on their performance.

When he'd finished, Dorrie took a deep breath. "I accepted a challenge for a sport fencing bout. A real one. Three touches wins." She thought it best not to mention what was at stake.

"Oh, how exciting!" cried Mr. Kornberger, throwing back his cloak and taking hold of the hilt of his sword.

"Excellent!" said Marcus.

"That's crazy," said Lavinia, giving Marcus an irritated look. "None of us know anything about real fencing. We're actors. We wear costumes. We use fake swords and entertain tourists."

"I know some moves!" objected Dorrie indignantly.

Mr. Kornberger beamed at her. "And the name of the rogue who will face you?"

Dorrie took a deep breath. "Tiffany Tolliver."

"Maybe not so excellent," said Marcus.

"Tiffany's going to the Junior Olympics!" screeched Lavinia.

Mr. Kornberger raised his sword encouragingly. "What Dorrie lacks in actual sport-fencing experience, she'll make up for in dramatic flair!" He lowered his sword and cleared his throat. "But Lavinia, why don't you run across the street and get the library's copy of *Fencing for Dummies*. Oh! And ask Amanda for *Classic Swashbuckler Films of the 1930s* by Derwood Honeycutt. That ought to be an inspiration." He turned to Dorrie. "What time is your appointment with destiny?"

"Uh, Tiffany said three o'clock," said Dorrie, hoping they were talking about the same thing.

"But that's just when the Melee starts," complained Lavinia.

"So, go watch the Melee!" cried Dorrie.

"Never," said Lavinia.

For an hour, Dorrie practiced with Tiffany's sword while Lavinia read sport-fencing rules out loud; Mr. Kornberger leafed through Mr. Honeycutt's book, exclaiming over pictures of actors brandishing swords on ship decks and castle draw-bridges; and Marcus and Justin shouted out random pieces of often-contradictory advice. This seemed to irritate Moe, who threw himself against the sides of his cage so that it rocked on its wheels until Rosa calmed him by wedging a half-eaten turkey drumstick through the cage's bars.

"God's dentures," said Mr. Kornberger, catching sight of his watch. "It's 1:45! I have to pick up my mother at the race-track." He crammed his feathered hat down onto his curls and saluted Dorrie smartly. "I to the bookmobile and you to the ramparts! If I don't get back in time to cheer you on, just put lots of spirit in your attack and have a good time. Oh, and feel free to vocalize. No rules against that, and I think vocalization really releases the swashbuckler within."

"Aaargh, me hearty!" Marcus crowed, clapping Dorrie on the back.

Dorrie was glad Mr. Kornberger had no idea what was riding on the bout. As soon as he disappeared, she told the others.

"Okay," said Marcus. "You should have talked to Mr. Kornberger's mother first, because I don't think you understand this whole betting thing. You're supposed to have at least a fifty-fifty chance of winning before you agree to a straight win-lose bet like that."

Dorrie fixed him with a furious glare and slung her duffel bag over her shoulder. "I think I do have a fifty-fifty chance of winning!"

"A hundred percent chance!" wheezed Rosa stoutly, puffing on her inhaler again.

✳ ✳ ✳

At three o'clock, Dorrie, Marcus, Lavinia, Justin, and Rosa, with Moe's cage trundling along behind her, crossed the park. Rounding the back corner of the bathrooms, they emerged into a little hardscrabble area out of the traffic of festival visitors. Tiffany was already there, sitting on a picnic table with her friends on either side of her and another sport fencing sword balanced carelessly over her shoulder.

She got to her feet. "Let the no-rules bout begin."

The Academy students shifted uneasily and exchanged glances.

Dorrie's hands tightened around the strap of the duffel bag. "A no-rules bout?"

"Unless you're too scared," said Tiffany. "I thought you liked realistic."

Before Dorrie could answer, Tiffany jumped off the table, teeth bared, and thrust the tip of her blade in the general direction of Dorrie's face.

As the Academy students scattered in surprise, Dorrie instinctively raised her own sword. Though she managed to keep Tiffany's blade away from her head, it came down hard on her hand. Yelping, Dorrie stumbled backward, falling over Moe's cage and toppling it. In slow-motion horror, Dorrie watched the door fly open and the mongoose streak away with an angry yowl. Tiffany and her friends broke into wild laughter.

"No, Moe!" shouted Rosa, scrambling after him, her inhaler bouncing to the ground. "Come back!"

Lavinia, Justin, and Marcus fanned out in pursuit as the mongoose disappeared around the corner of the bathrooms. Dorrie heaved herself to her feet and began to sprint after them.

"Nice chicken-out!" jeered Tiffany.

"It's not a chicken-out," called back Dorrie as she skid to an indecisive halt. "I have to help catch him. I'll be right back!"

"I'll give you ten minutes," Tiffany yelled after her as Dorrie, running again, reached the bathrooms. "If you don't come back, then it's a total forfeit."

Still holding the borrowed sword, Dorrie took off again.

"And then I'll still come after you to get my points," bellowed Tiffany.

Dorrie dashed around the corner and back out into the festival crowd. None of her friends were in sight, but people had begun to run around in panicked circles, lifting their knees high.

CHAPTER 3

THE DISAPPEARING FLOOR

M OE!" DORRIE CALLED DESPERATELY, catching sight of
the mongoose streaking toward the street.

She darted after him, nearly colliding with Marcus.
"Really?" he panted, running alongside her, "Park mayhem
isn't enough for him?"

The mongoose crossed the street amid squealing traffic and
bounded up the steps of the Passaic Public Library. Tail twitching,
he twined through the legs of a man trying to edge through the
library's front door with an armload of books, and disappeared.

"Scuggans will kill us for this!" Dorrie cried as they shot
across the street after Moe. She raced up the library steps two
at a time, her duffel bag bouncing on her back.

"You maybe," Marcus shouted from behind her.

Inside the library's main reading room, Dorrie stopped
short, and Marcus plowed into her. Moe was nowhere to be

seen. At the circulation desk, Mr. Scuggans, thickest in the middle and tapering at both ends, stood with his back to them, stapling a xeroxed photograph to a bulletin board lined with other photographs. A large sign above them proclaimed: "Do *not* check books out to these persons." A sizeable gap existed between the words "these" and "persons." As Mr. Scuggans's head swiveled to one side to scrutinize, his hair slid to the other side like a fried egg on a hot skillet.

"So he *does* wear a toupee!" Marcus hissed in Dorrie's ear.

While Mr. Scuggans readjusted it, Dorrie and Marcus hustled for the cover of the Romance section and then slunk in different directions, whispering Moe's name.

Dorrie saw him first, digging hopefully in a large flowerpot. Before she could snatch him up, the majestic honking of a goose began to blare from the phone in her pocket in echoing blasts. Moe shot off behind the circulation desk in a cloud of dirt, as Dorrie clawed for the phone's off button. Abrupt silence followed, as if the visiting goose had been shot out of the sky.

"What. Was. That?" Mr. Scuggans demanded in a deadly voice.

Red-faced, Dorrie slowly eased into view, Tiffany's sword behind her back.

Mr. Scuggans glowered at her, his lips drawn up into an unamused bundle. "I should have known."

Dorrie's eyes darted furiously to where Marcus stood,

pressed against a bookcase, knowing he particularly enjoyed programming her phone to ring in unexpected ways. Marcus only pointed delicately to a spot over Mr. Scuggans's head. Moe was crossing the top of the bulletin board's thick frame.

Mr. Scuggans drummed his flabby fingers on the countertop, his eyes boring into Dorrie's. "I don't suppose you have something for me?"

Moe provided an answer of sorts by flinging himself down onto the circulation desk in an explosion of stubby pencils and scraps of notepaper, and then immediately bouncing out of sight again.

Mr. Scuggans jumped a foot in the air, his eyes bulging. "Was that some sort of...of...RAT?" he hissed in a terrible voice.

"Not. Exactly," said Dorrie.

Marcus dived for the mongoose and hit the magazine rack hard. It overturned, sending magazines slipping and sliding all over the floor.

Mr. Scuggans snatched up his stapler and pointed at the door. "Remove it from the library's premises! At once!"

"There!" hollered Dorrie, pointing with Tiffany's sword, as the non-exactly-a-rat materialized on the back of a chair.

"Is that a weapon?" cried Mr. Scuggans, slamming the stapler back down on the counter.

As if Mr. Scuggans's stapler-banging had loosened something essential in the old building's electrical system, the lights overhead began to dim and glare in rapid succession. Dorrie and Marcus lunged for Moe at the same time, nearly knocking heads, and missed him as he leaped to a new perch. Just then, Amanda rushed into the reading room through the staff-room door, her chest heaving, her face alight.

"Out! All of you!" shouted Mr. Scuggans.

With a high-pitched howl, Moe streaked past Amanda and disappeared into the staff room.

"We'll catch him! Don't worry," Dorrie shouted. She and Marcus surged through the staff-room door after the mongoose, almost knocking Amanda over.

As Dorrie slammed the door shut behind them, she had just time enough to see dismay replace Amanda's joyful expression.

"Lock it!" Marcus panted. "Before Darth Scuggans brings a death ray in here or something."

Dorrie turned a heavy dead bolt. The room held a sofa, a few desks, a coatrack, and a tiny refrigerator. In one corner, a broom closet stood ajar, its door hung with mops and bags of rags. A crash came from inside the closet, and a plastic bucket came rolling out.

"He's in there!" Dorrie said with relief.

Marcus and Dorrie converged on the closet. Inside, cans of paint and Lysol, and buckets of rags and sponges crowded the closet's shelves.

Marcus pulled the door shut behind them. "Hah! Cornered!"

"Ow!" Dorrie cried as Marcus stepped hard on her foot. "I can't see a thing."

Something metallic tumbled off a shelf and crashed to the floor.

"3PO!" shouted Marcus. "Shut down all the trash compactors on the detention level!"

"Not now," cried Dorrie. Feeling blindly for Moe, and feeling more than a little nervous that she'd find him when his teeth sank into her hand, Dorrie slowly realized that she could now make out the dim shape of a mop head against the back wall. Light seemed to be shining through a crack in the back corner of the closet. A pounding began on the staff-room door.

Dorrie slapped at Marcus. "Look!"

Marcus slapped back at Dorrie. "Look?"

Dorrie faced him toward the sliver of light. Warm air seemed to be flowing out of the crack. When Dorrie put her hand on the back of the closet to steady herself, the wall gave way, swinging slowly to one side on silent hinges like a door.

"Whoa," said Marcus.

They were staring into a small windowless room with five walls. Bookshelves rose up to the ceiling on four of them. On the fifth, velvet curtains tied back with thick silk cords framed a little alcove. In it, a broad table, stacked with papers, stood on carved legs. Above the table hung a collection of portraits, most no bigger than a box of cereal. Nearby, two leather armchairs and a hairy ottoman wore a thin pall of gray dust. Above it, a glass ceiling lamp hung from a chain giving out a golden glow.

"What is this place?" Dorrie whispered, the dull pounding on the staff-room door suddenly seeming like a distant affair that didn't concern them.

Dorrie took a few steps into the room, her imagination pricked and thrilled. Beneath the dust at her feet, lines darker than the wooden floor criss-crossed and joined other lines, passing through small circles, pentagons, triangles and other shapes in a complicated pattern that seemed to blossom from a small star shape in the room's center.

Catching sight of Moe perched on a bookshelf daintily cleaning a paw brought Dorrie back to her senses. "We've got to get back to the park," she cried aloud, lunging for the mongoose, who leaped onto a higher shelf.

"And face Scuggans at peak frenzy?" protested Marcus, settling himself in one of the soft armchair and putting up his feet on the ottoman. "Why?"

"Because Tiffany said if I didn't get back in ten minutes, I forfeit, which means I'll have to wear the T-shirt."

A sudden jolt knocked Dorrie violently sideways off her feet to land sprawling on the floor. Falling, she felt the way she had once at summer camp when the rowboat she'd been standing in collided with a dock piling. Her phone flew out of her pocket and spun across the floor. A stillness took hold.

"What was that?" gulped Dorrie, holding tight to Tiffany's sword.

"Scuggans coming after us with a wrecking ball?" guessed Marcus, clinging to the armchair.

They listened hard but heard nothing except for their own heavy breathing. Then, slowly, with a creaking groan, the floor beneath Dorrie's feet began to bulge, as though it sat on top of an inflating lung. Dorrie and Marcus leaped back. With a complaining sigh, the floor settled back down.

"And what was that?" Dorrie whispered.

Before Marcus could answer, the floor began to bulge again, this time higher. Bits of the fancy inlaid wood cracked and creaked, popping out of place and skittering away, revealing rough wooden planks that bent with the bulge as though made of rubber. Dorrie and Marcus flattened themselves against a bookcase, heads in their arms, Dorrie waiting for an explosion. But none came. Looking cautiously out from beneath an elbow, Dorrie watched the bulge deflate. Where the rough wooden planks had been visible, a glassy black puddle now lay, steam drifting and curling across its surface.

Suddenly, the puddle's edges jerked outward, sending a new wave of disintegrating parquet beneath Dorrie and Marcus's feet. Dorrie cried out as she felt herself being sucked into the puddle's steaming center.

Chapter 4

Another Place Altogether

DORRIE THOUGHT SHE MIGHT be screaming but could hear nothing. She thought she might be pumping her legs madly against the pulling current and clinging to her sword, but those motions only felt like ideas. The heat was real. She howled as her skin seemed to dissolve into a sea of blistering bubbles, each carrying an impossible cargo of burning darkness. She felt her hair crackling with fire. And her fingertips melting away.

As quickly as the heat and dark had absorbed and filled Dorrie, they now released her, leaving her with the distinctly unsettling impression that she was plummeting downward. Her eyes and mouth flew open.

Far below, but rushing toward her at a fantastic clip, lay a long rectangle of mossy green. Its uneven surface gleamed with little winking lights. Dorrie's brain insisted on thinking: *When*

I hit, I'm going to split open like a bag of flour. She squeezed her eyes tight against the coming impact and the whole messy idea, but instead of the end of everything, she felt a terrific splashing jolt and then a deep desire to sleep. She drifted happily, motionless, ready to dream,

Something snaked around her waist. Dorrie felt herself pulled free of the wet and dragged up onto something smooth and hard. With a great effort, she opened her eyes. Marcus, his dripping hair plastered across his forehead, knelt beside her, staring anxiously into her face. Dorrie took a long, damp, chokey breath, and pushed herself upright.

"Are you all right?" asked Marcus.

"I...I think so." In her sopping clothes, Dorrie's limbs still felt heavy and tired, her thoughts thick and confused. A throbbing in her hand caught her attention. It was wrapped tightly around the hilt of a sword, purply-blue with bruises. *Tiffany.*

Dorrie looked around. She was sitting beside a long, rectangular pool of water she'd never seen before. A forest of tiled pillars stood along its edge. From high overhead, an angry chittering sound made Dorrie tilt her head back. The pillars, she now saw, held up a high, white ceiling dotted with gold stars and suns. Dead in its center, a jagged hole interrupted the ceiling's smooth expanse. From a broken-off piece of wood at its edge hung Dorrie's duffel bag, and on the duffel bag perched a furious Moe. The edge of the hole glowed with cold, blue-white light. Through it, Dorrie could see the room where they had briefly stood with its portraits and overstuffed armchairs.

Marcus sighed over Moe's furious accusations. "Whatever just happened, Scuggans is going to completely blame us for it."

Dorrie staggered to her feet and wrung out the bottom of her soaked dress.

"You're welcome on the whole saving-your-life thing," said Marcus, beginning to wiggle out of his pajamas bottoms.

"What are you doing?"

"Getting comfortable. They're heavy!"

"We can't get comfortable! We have to get back to the park!" She cupped her hands around her mouth. "Mr. Scuggans!" she hollered into the hole at the top of her lungs.

"Don't call him!" hissed Marcus, scuttling behind a pillar. "Have you not heard of plausible deniability?" He twisted a river of water out of his pajama bottoms. "Let's just *quietly* look for a way out."

Off-key singing put an end to Marcus's suggestion-making.

Dorrie's hands flew to her head. Not just because of the singing's abominable quality, but because a buzzing had started deep inside her ears, as though a family of bees had moved into her skull.

"What is that horrible sound?" cried Marcus, slapping at his ears.

Dorrie spun around, grimacing. "Which one?"

The singing seemed to be coming from behind a tall, narrow set of mottled greenish-blue doors. Dorrie sloshed toward them in her waterlogged boots and pushed. The doors barely moved. "Hello!" she called out loudly into the crack. Bracing herself, grunting, her feet slipping, she pushed harder until the door swung all the way open.

Panting, she stared open-mouthed. Flickering light from torches set in wooden holders along the walls illuminated the low, cracked ceiling of a narrow corridor that turned sharply farther on. Flagstones covered the floor. "Marcus?" she said slowly into the new silence. She felt him materialize damply behind her.

He stuck his head inside the corridor. "This is so vampire lair."

"Don't *say* that!"

They squeezed through the doorway together. The air felt much colder here. A chill pressed upward from the flagstones, and a shiver twitched Dorrie's shoulders. Bicycles and hand-carts lined the walls. Pairs of the strangest roller-skates Dorrie had ever seen sat in a row on a shelf. Each leather boot sat atop two-foot-high wheels that looked as though they'd been torn from the frames of tiny bicycles.

"Roller-skating vampires. Definitely. Probably Mr. Scuggans's relatives." Marcus stuck his hand into the nearest torch flame. "Real fire," he yelped, snatching it back.

Urgency drove Dorrie forward down the corridor at a run,

her breath making little clouds, her wet clothes feeling clammy now against her skin. "Is anybody here?"

Nobody answered. Between two of the torches stood a low, splintery doorframe. Dorrie sidled up to one side of it and peeked in. Rack upon rack of what looked like rectangles of stone or clay filled a low-ceilinged room.

Marcus ducked his head and went through. Dust rose in puffs around his wet shoes. "Oh, this is totally where they sleep."

"Quit it!" hissed Dorrie, edging slowly into the room after him. Almost immediately, she felt enveloped in dry warmth. Across the room, another low doorway opened into a starkly different room, all whites and golds with a checkerboard floor, its walls lined with books.

She ran her eyes dazedly over the racks of heavy, dusty slabs nearby. "This must be another part of the library, but what are these things?" She gently touched the edge of one of the thick rectangles. It felt warm and rough beneath her fingers. Tiny marks had been dug into its surface. Tiny marks that seemed, as she stared at them, to tremble and move. She leaped backward, wondering if she'd disturbed a nest of ants or roaches or something worse. She didn't have time to check.

"The pleasure of loooove lasts only a moment," warbled the still-distant voice again in a plaintive slur, the words now more distinct. "The sorrow of love laaaaaaasts a lifetime."

"Here! We're here!" yelled Dorrie, her ears filled with angry buzzing again.

The voice seemed to be coming from behind a pair of highly polished wooden doors with brass knobs. Dorrie and Marcus scuttled toward them.

"Wait!" Dorrie called as the singing abruptly ceased, along with the buzzing in her ears. She twisted the doorknob. Though she'd only crossed the room, Dorrie felt as though she'd run miles carrying an armful of bricks. When she finally succeeded in wrenching the door open, she gasped.

A far larger and airier room lay on the other side. Along the room's edges, tall stone figures in swirls of sculpted cloth looked down from pedestals set between banks of gleaming wooden bookshelves packed with leather-bound volumes. A dozen sets of doors—just like the ones they'd come through— interrupted the bookshelves at regular intervals. A wrought- iron and wooden balcony ran around the walls above the statues' heads.

More books lined every inch of the soaring walls between the balcony and a vaulted ceiling painted robin's egg blue. Thin golden lines connected glinting stars into wheeling constellations. Elaborate chandeliers bright with a multi- tude of white candles cast a wavering light. The silent room smelled of old leather and pencil lead and…Dorrie sniffed carefully…oranges.

Marcus shouldered past Dorrie. "Book-loving vampires."

"How come nobody ever showed us this part of the library?" whispered Dorrie, taking in the wide tables that marched up the center of the room in two straight rows, each holding a green-hooded lamp. "And where are all the people? Shouldn't there be people?"

Marcus pointed at a broad, polished oak desk on top of which stood a chalkboard propped on an easel. It was covered with what looked like scribbles. Dorrie blinked and rubbed her eyes. Now she could see that the scribbles were letters. They spelled out: "Staff Meeting in Progress. For Assistance in a Research Emergency, please dial Petrarch 5-8105." Next to the sign stood the kind of telephone that Dorrie had seen people use in old black-and-white movies.

"Does this count as a research emergency?" asked Dorrie.

Marcus helped himself to a piece of hard candy from a glass bowl sitting on the desk. "Sure, why not. 'How do we get out of here?' is a question."

Dorrie reached for the strange phone.

Marcus caught her arm. "You do know we've been down here way longer than ten minutes, right?"

The realization that she'd lost to Tiffany without even getting the chance to try and beat her almost brought Dorrie to her knees. She'd failed in the most frustrating way. She covered her face with her hands. "Poor Mr. Kornberger."

"Don't worry," said Marcus, pulling tiny drawers in and out of a heavy cabinet that stood beside the desk. "He probably won't even notice that you're wearing it." He ran his finger over the cards that filled one of the drawers. "What is this thing?"

Dorrie wiped her nose, which had gone all damp and drippy, and walked slowly toward the nearest bookshelf. No longer in a tearing rush to return to the park, she gave in to her desire to really take in the grand room. She ran her fingers over the soft spines of the nearest books.

"Old penny, dirty dog, coffee, mud," Dorrie murmured, giving the colors of the leather bindings names. Nearby stood a stepladder, a sprinkling of orange peels littering the floor around its feet. Dorrie lifted a book from where it sat facedown on the top step, propped her sword up beside the ladder, and sat down on the stepladder. The book's muted green cover felt thick and soft. Gilt letters glowed upon it. With a small cry, Dorrie let the book tumble to the ground.

"What?" said Marcus from where he stood spinning a globe.

"The letters on that book. They moved! They…they… squirmed."

Marcus hurried to her and retrieved the book from the ground. "What are you—" He broke off sharply, almost dropping the book again himself. "Whoa."

"See!" With a sharp intake of breath, Dorrie watched the figures that made up the title writhe and finally leap into focus as letters she recognized. *Index to 14th Century Angry Letters Left on Tables by Girls Planning to Run Away from Home.* With trembling hands, she flipped open the volume.

"So many," murmured Dorrie. Her eyes ran down the list of entries to the last one on a page that smelled strongly of oranges. After more twisting of symbols, it read: "Mohamad, Saffiyah. Baza, Kingdom of Granada, March 11, 1350. 'To My Parents Who Just Don't Understand.'"

"This place is weird," said Marcus emphatically and with great pleasure. Dorrie and Marcus exchanged a look of tense excitement, their eyes alight.

Dorrie carefully closed the book and pushed it into the gap between *Index to 14th Century Novels, Poems, and Other Fictions* and *Index to 14th Century Treatises on Physics.* She let her eyes dart back and forth across the bookshelves, her heart beginning to pound, as over and over again, squiggles became words before her eyes.

She heard a jingle and spun around to see Marcus swinging open a wrought-iron door set in something that looked like an enormous, ornate version of Moe's cage. A large key dangled in the door's lock.

Marcus stuck his head inside. "Come look at this."

The back of Dorrie's neck began to prickle. "Marcus, I don't think we're supposed to go in there." She crept to his side.

Inside the cage stood a long, battered table upon which lay

thick, red books chained to it at intervals. Dorrie and Marcus edged farther into the room and peered at the closest book, which looked worn, its title faded. Dorrie squinted at it, not shocked this time to see the letters wiggle and rearrange themselves until they stood out as clearly as anything she'd ever read. *The History of Histories.*

In fact, all the books on the table bore the title *The History of Histories.* As Marcus reached out to open one, Dorrie seized his arm. Somewhere nearby she'd heard a faint stirring, almost a whispering. "Marcus, don't," she hissed, frozen, her heart banging.

He shrugged her off. "Chillax. It's a library. We're just browsing."

"Yeah, in somebody's locked safe. C'mon, we've still got to find a way out."

Marcus ignored her, flipped open the volume, and began to leaf through its pages. He held a page up at an angle to catch the light better. "321 PLE—whatever that is—January 27— okay, got that." His eyes drifted down the page. "Check this out... 'On this 14th day of November, 1725, in Cambridge, England: Foiled, a plot to murder Thomas Woolston, author of *The Moderator.* Lybrarian: Dame Henrietta Banks. Keyhand: Colin Headly.'" Marcus snickered. "It sounds so James Bond. The whole page, the whole book is full of these little—"

He got no farther, for at that moment a figure staggered

upward into view on the other side of the table, his long hair a wild cloud of tangles, and the remnants of a dirty and torn cloak hanging askew off his cadaverous body. His chin glistened with wetness and gelatinous globs.

Screaming, Dorrie and Marcus reeled backward to the accompanying sound of thick paper tearing. The gargoyle of a face across from them broke into its own piercing cry, its scarecrow arms flying upward, releasing a fusillade of oranges. Dorrie felt herself pelted with them as she crashed backward into the iron barred door. The figure flung his upper body across the table, arms outstretched.

Tripping and sliding on the oranges, Dorrie and Marcus streaked for the nearest doors and exploded through them. On the other side, they pounded down a long, carpeted corridor papered in violently fuchsia bouquets, which became a curving stone stairway that wound upward in dizzying circles. It ended in another corridor, this one tiled in green and white diamonds. Hearing a crash from down in the stairwell, Dorrie grabbed Marcus's arm and they fled to the left, passing closed curtain after curtain.

Suddenly, whizzing past a curtainless stone archway, Dorrie glimpsed a heavy man in a brown robe hunched over a desk, a short fringe of hair hanging low on his otherwise bald head. Fear stabbed through her as she imagined him leaping off his stool to join the chase. Dorrie and Marcus ducked through an open door farther on and scurried past racks of what looked like half-used rolls of paper towels. Another door let them into a bright, bare corridor—this one grandly floored in polished marble.

Exhausted, Dorrie wrenched open a plain-looking wooden door and slipped through it with Marcus right behind. They pushed it softly closed behind them and slumped down, their backs against it.

"Now that was a research emergency!" panted Marcus.

Dorrie slowly took in the room. A cheery fire burned in a little brick fireplace, lighting up a collection of old-fashioned-looking couches and chairs. Glass-fronted bookcases lined the room on three sides. A marble mantel hung over the fireplace, and upon that stood two carved busts, one of a man's head and one of a woman's. In front of the fireplace, plates of steaming food sat alongside a pitcher on a low table. Dorrie was about to peer beneath the table to make sure no one was lurking when she caught sight of something white and floppy in Marcus's hand.

She felt the blood run out of her face. "That's not from the—"

"Book?" Marcus finished, shaking the hair out of his eyes. "More or less."

"You ripped a page out of the book!"

"Not on purpose!"

Marcus collapsed in a sprawl on the floor, the page crumpling beneath him. "I need a nap," he groaned. "A year-long nap."

"Don't squash it!" hissed Dorrie, expecting to be discovered any moment. "Roll it up, at least, or something!"

Marcus heaved himself off the page as though it cost him all the energy he had left. Slowly he began to roll the page up.

Another wave of the sleepiness she'd felt in the pool hit Dorrie. With it came a madly intense urge to orient herself, to see the streets of Passaic, to know exactly how far they'd traveled from beneath the Passaic Public Library. She staggered clumsily to her feet and, pulling Marcus reluctantly along with her, tottered toward a window that stood between two bookcases. She tore aside the silky green curtains and gave a little cry.

"This is impossible," whispered Dorrie hoarsely.

Marcus swayed beside her. "This is definitely not Passaic."

Chapter 5

Petrarch's Library

THE PANIC THAT DORRIE had been staving off now exploded within her, electrifying her fingers. She clung to the window's sill, anchoring herself to its solidness. Nothing was as it should be. Instead of looking down on one of Passaic's worn and potholed streets lined with its familiar saggy-stooped duplexes and corner convenience stores, Dorrie saw spread below her a vast patchwork of rooftops. Slate tiles and wooden shingles and straw thatch and blued copper lay against roofs of every pitch and style.

The buildings they sheltered connected to one another in a vast jigsaw puzzle that included open fields, pebbled courtyards, and gardens with tinkling fountains. A stone tower seamlessly gave way to a wooden farmhouse, which farther on became a timber and stucco hall, which fit snugly against an immense sort of palace heavy with stone carvings and glistening windows.

Stone gave way to bamboo. Stucco gave way to mud bricks. At a great distance, beyond a band of gnarled trees and rough rock outcrops, Dorrie saw what looked like a sun-scaled sea.

Voices in the hallway made her ragged breath catch, and she and Marcus turned frightened eyes on each other. The voices came closer; the knob on the door they'd used began to turn. In a blur, Marcus shoved the roll of paper he held down a thin brass tube with a flared opening that rose out of the floor nearby.

"Can't have a mission meeting without proper nourishment," said a big-boned man with an extra wobbling chin as he came through the door carrying a laden tray. Curly puffs of reddish hair grew with a great amount of spirit from either side of his head, as if trying to make up for the fact that not a hair grew from the top. Two girls about Dorrie's age trailed him, each holding their own trays.

Seeing Dorrie and Marcus, they both stopped dead. The first girl wore an expression of great wonder and a yellow hair band that held back an abundance of dreds. The second stared at them with narrowed, suspicious eyes from beneath dark bangs, the rest of her hair having been cropped at the ears. Having lifted a sardine from one of the plates he carried, the man was in the process of dropping it in his mouth with great relish when the first girl nudged him.

Catching sight of Dorrie and Marcus, he lowered the sardine. "Well, who in the name of Seshat are you?"

His words rattled and buzzed in Dorrie's ears.

"Han…" slurred Marcus.

Dorrie, who felt as though her brain had begun to spin inside her skull like a globe, gave Marcus points for quick thinking.

"Solo," added Marcus. He pointed at Dorrie. "Chewbacca."

Dorrie took some of the points she'd awarded Marcus back. Then, though she had never before fainted, Dorrie had a strong feeling, as her knees turned jellyish, that she was about to do just that.

The man dropped the tray on the table with a crash and hurried forward, catching Dorrie just before she slumped to the ground. As he carried her to a couch, a young woman with the longest hair Dorrie had ever seen appeared in the doorway, a bouquet of flowers in her hand.

"These zinnias will cheer up—" Catching sight of Marcus slipping to the floor, his eyes closed, she abandoned her thought and, tossing the flowers aside, hurried toward him, though not in time to keep him from landing with a heavy thud.

"Slip shock, Egeria, I think," said the man as the woman stooped over Marcus, feeling his hands.

"Slip shock?" exclaimed the short-haired girl. "But there are not supposed to be any new archways opening for years and years."

"They're soaking wet," the man said as he gently laid Dorrie down. "They need warmth and cloversweet."

The short-haired girl spoke again. "But they might be enemies! Maybe even Foundation."

Dorrie's heart began to thump wildly. She felt as though her blood was turning to ice water.

"Manners, Millie," said the man. "They could also be friends." He held out his hand to Dorrie. "Phillippus Aureolus Theophrastus Bombastus von Hohenheim."

With great effort, Dorrie managed to get her hand into his.

"I get called Paracelsus sometimes too, but Phillip does for most people."

"I'll go get Mr. Gormly!" said Millie sprinting for the door.

"Never mind Mr. Gormly," said Phillip, sounding irritated. "Go get some dry clothes from the circulation desk, and Ebba, you'd better fetch Ursula. Tell her, 'Slip shock.'" Both girls vanished through the door.

"Slip shock has a way of sneaking up on a person after a trip in," said Phillip, his thick eyebrows waggling. They sat over a pair of kindly eyes. "You'll be right as rain soon enough. In the meantime, you may feel confused, deathly tired, and as though your arms and legs had been run over by mill wheels."

Dorrie thought he sounded quite cheerful about the whole situation.

Together, Phillip and Egeria half walked, half carried Marcus toward another couch. As disoriented as she was, Dorrie couldn't help noticing that Marcus was making their job a lot harder than it had to be by giggling, trying to stroke Egeria's hair as if she were a cat, and gazing into her face as though he'd lost something in it.

"Also, your brain may feel a bit overworked," said Phillip, his voice still buoyant. "As if you're listening to a foreign language and instantly translating it into your own. Which, of course, you are. Assuming your mother tongue isn't Latin." He looked at Dorrie thoughtfully as he helped lower Marcus onto the other couch. "You do bear a vague resemblance to a milkmaid I met in Umbria once."

Curling up in a ball on the couch, Marcus closed his eyes, sighing and mumbling. Dorrie didn't know what to make of Phillip's words, but it had occurred to her that the shapes his mouth made as he spoke didn't match up with the words she was hearing.

"I'll go tell Mistress Wu what's happened," said Egeria, striding out of the room. She almost collided with a stout woman with black corkscrew curls who was carrying a basket in each hand, Ebba trailing after her. The woman set down the baskets. Giving Dorrie an efficient smile, she pulled a blanket out of one of the baskets and laid it on top of her.

With quick movements, she dug in the second basket until she'd unearthed a lidded jar and a goblet. She poured out an amber liquid. "I'm Ursula," she said, handing Dorrie the full goblet. "Drink this. It'll help you recover."

Dorrie touched the rim of the goblet to her parched lips tentatively. If Passaic could disappear, what would happen to her if she took a sip? Would she turn into a toad or vanish in a puff of lavender smoke? Would she be Ursula's prisoner for life? She hesitated and then, desperately thirsty, she drank, half waiting for webbing to grow between her toes. The cool liquid tasted of summer grass and the sweetness of flowers.

Marcus stirred. Phillip hurried over to him with another blanket, while Ebba, looking shyly at Dorrie, began to tug on one of Dorrie's wet boots.

As Phillip spread the blanket over Marcus, a grin that Dorrie thought looked appallingly idiotic spread slowly over her brother's face. He reached out his arms toward Phillip, his lips rummaging around in a kissy sort of way. Opening his eyes, he froze for a moment and then snatched back his arms, closing his mouth with a snap. "Dude, you are not the person I was dreaming about."

"My apologies," said Phillip.

"She was about seven feet tall," Marcus said with soggy admiration. "With chocolate cherry, mermaid-forever hair and purple eyes."

"That would be our Egeria, though I'd have to say her eyes are more of a blue." Phillip wiggled his bushy eyebrows at Ursula. "Might want to pour him a double dose."

As Dorrie sipped from the goblet, she saw for the first time that Ursula's left eye nested in a birthmark that flowed like a spill of red wine across her eyelid and temple to disappear into her hairline. Dorrie automatically looked away.

"It's a birthmark," Ursula said matter-of-factly, clock-spring curls bouncing around her pale face. "You can look if you'd like. Some people have noted it bears a startling resemblance to a sleeping cat."

Phillip snorted. "Yes, right before those charming commentators tried to set you on fire."

"Set you on fire!" repeated Dorrie, shocked.

Phillip peered over Ursula's shoulder at Dorrie. "Curiosity almost killed our lovely Ursula cat."

"More like a lack of curiosity," sniffed Ursula.

Dorrie decided they must be sharing a private joke.

Marcus worked himself more deeply into the cushions. "Maybe her eyes were more of a violet than a purple."

"There's a *hole* in the ceiling over the baths!" announced Millie, tearing back into the room, her eyes ablaze. "There's a room on the other side but it doesn't look like a proper archway at all!"

Phillip and Ursula stared at each other for a long moment, and Ebba's eyes grew round.

Millie tossed the clothing she held on a chair. "Oh, and there's some weasel thing in the water swimming round in circles!"

"Really?" said Ebba, letting go of Dorrie's boot and clapping her hands together, her face bright. "A weasel? Are you sure?"

"I don't know," said Millie, supremely indifferent. "It's long and wet, and it's showing its teeth a lot."

"It could also be a stoat or a marten," said Ebba. "Did its tail have a black tip? A stoat almost always has one, and a weasel hardly—"

"It's a mongoose," interrupted Dorrie, feeling more clearheaded.

Everyone but Marcus stared at her for a moment.

"Right," said Phillip finally, turning to Ebba and Millie. "Well, go fish it out!"

Ebba and Millie dashed away again. A hope crept through Dorrie. If the hole was still there, then no matter what she had seen through the window, perhaps Passaic was still on the other side of it. Poor, horrible Moe. She'd forgotten all about him.

"Where are we exactly?" Dorrie forced herself to ask.

Ursula gave Dorrie a keen, penetrating look as she poured a second goblet-full of liquid from the jar. "You don't know?"

Dorrie shook her head.

Ursula looked intently at her a moment longer, then at Phillip, who nodded slightly as she handed him the goblet. "You are in Petrarch's Library. I'm Ursula, director of the repair and preservation department here."

"The one for humans," said Phillip, winking at Dorrie as he carried the goblet over to Marcus. "You wouldn't want Master Al-Rahmi mucking about in your health with his whiffy glues and inks."

"Who's Master Al-Rahmi?" asked Dorrie, feeling that she was navigating a maze.

Ursula screwed the lid back on the jar. "Director of Petrarch's Library's *other* repair and preservation department. The one for books and scrolls and tablets, that sort of thing."

Dorrie set her goblet down. "But what *is* Petrarch's Library?"

Before Ursula could answer, Marcus sat bolt upright as though he'd just that moment solved the mystery of the universe's existence. "Maybe she just smelled like purple."

Dorrie rounded on him. "That's all you're wondering about?"

"Aren't you?"

"What? No, you idiot!" She seemed to finally have his attention. "We fell through a floor into a swimming pool, and if you didn't notice, that's not Passaic outside that window!"

He blinked at her. "Why can't *our* library have a pool?" He sank back into the cushions. "And a girl with mermaid-forever hair."

"The Romans, bless them," said Phillip. "Sheer genius mixing libraries and swimming pools."

"The Romans?" said Dorrie, feeling utterly frustrated. "What do the Romans have to do with anything? I just want to know where we are and—"

"Oh my," said a voice from the doorway.

Dorrie turned to see a solid, broad-shouldered woman in a long, red silk tunic leaning on the doorframe and breathing like a spent racehorse, an enormous pillow of black hair atop her head.

"Unexpected guests, I think, Mistress Wu," said Phillip pleasantly.

"Oh dear," said Mistress Wu, mopping at her face with a handkerchief. "I came as soon as I could. Egeria's moved the mission meeting into the Serapeum, so we shouldn't be bothered here. What a simply terrible fall it must have been for them. Are they quite all ri—" She stopped mopping and talking, a look of pure horror on her face. "Oh, how awful of me," she said, looking first at Marcus and then Dorrie. "How terrible to be spoken of as though one isn't in the room. Do forgive me!"

"I'm sure they're over it already," said Phillip. He turned to Dorrie, his eyebrows dancing. "Mistress Wu is the assistant to Hypatia, our director of administration, who is away in…on a trip at the moment."

A crooked cushion on a chair seemed to seize Mistress Wu's full attention. Her hands had reached out to straighten it when Phillip cleared his throat. "They're just wondering where they are at the moment."

Mistress Wu pulled her hands back, looking instantly devastated again. "Oh! Oh, of course you would!" She laid her hand on her heart. "Why, you must be almost mad with anxiety at this turn of events."

At Mistress Wu's words, Dorrie, who had not in fact been

feeling mad with anxiety, now felt its little flames set fire to the bottom of her stomach.

"That is…unless you're…um…well….no…no…you couldn't…" The words she'd uttered seem to induce excruciating embarrassment in Mistress Wu. Rather than finish the thought, she pounced on the crooked cushion and straightened it with a kind of profound relief.

Phillip took a seat and leaned toward Dorrie and Marcus. "Before we tell you about Petrarch's Library, would you mind first telling us how you came to be swimming in our Roman bath?"

Warily, Dorrie began. "We were chasing Moe—that's the mongoose—through the Passaic Public Library."

"Naturally," said Phillip, his eyebrows working up and down.

"He got loose at the Pen and Sword Festival," added Dorrie for clarification, so Phillip wouldn't think they were nuts.

"The what?" asked Mistress Wu.

"The Pen and Sword Festival," repeated Marcus, doing his part.

The adults still looked confused.

"It's like a Renaissance fair," offered Dorrie.

"Like a market fair, you mean?" asked Ursula.

"Well, you can buy pretend swords and pretend corsets and mead and stuff," said Dorrie. "But mostly it's for dressing up and pretending to be, you know, back in the Renaissance."

"Extraordinary," said Phillip. "Go on."

Dorrie remembered the mop closet. "We chased Moe into this weird room in the back of a closet, and…the floor in the room just sort of exploded."

Marcus sat bolt upright again. "Then there was this beautiful girl!"

"Yes," said Phillip. "I think we've covered that part of the story."

"And we found ourselves here," said Dorrie, feeling it was just as well that Marcus had skipped past their wanderings and the little matter of the page torn out of the book. "So what's Petrarch's Library?"

Ursula began to repack her basket with brisk little movements. "Petrarch's Library is the headquarters of a secret society."

"A secret society?" repeated Dorrie.

Mistress Wu looked thoroughly unnerved and began to mop at her face madly again. "Ursula dear, I'm not sure Francesco would like us just blurting that out."

Ursula stopped rearranging the basket. "I don't see how we can keep it from them, given the circumstances, do you?"

Mistress Wu nervously twisted her handkerchief into the thinnest of sodden snakes. "I suppose we don't have a choice, do we?"

"A secret society of what?" said Marcus, who finally seemed to have recovered some of his senses.

Ursula, firmly screwed the lid back on the jar of clover-sweet. "Lybrarians."

Chapter 6

The Lybrariad

MARCUS SNORTED. "LIBRARIANS?"

"The Lybrariad, by name," said Mistress Wu, moving one of the busts on the mantel an inch to the left and then two inches to the right.

"Why would a bunch of librarians need a secret society?" said Marcus, apparently feeling the full fog-clearing effect of the cloversweet. "Plotting revenge on people who don't return books on time?"

Mistress Wu paused in her bust shifting. "Oh dear, I suppose we really should do more in that area."

"But we have other much more important goals," said Phillip.

Dorrie looked from Phillip to Ursula. "Like what?"

"Turning well-trained lybrarians out into the world, for one," said Ursula.

"You train librarians?" said Marcus, as though such a pursuit was a complete waste of a secret society.

"That's part of our work," said Ursula, picking up the clothes that Millie had thrown on the chair. They turned out to be bathrobes. The first, a very large one made of red plaid flannel, she handed to Marcus. The second, a long one made out of a soft, light-blue nubby material with brown fur on the cuffs and collar, she handed to Dorrie.

Dorrie thought of Amanda checking out books, and Mr. Kornberger helping her find things on the shelves, and Mr. Scuggans terrorizing patrons with his overdue notices. "But why would you need to train librarians secretly?"

Phillip tore two hunks of bread off a loaf on the table and laid them on small plates. "Because lybrarians, at least the ones we train, are doing more than it looks like they're doing."

"It looks like they're doing the shushing thing," said Marcus.

"And with great panache, no doubt," said Phillip, buttering the hunk of bread generously. "But in addition to trying to make the world a quieter place for those trying to read and think, our lybrarians are also trying to keep people from having their tongues cut out or being thrown into jail or set on fire for scribbling the wrong thing on a piece of parchment. Not to mention keeping their writings from being destroyed or locked away."

Dorrie stared at Phillip in disbelief, trying to imagine Mr.

Scuggans putting down his fine announcement bullhorn long enough to even help someone eat a pie.

"Where?" said Marcus. "I mean, where are people still getting their tongues cut out for saying stuff, and who's still scribbling anything on parchment?"

"Oh, you'd be surprised," said Phillip, handing Marcus and Dorrie each a plate.

Dorrie took hers slowly and glanced out the window, the hairs on her neck rising. "Why can't we see Passaic from that window?

"Ah, now we've come to it," said Mistress Wu, a new torrent of sweat breaking out on her forehead.

Ursula bustled to the window and pushed the curtains back fully. The blue of the sky had deepened into dusk since Dorrie had last looked through it.

Ursula took a deep breath. "Do you know what a hub is? The center of a wheel, say?"

Dorrie and Marcus nodded.

"Petrarch's Library is a sort of hub," said Ursula. "Its spokes, however, aren't the wooden rods of a wagon wheel. No. Its spokes are the four hundred or so smaller libraries that connect to it."

Phillip buttered a piece of bread for himself. "One Spoke Library sits in Passaic, and another sits in Peking, and another in Paris. You see?"

A wild beating had started up in Dorrie's chest. "But Paris and Passaic are miles and miles apart."

"And yet, through Petrarch's Library you can get from Paris to Passaic in a matter of minutes." Phillip sniffed. "Assuming you can find a bicycle when you want one, or a pair of roller-skates in a pinch."

"Majestic," said Marcus with deep fervor.

"Majestic?" repeated Dorrie.

"Oh, I meant to tell you," said Marcus. "I've left 'awesome' behind."

"Always a sad thing to be left behind," sighed Mistress Wu. "People even leave libraries behind, you know. Just abandon them to the cruelties of mice and wind and rain and torch-bearing philistines." Her eyes began to well fabulously. "Petrarch's Library is more full of Ghost Libraries than Spoke Libraries. Oh, yes," she added vehemently, as though Dorrie and Marcus had expressed some doubt upon the matter. "Ghost Libraries are constantly crashing into us here. Squeezing in. Making places for themselves where it suits." She suddenly sounded querulous. "Always changes the layout of Petrarch's Library. Very confusing for us." She sighed again. "But you can't blame them, poor things." Now tears collected again in the corners of her eyes. "Fallen to wrack and ruin in their own times and places." She dabbed at her eyes with her handkerchief.

"It's true," said Phillip cheerfully. "One day, it's two lefts and a right to get to the loo, and the next day, you're lucky if you can find the thing at all." He began to fidget in his seat as if in discomfort. "Excuse me." He dug two oranges out of a loose pants pocket. Dorrie started, forcibly reminded of the frightening figure who'd surprised them in the room with the *History of Histories* books.

Phillip held them up to Ursula. "Found these on my way over."

Ursula raised her eyebrows. "The Archivist, no doubt."

"Who's the Archivist?" said Dorrie, avoiding Marcus's eyes and trying not to sound too interested.

"One of our resident lybrarians," said Phillip. "In charge of the *History of—*"

"A very old man who once a year drinks far too much Madeira wine and gets maudlin," Ursula cut in crisply.

Phillip pulled a third piece of fruit out of his vest pocket. "When the Archivist gets maudlin, the corridors tend to fill with bad singing and oranges. Lots of oranges. He reads them out by the dozens."

Dorrie and Marcus looked at Phillip blankly.

Phillip tossed an orange to each of them. "I'm sorry. I mean, he reads the oranges out of a book. A French novel, in this case. Terrible plotting but a beautiful description of an orange near the end. That's how we get a good deal of our food around here."

"*What!*" cried Dorrie and Marcus in unison.

Phillip waved at the laden table. "Took me an hour and a half to read all that out. It's amazing what the right reader can get out of a book. And if I do say so myself, I have something of a knack when it comes to meats and sauces."

Dorrie looked at the bread beside her with new wonder.

"If we're quite done discussing oranges and sauces, there's one other fact of great importance we haven't yet shared," said Ursula.

Something in Ursula's tone sent a wind kicking up in Dorrie's chest.

Ursula played with the pocket on the long, yellowed apron she wore. "The Spoke Libraries don't just connect Petrarch's Library to far-flung places." She found Dorrie's eyes, and then Marcus's in turn. "They connect Petrarch's Library to every century that has passed since the invention of the written word."

Dorrie held tight to the edge of her blanket. "You mean you can get from—"

"500 BCE to 1611 CE?" finished Phillip. "Ancient Egypt to twelfth-century Byzantium to eighteenth-century Japan? Yes."

"Monumental!" shouted Marcus, sending a slosh of cloversweet flying from his goblet.

"You can tell the Spoke Libraries from the Ghost Libraries," said Mistress Wu, "because the Spoke Libraries form on the other side of conveniently labeled stone arches. Tells you what lies on the other side."

Phillip scratched his head. "Except for yours, apparently."

"We saw an archway like that!" cried Dorrie, "There was a man on the other side. He looked like some kind of monk."

"Ireland, 812 CE, most probably," said Phillip. "Tell us, what century are you from?"

"The twenty-first," said Dorrie, feeling bewitched. Ursula's long apron with its big pocket and Phillip's embroidered vest and Mistress Wu's long silk tunic made a new kind of sense. Suddenly, a vision of Tiffany's jeering face smashed through the magic stained glass of the moment. And then the faces of her parents, faces pinched with worry. Who knew what revenge Tiffany was going to take on Dorrie for disappearing. Her parents had probably called the police.

Setting her bread aside, Dorrie pushed the blanket off her legs. "We have to leave. Now."

"Now?" said Marcus, outraged. "But it's just getting interesting!"

"Nobody knows where we are!" Dorrie turned to Phillip. "How do we get back into Passaic?"

"Oh, but you can't," said Mistress Wu, sounding as pained as if she were being forced to strangle kittens. "You simply can't at the moment."

Dorrie suddenly did feel mad with a great jag of Mistress Wu's anxiety. "Why not?"

"Well, for one thing," said Phillip, "it sounds like we'd have to shoot you back through the hole with a cannon, and we don't have one of those on hand at the moment. Even if we did, right now you'd just sizzle against the hole rather magnificently and fall back into the pool in a deadish sort of way. The hole will be far too hot to travel back through until at least tomorrow—"

"Tomorrow!" cried Dorrie and Marcus together.

"Or a day or two after that."

"But our parents will think we've been kidnapped or something," said Dorrie.

"Well, there you're in luck," said Ursula. "Time has all but stopped in your Passaic for the moment, at least for those of us here in Petrarch's Library."

"Premium!" cried Marcus.

"For how long?" said Dorrie hoarsely.

"For the next four weeks or so," said Phillip, "or whenever you return to Passaic. Whichever comes first."

"Whichever comes first?" repeated Dorrie softly.

"I promise," said Phillip. "No one in Passaic has even noticed that you're gone."

Dorrie's heart beat slowly and hard as she closed her eyes and saw the pandemonium she and Marcus had left behind at the Pen and Sword Festival. Again, she saw herself falling through the floor of the Passaic Public Library and, at that very moment, all the shouting and running and sword-waving in the park coming to a grinding halt.

She caught her breath as a horrible, wonderful realization blossomed. Perhaps Tiffany still awaited her return and Dorrie hadn't forfeited anything to her yet. She hadn't yet lost the bet. And in the meantime—she looked out the marvelous, impossible window—there was all this.

"I'm so very sorry," said Mistress Wu, mournfully. "It's just how the Library works!"

Dorrie met Marcus's enthusiastic eyes with her own eagerly blazing ones.

"There's another matter," said Ursula. "The Lybrariad depends on Petrarch's Library as a secret headquarters from which to do our work." Her eyes flicked to Dorrie's hands and back so quickly that Dorrie wasn't sure she hadn't imagined it. "Now that you've found us, we need time to come to some decisions."

Dorrie reached for breath which with to speak. "What kind of decisions?"

"There are things you'll need to be told, things you'll need to understand about your situation," said Ursula carefully.

Mistress Wu wrung her handkerchief. "I've sent word to Hypatia. Once she returns, we can figure out what to do. Also,"

—she straightened up a line of sardines on their platter— "Francesco will want to speak with you."

Something in her tone made Dorrie's fears surge back past her wonder. "Who's Francesco?"

Ursula looked at Dorrie steadily. "Francesco D'Avila is our director of security. He's out of library, as well, at the moment. Dealing with more of that nasty Inquisition business."

"He can detect a threat just about anywhere," observed Phillip archly.

"Francesco is one of us," said Ursula. "A lybrarian. A good man."

"Deep, deep on the inside," said Phillip under his breath.

CHAPTER 7

SWORDS IN THE STACKS

I T WAS DECIDED THAT Phillip should keep Dorrie and
Marcus company for the night while they recovered.

"Though I daresay Francesco won't appreciate that we let
them sleep in the Mission Room," said Mistress Wu as she and
Ursula departed.

While Phillip lit a lantern in the darkening room, Dorrie
and Marcus sat in the bathrobe and dressing gown that Millie
had brought and feasted on the platters of food. Their wet
clothing hung over the fire screen, dripping and steaming
pleasantly. After stuffing themselves full of onion soup, sardines, slice after slice of yellow cheese, and a staggering number
of eclairs, Dorrie felt a deep weariness stealing over her. Phillip
turned down the lantern and settled himself in one of the fat
armchairs beside the fire. Dorrie and Marcus eased themselves
down beneath their blankets.

Watching the fire's dancing flames, still and quiet at last, Dorrie realized that her fingertips still felt faintly warm and had not really stopped feeling that way since she had come through the hole. She drew the hand that Tiffany had bashed out of the blankets. A crescent of blue-black darkness had formed at the base of her thumbnail. She tucked her hand back under the blankets and stared again at the fire.

She and Marcus truly were…*elsewhere*…with no Miranda to shout for her imaginary dog and no dinner pots to wash with her father and no familiar blue comforter with the hole that sighed feathers over her. And no chance of her mother easing open the door to whisper, "Good night, Sweet and Sour." But she and Marcus had stumbled upon something incredible, and it hadn't cost her even her bargain with Tiffany Tolliver.

Dorrie thought about the Irish monk on the other side of his archway. When she'd dashed past him, had he really been sitting in an entirely different time? One filled with oxcarts and court jesters and bows and arrows? Her head hurt pleasantly at the thought. Back in Passaic, now was now, the past almost a dream, and the future unknowable. In Petrarch's Library, now must be something else entirely.

Despite the shadow cast by the unmet director of security, a small thrill spun through Dorrie's chest. She fell asleep, leaving any farther thinking in the room to the mouse hunting for crumbs in a shadowy corner.

✳ ✳ ✳

After what seemed like mere minutes, Phillip woke Dorrie with a little shake and the news that she and Marcus had slept half the morning away, that he would soon have to leave on business outside Petrarch's Library, and that Ebba was on her way over to keep them company until Hypatia returned.

Dorrie stretched. "What should we do while we wait?"

"Well, I suppose you could curl up and read a book. We've got a few of those around. Or count dust motes. Or wash the windows in here." He gently shook Marcus, who responded with all the animation of a sack of sand. "Of course, if you're the sort of person who would prefer to explore the Library, well, there's no accounting for taste."

Dorrie grinned at Phillip and took over the job of waking Marcus. As she used her fists to pound her brother into groggy awareness, Phillip crouched by the fire and pushed a little three-legged iron pot deeper into the flames. "I'll eat a lot of things out of books, but I draw the line at coffee."

In the morning brightness, Dorrie noticed that over the mantel hung an enormous black chalkboard painted with a grid of white lines and words crowded in between the lines. At the top, large letters shifted and swam like eels before Dorrie's eyes, finally spelling out the words "Mission Docket."

"Why do the words in this place *do* that?" asked Dorrie.

Phillip glanced at the blackboard. "Ah, one of the Library's useful peculiarities. Instant translation. If I say or write it in Latin, you hear or see it in..."

"English," said Dorrie, catching on.

Phillip poured the steaming coffee into a mug. He held up the iron pot, beaming. "Coffee, anyone?"

"Sure," said Marcus, as though he drank it every day at home.

Phillip poured a second mug full and handed it to Marcus, who took a substantial sip. An instantaneous facial paralysis seemed to strike him. As soon as Phillip turned away, Marcus promptly spit the coffee back into the mug.

"Hand me that book of Basho poems, will you?" Phillip said to Dorrie, jerking his chin toward a thin volume with a marbled paper cover that sat on the cleared table. "Ursula brought it over when she realized you were going to sleep right through breakfast. Her own copy."

Dorrie passed the book to him. Phillip settled himself comfortably back in his chair and flipped through the book's pages. "You can't beat haiku for the quick breakfast." He stopped at a page near the back. "Ah! Here's just the thing." With the fingertips of one hand resting gently on the open book, Phillip cleared his throat. Seeming to focus all of his attention of the page below his fingertips, he began to read out loud. "Coolness of the melons, flecked with mud, in the morning dew."

Dorrie stared as Phillip began to draw his thumb and

forefinger together on the page as if trying to get hold of the end of a thread or the head of a pin. Something seemed to be growing between them. Dorrie gasped as the little book seemed to stretch and flex. In another moment, Phillip had eased a pale green melon from its pages and set it on the table. He looked up into Dorrie and Marcus's flabbergasted faces.

"Quite a nice one! Fruit isn't really my forte." He picked up a knife and jabbed it toward a basket sitting on the hearth. "Ursula brought those as well. Help yourself. She had to go back to the repair and preservation department. The Archivist came crawling in with a pounding headache about dawn and needed her attention."

Marcus reached into the basket and helped himself to a flat rectangle made of nuts and seed and bits of fruit, all held together in a sticky amber glaze.

"Will the archivist guy be all right?" asked Dorrie.

"Perfectly," said Phillip, cutting the melon into pieces.

Dorrie looked up at the words written below "Mission Docket." "Imperiled Subject...Nature of Threat..." she read out loud, enjoying the sensation of watching the initially unreadable yellow letters coil and straighten to form words she could comprehend. "Wheren...Assigned Lybrarian...Outcome."

Her eyes traveled down the names below the heading "Imperiled Subject." She read the names silently: "Simon Morin, Casimir Liszinski, Su Shi, Katharina Henot." The column labeled "Nature of Threat" was almost too horrible to read. Dorrie's eyes skittered over words like "beheaded" and "burned at stake" and "tortured."

"So all these people," said Dorrie. "They're the ones in trouble for writing something?"

"That's right," said Phillip, wafting the steam from the coffee toward his nose. "Wrote something someone didn't like." He took a small sip. "It's always the limericks that seem to get people in the most unexpected trouble."

Dorrie's eyes caught on the last name listed under "Imperiled Subject." Petrarch's Library. Her eyes ran across the words that filled the little boxes next to that entry: "Persistent Inquiries by Person Unknown, Timbuktu…1597…Kash…Ongoing."

"Petrarch's Library is an imperiled subject?" asked Dorrie.

"Oh, not to worry," said Phillip. "It makes the list regularly. Rumors of imminent discovery. Innuendo. People seek it like lost Atlantis. Our director of security is a great one for thoroughly checking out each and every whiff of a threat to our inconspicuousness or any plots against us."

"What *are* these?" exploded Marcus, staring at what was left of his sticky bar, a look of utter satisfaction on his face.

"Ambrosia," said Phillip. "One of our lybrarians reads them out when she's worried, and she's frantic about her friend Socrates."

Dorrie's eyes flashed to the Mission Docket. *Socrates.* She'd just seen that name on the board…near the top.

Marcus shoved the last of the bar into his mouth. "It must be such a bummer to be named Socrates."

"How so?" asked Phillip.

"You tell people your name," said Marcus, "and all anyone can think about is *the* Socrates."

Phillip pulled a piece of ambrosia out of the basket. "Well, I am thinking about *the* Socrates."

"See!"

Phillip lifted one eyebrow. "Yes but that's because I'm also *talking* about *the* Socrates."

Marcus stopped chewing. "Socrates, the ancient Greek philosopher. Socrates who had to drink the poison hemlock. Socrates who was big into asking questions?"

Phillip put his mug down. "Otherwise known as the Socrates of Athens who was charged with impiety, made to stand trial, argued his own defense, was found guilty, and sentenced to drink a pretty goblet full of the stuff. Yes, the one and only."

"Isn't it a little late for worrying?" said Marcus. "I mean, didn't that all happen thousands of years ago?"

"You forget," said Phillip, crossing one leg over the other. "From Petrarch's Library, one can walk into an Athens in which Socrates hasn't yet drunk the hemlock."

A knock sounded on the door.

"Come in," boomed Phillip.

Ebba, the girl they'd seen the previous day, poked her head around the door. She smiled shyly at Dorrie and Marcus.

Phillip packed up the coffeepot and mugs. "You can find Ursula over in the repair and preservation department, if you need her. Ebba will take you to the Apprentice Attics and find a room for you there. It's been a pleasure to meet you. When I return, we must talk about the state of alchemy—I mean, chemistry—in the twenty-first century." He hurried out the door.

After they'd changed from their bathrobes back into their clothes, they met Ebba out in the polished marble hallway.

Ebba smiled uncertainly at Dorrie and Marcus. "So how do you feel about bicycles?"

They only had to walk a short way until they found four of them parked in a jumble by a broad brick stairway. Stuffing their robes in Ebba's satchel, they pedaled along behind her, making a dizzying number of turns. Through open doorways and passing them in the corridors, Dorrie glimpsed people in turbans and people in bowlers. People in hoods, fezzes, bonnets, colossal wigs, and straw sombreros. People in saris and gum boots, bow ties and kilts, habits and high-heeled shoes, kimonos, bloomers, robes, doublet and hose, fringed leather, gowns of every length, and trousers of every sort of cloth. Often in very odd combinations. Many stared at Dorrie, and she couldn't help but stare right back.

At the top of a flight of stairs, they left the bikes leaning against a wall.

Ebba turned suddenly. "I know you're there, Kenzo."

A younger boy with lank black hair and ears that stood out like sugar-bowl handles leaped out from behind an enormous urn and scowled. "How?"

"I could hear you breathing."

The boy joined them as they trooped down the stairs, staring at Marcus with astounded bright eyes. "Is it true you busted a hole into Petrarch's Library?"

Ebba looked embarrassed. "Kenzo, don't accuse them of that."

"I'm not accusing. I'm just asking."

"No, we just fell through one that was already there," said Marcus. "At least that's what we're going to tell Scuggans."

"So, do you live here?" Dorrie asked Ebba, as they turned a corner into a room hung with tapestries and filled with heavy wooden trunks.

"Of course," said Kenzo, looking at Dorrie as though she'd just fallen a few notches in his estimation.

Ebba pushed her yellow headband back. "Kenzo, they've never been here before. They don't know." She led them up a narrow set of wooden stairs. "Kenzo lives here with his mother in some rooms off the Dutch Royal Archives Library. She works in the reference department."

"Ebba's an apprentice," said Kenzo. "I'm *going* to be one. Maybe next year."

"Apprentice what?" asked Marcus.

"Lybrarian," said Kenzo. "What else?"

Ebba stopped on the landing and looked at Kenzo sternly, her hands on her hips. "Aren't you supposed to be helping with lunch?"

"Okay, okay," said Kenzo, kicking the spindles as he made his way back down the stairs.

"How did you and Kenzo get here?" asked Dorrie, as they continued up the next flight of stairs, wondering if they had also plunged accidentally into Petrarch's Library.

"Kenzo came here when he was just a baby, after his mother had to leave Japan. The Lybrariad rescued them. I was born here. Lots of people live here who aren't lybrarians. Refugees, mostly. Or the children of refugees. My parents were from Timbuktu, but now they live out in Haven, the village on the other side of the island. I spend some time here and some time with them."

As they rounded a corner to a carpeted corridor, Ebba almost ran into a tall woman who had just emerged from a stone archway without looking. "I beg your pardon, Ebba," the woman said, looking distractedly at them for a moment before moving on. She was dressed all in white, the cloth hanging in a loose drape over one shoulder. A thin circlet pressed down on her long, gently curling dark locks, which were pulled back into a loose bunch at the back of her head.

Dorrie looked back at the archway and caught her breath. Above it, between two images of a sword crossed with a quill pen, the words "Athens, 399 BCE" glowed. Beyond the archway stood a small white room with a table against one wall, upon which stood a rack of scrolls and little clay pots. Along the top of the walls, dolphins made of bits of blue tile cavorted. "That's a Spoke Library in there, isn't it?" breathed Dorrie.

A tinkling sound caught Dorrie's attention. Two rough stone ledges protruded from the stones on the left side of the archway. The bottom one stuck out farther than the top one, and upon each stood a large clay pot. Water trickled from the higher pot into the lower pot through a clay tube.

"It's a water clock," said Ebba, peering into the lower pot. "Every hour, the water level rises to another line." She pointed at a set of deeply etched marks in the clay. "See?"

Beside each mark, figures danced, and in another moment, Dorrie could read "9 a.m." and "10 a.m.," hour by hour up to the top of the pot, which read "12 p.m."

"All the archways have a clock on the left and a calendar on the right," said Ebba. "So we know what time it is out in the Spoke Libraries. Sometimes time runs slower or faster out there than it does in Petrarch's Library."

Dorrie looked back down the corridor where the woman

in white was just disappearing around a corner. "So she just walked out of a whole other time."

"Well, yeah," said Ebba, as if Dorrie had just announced that eyes were for seeing.

"Then how come she looks like she just came back from getting a cavity filled?" asked Marcus. "I mean, she just rode a time-space-continuum roller coaster."

"Is she the one who's friends with Socrates?" asked Dorrie.

Ebba looked surprised and then worried. "How…how did you know?"

"Phillip told us about her, and we ate some of her ambrosia."

Relief flooded Ebba's face. "Oh. Yes, that's Aspasia. She's been trying to convince the city of Athens not to bring Socrates to trial, but I don't think she's getting very far. For now, the history books tell us that he'll be summoned to appear before the legal magistrate in about a week. A citizen is going to charge him with the crime."

"The impiety thing?" asked Marcus.

"Exactly. For saying that the moon and the sun are rocks rather than gods, or something like that. Oh, and also that the stuff he says is making people do bad things."

"Like what?" Marcus snorted. "Ask irritating questions?"

Dorrie felt a snort of her own indignation coming on. "Yeah, how can you *make* someone do something with words, unless they're under some kind of magic spell or part zombie or something?"

"Or you get the person to agree to a stupid bet," said Marcus, his expression one of freshly laundered innocence.

Dorrie shot him a thoroughly unlaundered look of irritation.

Ebba looked from Dorrie to Marcus. "You're not really enemies of Petrarch's Library or part of some new Foundation out to destroy us or anything, right?"

"What? No!" said Dorrie. "We'd never even heard of Petrarch's Library before yesterday."

Ebba grinned. "I didn't think so."

They continued down the hall. "So, how exactly do the librarians here keep people from, you know, being set on fire for saying the wrong thing?" Dorrie asked.

Ebba looked confused. "Oh, lots of ways. It depends on the situation."

"Maybe their stubby little pencils are really fire extinguishers," said Marcus.

"But librarians…" Dorrie chose her words carefully. "They put books on shelves and check out books, or help you find something out. They don't seem very…" She took a deep breath. "Strong or brave or the kind of people who'd know how to do, well, daring things like that."

"Oh, no," said Ebba, stopping short and looking shocked. "A properly trained lybrarian is one of the most fearless and fearsome beings in the world!"

"Fearsome?" said Dorrie, trying not to sound doubtful.

Ebba must have heard the dubiousness in Dorrie's voice anyway. "They're wonderful at finding out things and slipping around undetected and getting the right information into the right hands. And of course they're all masters of..." She looked from Dorrie to Marcus. "The Lybrariad thoroughly trains them! Come on, I'll show you." She launched herself forward at a run with Dorrie and Marcus pelting after her.

After a series of hallways and stairways and confusing turns, Ebba finally slowed down and then barreled through a set of battered brown doors.

Marcus elbowed Dorrie. "It's going to be librarians learning how to yell at people for bringing soda into the library. I know it."

"Shhh," hissed Dorrie, pushing open the doors.

They found themselves standing on the edge of a large room that rang with the sound of heavy sticks being whacked against one another, and the shouts and grunts of people kicking and punching in unison in one of the room's far corners. Spears and swords of every conceivable size and shape hung from the walls in great profusion.

"Those are librarians?" cried Dorrie, so loudly that a few people in the process of hauling themselves up long ropes hung from the ceiling stopped climbing and stared at her for a moment.

Marcus's mouth hung open.

Ebba turned to them, her face proud. "This is the Gymnasium, where the lybrarians learn their combat skills. In case they hit a brick wall with the research and stealth. And *only* for defensive use."

"Combat skills," repeated Dorrie, sounding very much like Marcus murmuring about Egeria's mermaid-forever hair.

Dorrie's fingers tingled, and her pulse quickened as not far from where they stood, a man in breeches and a billowy white shirt forced a woman in a long gown backward with a blindingly fast succession of sword thrusts and parries. A knot of string held back the man's thick, dark hair. For a moment, his blade and that of the woman came together in a quivering cross. His nose loomed over his face like a monument. It sucked mercilessly at Dorrie's attention.

The woman grunted and the swords slid against each other, first in one direction and then another. The woman tried to thrust, and the man blocked her blade and began to drive her backward again with the casual attention of a shopper pushing a grocery cart. They moved nothing like Mr. Kornberger did when he demonstrated a move. They were a hundred, a thousand times better!

"They're ninja librarians!" crowed Marcus.

A staggering realization swelled and burst into a fountain of blazing sparks inside Dorrie's chest. Here in Petrarch's Library, her desire to wield a sword made a dumbfounding kind of sense.

Chapter 8
The Apprentice Table

B USY REPLAYING THE SWORD fight she'd seen, Dorrie hardly remembered the bicycle ride from the Gymnasium to where Ebba finally stopped and dismounted, leaning her bicycle up against a wall. Only when they emerged into a grassy, sunlit space the size of a football field did Dorrie come back to her senses. She blinked in the warm brightness.

"This is the Commons," said Ebba, spreading her arms wide. "It's kind of the center of Petrarch's Library."

All around the green expanse, the warren of Petrarch's Library rose to various heights. Sunshine poured down onto the Commons and most of the buildings, but patches of thunderous clouds hung low over a few spots in the architectural tangle. Beneath them, various mists and drizzles and soaking storms blew.

Ebba followed Dorrie's gaze to one of the downpours. "The libraries come here with their own weather. There's a perpetual snowstorm over at the Abbey Library of Saint Gall. The apprentices have snowball fights there on the first day of every month."

Ebba led them along a path of crushed shells that wound around clumps of trees and gardens of various sorts. "Some of the lybrarians like to garden."

As they walked along a hedge of hydrangeas, Marcus snorted. "If I could travel all over the time map, there's no way I'd waste my time messing around with daffodils and—" He broke off, his mouth open, staring over the hedge, and then whispered hoarsely, "There she is."

Dorrie craned her neck to see. "Who?"

"Egeria," choked out Marcus.

Dorrie stood on tiptoe. At some distance on the other side, Egeria, her hair caught up in a long braid, knelt with a group of people next to a raised bed full of bright green, fuzzy-looking plants.

Ebba pushed a branch aside. "Oh, yes, she's way into plants. That's her beginner European field-foraging practicum. It's the first one she's ever taught. She only just made lybrarian this past midwinter. I think she might be one of the youngest ever. She's only sixteen."

At that moment, Egeria looked up and waved. She had a smudge of dirt on her cheek, covering half of the spray of large freckles sprinkled on her nose. She came to them, smiling. "You've dried."

Marcus seemed to have relapsed into slip shock and just stared at her.

"Since yesterday, I mean," she added.

Dorrie and Ebba looked at Marcus in alarm as he began to laugh maniacally, his face turning a dazzling shade of red. He stopped as abruptly as he'd begun. "Nice, uh, garden," he choked out, sounding as though one of the larger statues from the Reference Room had been laid across his chest.

Egeria looked brightly around at the well-tended beds. "Oh, are you interested in plants?"

"Totally! Plants are just so...so..." Marcus worked his hands around in circles that Dorrie thought were meant to look enthusiastic. "Awesome!" He looked wildly around. "The way they grow up on those stems, with that wide variety of... shapes and smells and...roots and, and—"

Dorrie widened her eyes at him, shaking her head faintly from side to side to warn him that he had crossed into the land of total idiocy, but he seemed unable to extricate himself from his sentence. Before Marcus could embarrass himself farther, Ebba explained that they needed to get to lunch, and Dorrie hauled him on down the path.

At one end of the Commons, Ebba stopped at a two-story, timber-and-plaster building with a steep thatched roof. Diamond-paned windows stood open in the sunshine, and a dozen bicycles and handcarts were scattered around the entrance. A painted sign swinging over the massive wooden door read: "The Sharpened Quill."

Inside, cutlery clattered and voices rose and fell in conversation beneath a low-beamed ceiling. Heads turned toward them as they entered and the room quieted slightly, then returned to its original volume.

"The apprentices usually sit over there," said Ebba pointing to a long trestle table in a corner where a crowd of younger people sat. Kenzo noticed them immediately and began to wave at them wildly.

Millie, the other girl who'd discovered them, looked up from her seat nearby. Dorrie smiled tentatively at her. Millie looked straight at Dorrie for a moment and then, without smiling back, turned to speak to a girl sitting next to her. The girl, small and fragile-looking with long, dark hair and eyes like darting green fish, simply stared at Dorrie and Marcus.

Ebba pointed to the back of the room where a table laden with serving bowls and trays stood against the only section of wall not lined with rough-looking, saggy bookshelves stuffed with well-thumbed volumes. "You get your own food. Everything's over there. Come on."

When they arrived at the apprentices' table after filling their plates, most of those seated stopped eating and talking to stare at Dorrie and Marcus.

Ebba unslung her satchel. "Can you make some room?"

Nobody moved.

"She said make some room, Goggle Eyes," ordered an older girl with a little brown velvet hat perched on her head. In a rush of knocking knees and sliding plates, the apprentices crowded closer to each other. Millie and the girl with the darting eyes moved last and slowly and not very far. Ebba, Dorrie, and Marcus sat down.

"I'm Mathilde," said the girl who had spoken, sticking her hand out across the table. She had merry brown eyes and thick chestnut hair parted in the middle and pinned in two coils to either side of her head. To Dorrie, she looked a little older than Marcus, maybe fifteen.

"I'm Dorrie. Dorrie Barnes." She took Mathilde's hand, glancing at her brother. "And this is Marcus."

"So are you really keyhands?" sang out Kenzo, while the rest of the table froze, some going pink in the cheeks.

"What's a keyhand?" asked Dorrie.

"You don't know?" asked Kenzo, astounded. "Maybe you really are Foundation."

"Kenzo," Ebba said, shocked. "You're being rude again!"

"How is that rude?" Kenzo protested.

Mathilde waved a chicken leg. "Because anyone who isn't Foundation would be insulted at the question,"

"If that person even knew what you meant by 'Foundation.'" said Marcus.

101

Kenzo shrugged. "Millie said you probably were."

"Yeah, well, Millie says a lot of things," said Mathilde, looking pointedly up the table to where Millie sat. Millie gave Mathilde a hard look back. Mathilde resumed her introductions, pointing across the table at a giant of a boy with a lantern jaw and a shock of red hair. "That's Sven." The boy nodded in a morose sort of way. "That's Izel," she said pointing to the girl with the darting eyes who sat next to Millie. Lastly, she patted the boy beside her. His dark lashes were startlingly long. "Saul. Of Ye Olde Tarsus." She sighed melodramatically. "He doesn't think girls are much good."

A couple of the older apprentices farther down the table snorted. Saul put down his piece of toast and extended his hand to Dorrie and then to Marcus. "Don't listen to her. She likes to make fun of me."

Mathilde shook her head so that the gold and brown feather in her hat bobbed mischievously. "What about: 'But I suffer not a woman to teach, nor to usurp authority over the man, but to be in silence.' Paul in a letter to Timothy: First Timothy, chapter 2, verse 12." She leaned forward, nodding conspiratorially. "Paul was once named Saul. He changed his name."

"I'm obviously not THAT Saul. I would never write that and you know it!" Saul protested. He turned to Dorrie and Marcus. "I wouldn't. I really wouldn't."

Dorrie looked back at Saul, bewildered.

"Not yet," said Mathilde primly. She leaned toward Dorrie. "So wheren are you from?"

Around the table, the chewing of food largely ceased. Everyone at the table looked with rapt attention at Dorrie and Marcus.

"Shouldn't we let them eat before we start diving at them with questions?" protested Ebba.

"It's okay," said Dorrie. "But...what does 'wheren' mean?"

"Sorry," said Mathilde. "It's just a word we use around here. It means both 'where' and 'when' at once. 'Wheren are you going?' or 'Wheren are you from?'"

"We're from Passaic, New Jersey," said Marcus. Piously, he added, "A world-class city."

"What century?" blurted out Kenzo.

Dorrie could hear the apprentices holding their collective breath.

"Twenty-first," Marcus answered.

Excited murmurings rose from the table. Even Millie looked up.

"So is anyone living on Mars yet?" asked a tall, dark-haired boy.

"Not yet," Marcus replied, biting into his own toast. "But people have been to the moon."

"Told you!" said Kenzo loudly, elbowing the tall boy hard.

"Are people still listening to ragtime music?" Ebba asked.

Marcus stopped chewing. "Ragtime? Are you serious?" He

looked around the circle of expectant faces. "What's the last year that Petrarch's Library opens into?"

Saul shrugged. "1912."

Dorrie's mouth fell open. "So you don't know about anything that happened in the world after 1912?"

Millie looked daggers at Dorrie over the top of the newspaper she held. "And I doubt that you know about anything that happened before 1912."

Marcus leaned back, his arms folded behind his head. "Two words, people: electric guitar."

Now the apprentices looked at each other confused and amazed.

"Yes, but can women vote in any of the nations yet?" asked Mathilde.

"Of course," said Dorrie, suddenly wondering exactly how long ago women had started voting.

A surprised and pleased murmur traveled around the table.

Mathilde's eyes shone. "How wonderful!"

"Telepathy?" asked Sven. "Can people communicate by telepathy yet?"

"Uh," said Dorrie, "I don't think so." Sven looked so disappointed that Dorrie racked her brain for something that might impress him.

"We have cell phones," said Marcus. "Which is sort of the same idea."

Dorrie rolled her eyes. "They're nothing alike!"

"Sure they are," said Marcus. "With a cell phone, I can send a message to you even if you're miles away."

"How does it work?" asked Ebba excitedly.

Dorrie frowned. "It's not *real* telepathy! It's just people carrying cell phones."

The apprentices looked confused again.

"What's a cell phone?" asked Ebba.

Dorrie's face screwed up with the challenge of trying to describe it. "It's a... It's a..." She felt embarrassed as the apprentices waited with bated breath for her answer. C'mon, Dorrie, she thought to herself. You use one almost every day!

Instead of answering, Dorrie decided to ask her own burning question. "So do apprentices learn how to sword-fight and stuff?"

"Of course," said Millie, as though Dorrie had asked a particularly stupid question. "You can't serve as a lybrarian unless you've mastered a combat skill."

Dorrie's heart gave a glad leap, remembering the way the man and woman in the Gymnasium had made their swords positively dance. "Who teaches you?"

Sven mashed his peas into his mashed potatoes with artistic flair. "Mostly, the resident lybrarians."

"Their main job is to turn the regular old librarians who come here every year into true lybrarians," said Saul.

"If they can," said Mathilde.

"But we can train alongside them," said Ebba.

"And learn what exactly?" asked Marcus.

"How to pick locks," said Kenzo.

"How to snatch a magazine out of the middle of a stack of periodicals with the speed of a cobra," added Sven with just as much pride.

"It's very thorough training," said Saul.

Sven put down his fork and began to count off on his fingers. "There's cataloguing, deception and impersonation, publishing law, stealth and illicit entry, library organization, unarmed combat, research skills, armed combat, book repair, fire and explosives—"

Mathilde took a bite out of a large apple. "I think they get the idea."

Dorrie did. Sven's list had filled her with a giddy excitement that threatened to lift her right off the bench.

Kenzo seemed not to have heard Mathilde. "Patron relations, horsemanship," he said, now counting on his toes. "Water training, espionage, escape and concealment, meteorology, geography, field survival—"

"Stealth and illicit entry?" crowed Marcus. "Prime cut! This place is now my official personal paradise!"

"We shouldn't be telling them all of this stuff about us," Millie cut in harshly. "They really could be enemies."

Dorrie felt her face go hot as a sudden silence descended on the table.

Mathilde looked hard at Millie over her apple. "And you should do a little reading in *Martine's Handbook of Etiquette and Guide to True Politeness*. Didn't Mistress Wu ask us to treat them as guests?"

Millie's angry gaze swept around the table, avoiding Marcus and Dorrie. "I'm just looking out for the Lybrariad's safety. If Francesco was here—"

A sudden gust of wind blowing through the door of the Sharpened Quill made them all look up. Mathilde yelped and slid down in her seat, as though someone had suddenly yanked her feet down through a hole in the ground.

Dorrie watched a woman her own size stump sensibly toward the food table. She wore a white blouse with a high collar, a shapeless gray bell of a skirt that matched the color of her hair, and a string of pearly pink beads. An enormous pair of cloudy, gold-rimmed eyeglasses covered half her dewlapped face. Even from across the room, the eyes behind the glasses seemed to crack and spark with pale blue all-seeing fire.

"Have something overdue, Mathilde?" asked Saul, reaching across Kenzo's plate for the water pitcher.

"Something lost, more likely," said Izel, as though very sorry she had to be the one to share that fact.

"Well, don't all stare at her!" said Mathilde, disappearing

entirely beneath the wide planks of the table. Dorrie and the others turned back to face each other.

"Who is she?" asked Marcus.

Saul poured himself some water. "That's Mistress Lovelace. She runs the Library's circulation desk. If a lybrarian wants a sari to wear in India? Weapons, hats, maps, footwear, coin of the realm? He has to get it from her."

"He or *she* has to get it from her," Mathilde hissed from below. "Mistress Lovelace can probably smell me."

"Guilty terror does have a certain scent," Saul said, taking a bite out of a chicken leg.

Ebba grabbed Dorrie's shoulder. "Oh, I was supposed to give you something." She dug in her satchel. "Here." She pulled out two rectangles of stiff, creamy paper and handed one each to Dorrie and Marcus.

"What is it?" asked Dorrie as the microscopic writing covering the little card resolved into something she could read.

"Library card," said Saul. "Mistress Lovelace is very particular about issuing them promptly to guests and new residents." He glanced over at the director of circulation. "She's quite particular about just about everything, really."

Millie began to angrily cram her newspaper into her satchel, as if the issuing of library cards was some sort of final outrage.

Dorrie looked more closely at the card. On the blank line in the middle of the card reserved for a borrower's name, someone had written "Unknown Entrant No. 1" in a firm, cursive hand in violet ink. Three jam-packed typed paragraphs of a particularly tiny type filled up the rest of the card. Dorrie read the slightly larger typed words that ran around the four edges of the embossed card like a border: "Marking, staining, tearing, breaking, or otherwise causing damage to lent items is punishable by Library statute with fine or indentured servitude, and the circulation director will prosecute for all offenses."

Dorrie understood a little better now why Mathilde was under the table. She looked up at the apprentices. "I don't think I'd have the nerve to take anything out."

"You already have," said Marcus, plucking the card Dorrie held out of her hand and tossing her the other one. On the back of the new card were alternating columns marked "Lent" and "Returned." In the first box under "Lent," the same firm hand had written: "Blue dressing gown with fur cuffs and collar" and a date.

"She's not mean," said Ebba. "She, just, well…she doesn't make exceptions."

"Could you at least tell me when she leaves?" Mathilde said coldly from beneath the table.

"Could be a while," said Saul. "She's just settling down for what could be a good, long chitchat."

"A one-sided chitchat," purred Izel.

"Why one-sided?" asked Dorrie, looking over at the small, deeply tanned man who sat across from Mistress Lovelace.

Saul looked serious. He stuck out his tongue and made a scissoring motion with his fingers just below it. "Someone cut out the riding master's tongue."

Dorrie felt instantly sick. "That's awful."

A young woman with an armload of books had elbowed her way over to the apprentice table. She handed a folded-up piece of paper to Ebba. "Message for you," she panted before moving on.

Ebba unfolded it, and her brow furrowed. "Francesco's back." She looked up at Dorrie and Marcus. "The director of security. He wants to see you."

Another uncomfortable silence took hold.

"Bad luck that," Mathilde finally said from beneath the table.

Dorrie felt her mouth going dry. "I thought we were supposed to meet with Hypatia."

"I guess she's still not back," said Ebba, staring at Francesco's message.

Kenzo cocked his head to one side. "Millie said that Francesco will probably want to maroon you out on the other side of an archway. Maybe in Outer Mongolia."

"*What!*" Dorrie and Marcus said together. Dorrie's stomach lurched. From her close reading of the Passaic Public Library's entire collection of novels featuring pirates, she knew just what "marooned" meant. Being left behind somewhere with no way to return home.

"Don't listen to him," said Ebba, scanning the contents of the note. "Maroonings have only happened very rarely. Only when someone's found out about Petrarch's Library who shouldn't and might do it harm and…" Her words came to an awkward, stumbling stop.

A chill crept its way down Dorrie's spine.

Kenzo shrugged. "Outer Mongolia's not the worst—"

"I know you're not enemies," said Ebba, giving Dorrie a brave attempt at a smile. "He'll see that. It'll be all right."

Mathilde eased herself out from under the table, her gaze sweeping across the room. "You show them the way to his office and I'll try to find Mistress Wu."

"I've got a baaaaad feeling about this, Chewie," muttered Marcus.

Chapter 9
Accidental Keyhands

E BBA LEFT THEM IN front of a heavy, wooden door set in a curved stone wall with a torch flickering on either side. "His office is through the door and up the stairs."

Dorrie, her teeth on the point of chattering, nodded dumbly, as a man dressed in lederhosen roller-skated past them. Earlier in the day, she would have enjoyed guessing his home place and time, but now the word "maroon" blinked on and off in her head in red-drenched neon letters. If the director of security thought they posed a danger to Petrarch's Library, would he just decide to toss Dorrie and Marcus out into Attila the Hun's lap or into a medieval city full of Black Plague, never to return?

"I'll help look for Mistress Wu," said Ebba, her eyes wide and distressed.

When Ebba had skittered out of sight around a corner,

Dorrie grabbed hold of Marcus' T-shirt. "Should we run away? Try to hide until we can get back through that hole?" With no small horror, Dorrie realized she had no idea in which direction the room with the swimming pool and the hole lay.

Marcus pulled at his hair as if the tension on it would help him think better. "We haven't done anything wrong. We'll just explain."

Dorrie shivered. "Yeah, but what if he doesn't believe us?"

"I've *got* to see Egeria again!" bellowed Marcus.

Dorrie stared at him, boggled. "Marcus, we might never see Mom and Dad and Miranda again if we do the wrong thing!"

He pressed his fingertips to his temples. "Can I just have a minute to think here?"

The door swung open with an arthritic groan. Dorrie found herself face-to-face with a large man with stooped shoulders dressed in what looked like an old-fashioned police officer's uniform. A black egg-shaped helmet sat rakishly on his head. For a moment, sucking on a toothpick, he simply looked at them, while Dorrie's heart thumped with more and more force.

Finally, he doffed his helmet, one corner of his mouth crooking upward in a grin. "Mr. Gormly I am, and you don't look all that threatening to me, whatever the boss says." Dorrie thought she saw the man wink and felt a little rush of gratitude. Mr. Gormly led them up a narrow wooden stairway that wound round and round. She couldn't help but think that in fairy tales, no good ever seemed to come to people at the top of towers. She felt for Marcus's hand behind her. Remarkably, he let her squeeze it hard and even dig her nails into it a little.

Mr. Gormly led them into a gloomy circular room with one thin slit of a window. Heavy wooden file cabinets lined the walls. A man Dorrie supposed was the director of security sat writing at a small, scarred table. A dark moustache drooped thinly over the ends of his upper lip in waxed curves, and the graying hair on his head was pulled back into a tight ponytail. A black patch very much like the one that Rosa had worn in Passaic for fun covered one of his eyes. On the table lay a sword that looked a whole lot like the one Dorrie had borrowed from Tiffany and dropped somewhere in Petrarch's Library. Beside the table leaned her bag.

After a long moment, he stood, his craggy face grim, a long sword hanging at his side. His one visible brown eye bored into Dorrie's. "Who sent you?"

The dispassionate, measured manner in which he spoke made Dorrie's insides go icy. She had the distinct feeling that he wouldn't hesitate to throw her out the very skinny window if he felt she was a threat to Petrarch's Library.

"Nobody sent us," stuttered Dorrie.

"How did you make that hole?" Francesco demanded in his clipped, cold way, dangerous icebergs floating between the words.

"We didn't," said Dorrie, her voice a squeak.

Francesco stepped around the table, his heels pounding dully on the carpet, and halted in front of Dorrie and Marcus.

Without a muscle on his face moving, Francesco seized Dorrie's hand.

"Let go of her," cried Marcus, hauling on Dorrie's other arm.

"Hey!" shouted Dorrie, struggling to free herself as Francesco stared at her fingertips intently. Francesco let her go but only, thought Dorrie, because he'd finished scrutinizing her hand. Her terrified thoughts stampeding, Dorrie lunged for the sword on the table and pointed its quivering tip at Francesco. "Let us go! We don't want to be marooned!"

Francesco, looking utterly unfazed, stared stonily at her, his one visible eye visibly narrowing.

"Two words, Sister," said Marcus in a strangled voice, as Francesco changed the position of his left hand ever so slightly. "Stage. Combat."

Her breath rasping, Dorrie licked her lips, fighting to keep the sword steady.

"Dispensing the best of Petrarch Library's hospitality, are we?" said a voice from the doorway.

Keeping her sword pointed at Francesco, Dorrie whipped her head around. The man with the enormous nose whom she'd seen sparring in the Gymnasium now lounged in the doorway staring at Francesco. He looked unaccountably amused. "It's definitely a marooning you've decided on, have you?"

Francesco marched heavily back to his desk. "That would be a wonderfully simple solution."

The man in the doorway raised an eyebrow at Dorrie. "If you're going to start a sword fight, best not to do it with a blunt-tipped practice foil." He gestured quickly for her to lower her sword. Hastily, not knowing why she trusted him, Dorrie brought the tip of her blade down.

The newcomer's eyes fell on Mr. Gormly. "Ah, Mr. Gormly, I see you've agreed to serve in the new position of official Peeping Tom."

Though Mr. Gormly simply examined his fingernails, Francesco's eyes flashed. "Security guard in the service of the Lybrariad, if you please, Savi."

"A travesty," said Savi.

"A necessity in these days," growled Francesco.

"I came to talk to you about Kash."

"I'm busy at the moment."

"Perhaps you've noticed that he has not yet returned from his mission."

"And perhaps you've noticed that there's a gaping hole over the baths that looks nothing like an archway. In fact it looks like someone or something blew it into existence with a barrel of cosmic gunpowder."

"Hence the interrogation."

"Call it what you will. We have to consider the possibility that someone or some organization, possibly even a reborn Foundation, has succeeded in forcing a way into Petrarch's Library. Kash's intelligence warned us of just that possibility."

Savi looked Marcus and Dorrie over. "Funny, I would have expected the sword of a Foundation operative to be a touch sharper."

Francesco glared at Savi. "Spoken like a true cavalier." He gripped the pommel of his sword. "Make light of the danger if you must, but the security of the Lybrariad and its mission rests on my shoulders."

"But we're not a danger!" burst out Dorrie.

"So you say," replied Francesco grimly. "And yet, your little knitting needle there was found in the Reference Room." His eyes found Dorrie's again, pinning her with their intensity. "What did you want there?"

"We were just looking for a way out!" cried Marcus.

"I'm not sure I can afford to believe that."

Savi gave a hard little laugh. "Beware that in trying to oppose the Foundation, you don't join its ranks yourself, Francesco D'Avila."

Francesco's face drained of all color. He blew a hard breath through his nose. "Tread carefully around my honor, or you'll lose yours altogether."

A dangerous light seemed to flicker in Savi's eyes. "If my honor and I must ever part, and I don't intend that they shall, you will not be a factor."

"If you're quite through," said Francesco, "I have a job to take care of here."

His low tone sent ripples of fear through Dorrie's limbs.

"What about the whole 'innocent until proven guilty' thing?" cried Marcus.

"It's not fair to maroon us just because you don't believe us!" cried Dorrie.

"She does have a point," said a new voice.

"Hypatia," said Francesco, in a tone of surprised reverence.

Dorrie turned to see a woman with a headful of dark, loose curls streaked with gray gliding through the doorway, with Madame Wu panting behind her. Madame Wu stopped for a moment to straighten a stack of books on a file cabinet.

"May I?" said Hypatia, gesturing at Francesco's chair.

"Of course," he said, giving her room to pass. As she settled into the chair, Francesco eyeballed Madame Wu. "In my absence, you should have informed Mr. Gormly immediately of last night's events."

"Phillip and Ursula and I really didn't think it…"—here Madame Wu glanced back at Mr. Gormly—"necessary."

Francesco pulled at one side of his moustache. "I'm not sure any of you did any thinking at—"

"If you please, Francesco," interrupted Hypatia. She looked from Dorrie to Marcus with a patient, penetrating expression. Dorrie tried to keep breathing evenly and not stare at the thin silvery scars that meandered over Hypatia's dark face.

"What interesting circumstances in which to meet you. I'm Hypatia, current director of Petrarch's Library." She glanced at Francesco. "I know you have concerns, Francesco, and understandably so, but let's not jump to conclusions."

Dorrie looked into Hypatia's calm green eyes, wanting to trust her. "We weren't after anything in the Reference Room. We just wanted to find a way back out."

A small smile played on Hypatia's lips. "And who can blame you, really?"

Francesco dug his hand into Dorrie's bag and pulled out a red book. "And how do you explain your possession of this?"

Mistress Wu gave a little gasp.

"I know it's overdue," said Dorrie, wondering if these lybrarians shared Mr. Scuggans's abhorrence of irresponsible borrowers. "I was going to return it yesterday."

Hypatia looked at Dorrie oddly. "Overdue from what library?"

"The Passaic Public Library," said Dorrie. Even as she spoke the words, Dorrie uncomfortably absorbed the fact that the book, though red like the Passaic Public Library's copy of *The Three Musketeers*, in no other way resembled it. This book looked old, its leather cover cracked. Faded gold symbols had been dug into the leather to spell out a title. They weren't letters Dorrie even recognized. Francesco laid the book in front of Hypatia, who paused for a moment before flipping it open. She tilted her head, clearly disconcerted.

"That's not my book," said Dorrie hoarsely.

Hypatia slowly turned a few more pages. The pages were filled with faded, rust-colored writing, spelled out in the same unfamiliar letters. Sometimes the writing was loose and scrawling and sometimes crabbed, as if the writer couldn't decide whether the book had more than enough room for his or her thoughts, or not nearly enough. In the book's middle, someone had cut the shape of a five-pointed star into page after page.

"Then how did you come to possess it?" said Francesco grimly.

"I d–don't know," stuttered Dorrie, at a total loss for an explanation.

Francesco crossed his arms. "And we're supposed to just believe that as well?"

"If we were lying," said Marcus, "we'd come up with a much better story than 'I don't know!' Is it your book?"

Francesco said nothing.

Dorrie began to paw madly through her bag. "Where's *my* book?"

"And that would be…?" asked Savi.

Dorrie gave up on her search. "*The Three Musketeers.*"

"Ah, your fencing manual, I presume," said Savi, looking down his nose at her.

She blinked at him, not sure why he looked amused again. She had, in fact, paid close attention to the sword-fighting scenes in the book.

"So you have no idea how it came to be in your bag?" said Hypatia.

"No!" Dorrie cried. "All I know is that *The Three Musketeers* was in my bag when I left our house yesterday."

Hypatia closed the battered book and pushed it to one side, her fingertips lingering over its cover. She glanced at the other lybrarians briefly, an eyebrow up. "We'll set this matter to one side for the moment…"

Mistress Wu swiftly pulled a piece of paper out of a notebook she carried and thrust it in front of Hypatia's face. The director took it, gave it a quick scan, and then looked back up at Dorrie. "Chewbacca?"

A short-lived but unmistakable guffaw escaped Marcus. Dorrie shot him a desperate look.

Francesco curled his lip. "They think the situation is funny!"

"No, we don't think it's funny!" Dorrie cried, as beside her Marcus shoulders began to shake uncontrollably with silent laughter. She whirled to look at Hypatia. "It's just that my name isn't Chewbacca."

"Not Chewbacca," wrote Mistress Wu dutifully.

Here, Marcus had to cover his quickly reddening face with both hands as tears began to stream out of his eyes. Dorrie looked helplessly at Marcus and then back to Hypatia. "My name is Dorothea. Dorothea Barnes. And that," said Dorrie giving Marcus a baleful look, "is my brother, Marcus."

Marcus drew in a deep, shuddering breath, as if trying to call himself back from his hysterics.

"Ah," said Hypatia. "So not..." Here she again consulted her paper. "Mr. Solo?"

Another wheeze escaped Marcus, and he bent over double.

Hypatia put the paper down.

Even in her terror at the thought of being marooned at any moment, Dorrie felt idiotic. "We just weren't sure at first. We just didn't know whether—"

"—you could trust us?" finished Hypatia. "Thoroughly understandable."

Gratitude and relief filled Dorrie. "Exactly."

Mistress Wu shifted a stack of papers on the table slightly to line up parallel to the table's edge.

Francesco grabbed the edge of the table hard and leaned toward Hypatia. "The connection with the Spoke Library is all wrong. It's just a gaping hole. And where are its companion archways? They always form within days of the first. There should be six or seven others, and we shouldn't need a bloody zeppelin to reach the first one. Then this book coincidentally appears! Something is very wrong. We must consider the possibility that a newly strengthened Foundation is behind this, and that these two are in their witting or unwitting service."

"If you're going to keep accusing us of working for the Foundation," said Marcus, "you could at least tell us what it is."

Hypatia nodded slowly. "One upon a time, long before Petrarch's Library came into being, the Foundation had complete control of the written word wherever they ruled, and they held it jealously. By 1300 CE, a good portion of what you would call Europe, the Middle East, and Northern Africa was under the Foundation's complete sway."

"Then how come I've never heard of the Foundation or the Founders?" asked Marcus.

"Because the history you know," said Hypatia, "is not the history that has always been. It only seems that way to those living it."

Dorrie felt that the floor had turned into a water bed.

"The lybrarians spent many centuries chiseling away at the Foundation's power," said Mistress Wu. "Until it broke into pieces. History changed as a result."

Hypatia drummed her fingertips on the table. "Though the Foundation has receded from sight, and the world's memory of it has dwindled into legend, it's still possible that there are those who dream about its old power. Francesco's greatest fear is that someone might desire to use Petrarch's Library as a means of reasserting that power."

"That hole is proof that someone's gone beyond dreaming," said Francesco.

"Perhaps," said Hypatia. "Perhaps not." Gazing first at Dorrie and then Marcus, Hypatia picked a quill out of a pewter mug and ran its feather along her finger. "Has anyone yet explained to you what a keyhand is?"

Dorrie and Marcus shook their heads.

"Keyhands occupy a special position here within Petrarch's Library," said Hypatia. "For one thing, travel into and out of the Spoke Libraries is only possible with the cooperation of a keyhand." Hypatia put the quill down. "May I have some ink and a bit of paper, Francesco?"

Dorrie felt a pointed stillness enter the room, as though everyone in it but she and Marcus was thinking the same thought.

Francesco hurriedly handed Hypatia a bottle and a piece of rough paper from a drawer. Hypatia poured a drop of the ink on the paper and then looked up at Dorrie and Marcus. "Touch the ink and then try to make a fingerprint."

"Why?" Dorrie asked.

"It's not poisonous," barked Francesco.

Dorrie and Marcus each pressed an index finger down in the tiny spreading puddle of ink and then pressed their fingertips down onto a clean section of the paper. Dorrie leaned forward to look at the result. A chillness crept across her shoulders. The pressure of her finger had left a solid black oval on the paper. No pattern of whorls or lines. Nothing. She tried it again and again. Her fingerprint was gone.

Hypatia leaned across the table toward Dorrie and Marcus. "The first three persons to pass through a new archway in the moments after it forms attain the power to navigate that particular archway, and bring others back and forth with them. Losing one's fingerprints is a side effect of acquiring a keyhand's unique time-slipping abilities."

Dorrie's heart seemed to come to a jolting halt.

"What a colossal waste," muttered Francesco bitterly.

"So are we keyhands?" Dorrie felt a spasm of fear mixed with wonder.

"Falling through a hole, *if* that's what you did," growled Francesco, "does not make you keyhands!"

Mistress Wu patted at the back of her neck with a fresh handkerchief. "You see, usually, long in advance of a new archway forming, the Lybrariad chooses two very skilled and experienced lybrarians to become keyhands."

"In other words," said Hypatia, tapping the inky piece of paper, "you are keyhands in the sense that you now have a keyhand's ability to navigate an archway. You are not keyhands in that you do not possess the customary experience, wisdom, and skills typically possessed by those we train for the job."

"But why train only two lybrarians for the job?" asked Dorrie.

"Yeah," said Marcus. "You said the first *three* people through the archway get keyhand powers."

"Well deduced, well deduced!" cried Mistress Wu, beaming as though Marcus and Dorrie had ferreted out the answer to the riddle of the Sphinx. "And here's your answer: Because there's always someone just on the other side of the archway who quite likes the idea of people saying or writing what they please. We rarely have to search far for them, and they've almost all made capital keyhands." Her eyes shined. "It's as if they came looking for us in one way or another. We think they're why the archways open where and when they do."

"Did you come looking for us?" asked Hypatia, looking first at Marcus and then at Dorrie.

Dorrie's heart beat faster. She glanced at Marcus, who only gave her an almost unnoticeable shrug. Dorrie racked her brain. *Had she come looking for Petrarch's Library?* She glanced at Francesco's grim face, sweat trickling down her back. She had a feeling she and Marcus would be safer if she had but… "No," she finally said, simply unable to concoct a believable story beneath Hypatia's gaze.

"As if Petrarch's Library would open for a child," muttered Francesco.

"The fact that you have attained a keyhand's power," said Hypatia, "presents a bit of a problem for the Lybrariad."

"To say the least," said Francesco. "The sooner we get rid of these two and let the hole close, the better."

Dorrie and Marcus exchanged panicked glances

Savi looked stunned. "And abandon the twenty-first century?"

"How else to protect Petrarch's Library?" snapped Francesco. "We can probably take care of it by tomorrow."

Dorrie felt her knees begin to shake. She felt as though she were drowning in a nightmare ocean, her fate in the hands of others. She forced herself to think, to not go under. If she and Marcus were ever to get home again, they had to avoid being marooned. They had to at least convince the lybrarians to allow them to stay within the walls of Petrarch's Library, even if it had to be as prisoners. "Wait!" she cried out.

Everyone in the room looked in her direction. "Why maroon us when we could be useful to you? We could live in Petrarch's Library. We could do work. We could, uh…shelve books or mop floors or…"

"Yes!" Marcus threw a hand up in the air. "Genius idea from the little sister! I was just going to suggest that."

Mistress Wu looked horrified. "Oh, I don't think you—"

"Or we could…" Dorrie interrupted, desperate to convince them. An idea with stubby wings and a ridiculous ungainly body took clumsy flight within her. An idea fueled by her sudden realization that, beyond avoiding a marooning, there was a much, much bigger and more breathtaking goal to strike out toward. *Why couldn't...* She felt her heart catch fire.

"Why couldn't we join the Lybrariad? Why couldn't we become apprentices? Other kids do. You could train us so that we wouldn't be a danger to the Lybrariad. Then you could still do your work in the twenty-first century!" Dorrie stopped speaking, out of breath. She looked pleadingly from face to face.

Hypatia pushed the ink-stained paper to one side. Mistress Wu, her mouth open, didn't even check to see if it lay exactly perpendicular to the edge of the table.

"That is so ridiculous," said Savi, "that it almost makes a kind of sense."

Francesco rounded on him. "Are you mad? We know nothing about their characters. We have no guarantee that they would have the mettle to succeed. They have no particular concern for our principles!"

Marcus looked indignant. "I have never burned a book in my life! I mean, maybe I've written in a few. But only in pencil!"

Hypatia leaned back, as if to better take in everyone in the room and all that had been said. "First off, I'm very sorry that you've been under the impression that a marooning was being considered."

"It's not?" stammered Dorrie.

Hypatia raised her eyebrows slightly, a shadow of a smile playing on her lips. "In Petrarch's Library's centuries-long history, only two maroonings have ever taken place, and those for extremely good reasons. The Lybrariad has no current intention of doubling that number in one fell swoop."

A wave of relief coursed through Dorrie. She glanced at Marcus, who flashed her a sickly grin.

"No," said Hypatia, with a little half-smile. "If you were looking forward to the rumored trip to Outer Mongolia, we must disappoint you. Assuming you mean us no harm, the choice as it stands is only between sending you home and letting the hole close up, or leaving it open and maintaining some sort of relationship with you two." For a long moment she was silent and then, almost to herself, she murmured, "There would be much to lose by closing ourselves off from the twenty-first century."

Francesco whipped his head around to face Hypatia, a vein throbbing in his neck. "You can't seriously be thinking that such a…such a…risky scheme should be considered?" Each word sounded to Dorrie as though he'd chipped it separately out of a block of ice.

"It would be a bit of a mad gamble," admitted Hypatia.

"It would be outright folly," Francesco said through clenched teeth.

"It would be ninja-tastic!" cried Marcus. "I mean, for me."

"Ninja-tastic?" growled Francesco. "You're not in a storybook, boy. The lybrarians of Petrarch's Library risk their lives every day. Sometimes just so a madman can safely proclaim that the universe is ruled by a blind fairy or a dancing goat or a talking soup ladle."

"Dude, that is so cool," Marcus said.

"It's extremely dangerous is what it is," fumed Francesco, his hands gripping the edge of Hypatia's desk.

"But we'd get to travel across time!" said Marcus.

"You think it's such an adventure now," muttered Francesco.

To Dorrie's surprise, Hypatia slid her hand over Francesco's whitened knuckles and then turned her eyes on Dorrie and Marcus. "The powers of a keyhand are rare. Rare things are sought after. Often violently. I don't exaggerate when I say that continuing an association with us could put you in mortal danger. Tell me," said Hypatia, shifting her gaze to Dorrie. "Why would you want to make such an offer? Only to avoid a marooning?"

"And to have a chance to really use a sword," burst out Dorrie. "I've been practicing forever but I can't do anything real with it in Passaic. You know, anything that counts."

"May we assume then that the sword has failed to make a comeback in the twenty-first century?" asked Savi, his mouth twitching.

"Only for sport," said Dorrie, "or pretending in plays and stuff. But in another time I could really…" Her words trailed off as a breathtaking image of herself driving back a cloaked villain flitted in front of her eyes.

131

"I see," said Hypatia, after a moment.

Dorrie wasn't exactly sure why, but she felt somehow that she'd given a wrong answer.

"Hypatia," said Francesco, fixing her with an intent gaze. "It would be years until they could function as lybrarians, let alone and if *ever* as keyhands." He turned to Dorrie and Marcus. "Would you be willing to abandon your family and home for the duration of years of training? To stay always within in the confines of Petrarch's Library until we've trained you well enough to have some measure of confidence in your abilities not to guarantee our downfall?"

Dorrie's heart sank. "No. We couldn't."

"Of course! You'd want to have it all!" barked Francesco. "Time out in your Passaic to enjoy loved ones and your nice normal little lives, and then, when it was convenient, you'd deign to do a little training here." He whirled back to face Hypatia. "If they can't cut ties, they would present an incalculable daily risk to the Lybrariad's safety."

Hypatia looked steadily at Dorrie and Marcus in turn. "There's truth in what Francesco says. It might indeed be best for us to part ways." She sat up straighter and brought her hands together. "Well, Mistress Wu has called a full staff meeting for tomorrow morning. We'll discuss the situation and reach a decision then."

"That hole could be passable within hours," said Francesco.

"Confine them to the Apprentice Attics and set a watch on them until after the meeting."

Hypatia tapped the tip of her pen against the desk and swept her gaze heavily over Dorrie and Marcus. "Do I have your word that you won't attempt to return to Passaic until we come to a decision about how to proceed?"

Dorrie and Marcus nodded vigorously.

"Then, that is good enough for me. Mr. Gormly can show you to the Apprentice Attics. You can stay there for now." She drew the book that Francesco had pulled out of Dorrie's bag closer.

Chapter 10

A Little Night Music

Once out of sight of the tower door, Mr. Gormly took his helmet off and tousled his short curls. "Damn shame to have to wear a hat this uncomfortable for a job I don't even like." He tucked it under his arm as he led them farther along a corridor. "I'm no natural-born snitch, but it's this or live out in that dead crossroads of a village on the other end of the island, and I couldn't stand all that quiet. I'm a city man through and through."

Dorrie, her bag again over her shoulder and Tiffany's sword in her hand, glanced sidelong at Mr. Gormly. "Are you a lybrarian?"

Mr. Gormly laughed out loud. "I'm afraid folks around here don't think I'm lybrarian material." He said it as though it didn't bother him a bit. "But no lybrarian wanted to do internal security."

"Were you born here?" asked Marcus.

Mr. Gormly moved his toothpick from one side of his mouth to the other. "Refugee. The Lybrariad broke some of us out of a dungeon in Aberdeen, Scotland."

"A dungeon!" said Dorrie. "Why were you there?"

"Oh," said Mr. Gormly, making the toothpick disappear entirely into his mouth and then reappear. "Some of us tried to say that Scotland wasn't in need of the services of a king. Or a queen, for that matter. The crowned ones and their friends didn't like that. Quick as a wink, there we were, knee deep in dirty royal water, chained to a wall by our wrists."

Dorrie looked at Mr. Gormly with new respect as he led them along a little balcony that overlooked a bright room filled with evenly spaced back-to-back bookcases and loaded with straight-backed chairs and colorful globes set on wooden stands. He stopped in front of a modest little white door made of planks. "I know what it's like to be mistrusted." He set the ugly helmet back on his head. "Come to me if anyone gives you a hard time."

Dorrie nodded gratefully and felt for the door's black iron handle. Marcus pushed the door open. They poked their heads inside, and Dorrie was instantly enchanted.

She had been expecting something cramped and dark and maybe cobwebby, but the Apprentice Attics were nothing of the sort. True, the ceiling sloped, but its peaked roof soared far overhead. Lower down, great rough beams crossed at intervals, and from a few hung swings and climbing ropes. Sunlight slanted through three arched windows at the far end of the room.

Though the air here was cool, a fire crackled in a roughly made but generous fireplace in the center of the room, its unplastered brick chimney crooking upward through the beams and finally out through the planked ceiling. A circus of chairs and sofas and footstools were scattered about the room, some drawn up in clusters by the windows and the fireplace, and others around tables and desks. Mathilde and Ebba huddled together on the end of a sagging couch with Kenzo perched on its back. Izel sat by one of the windows, her neck craned to catch better sight of something.

"You're not marooned!" cried Ebba, jumping up. "Oh, I'm so relieved!" She looked instantly sorry to have chosen those words. "I mean, not that I really thought you would be but I just, uh—I mean you're not going to be, right?"

"Not tonight at least," said Dorrie. "We're supposed to stay here."

Marcus threw himself into an armchair. "Not that Francesco wouldn't *like* to maroon us."

Dorrie grinned and swung her bag off her shoulder, taking in the long row of sweaters and coats and capes that hung in layers from hooks on either side of the entrance, and the tumbling river of boots, shoes, fishing rods, and roller skates that flowed beneath the hooks.

"Here, I'll show you the bedroom you can have," said Ebba. "It used to be Egeria's, but now that's she's made lybrarian, she's got her own place."

"We'll take it!" burst out Marcus.

She led them to one of the doors that ran in two rows down the length of the room. Grinning, she pushed it open. "It's a bit of a squeeze."

Marcus had to duck to get through. Inside the tiny room, the ceiling started off low on the door side and slanted steeply to meet the opposite wall only a few feet from the floor. It afforded just enough height for a little round window. The room itself only had enough space for two narrow beds covered with patchwork quilts and a little table at the foot of each bed. On top of one stood a kerosene lamp with a glass chimney. Thick, square-headed nails had been bashed into the rough plaster here and there, and from one hung a thin silky scarf. On two others, the plaid bathrobe and the fur-cuffed dressing gown had been neatly hung.

Dorrie threw her bag on the bed nearest the blue dressing gown. Ebba flopped beside it. The mattress made a whispery sound, and the smell of straw wafted through the air. "The straw should be okay. Egeria was a pretty regular changer." She giggled. "If it was Sven's, you'd need fresh."

Back in the den, after Mathilde had pulled Sven out of his room and persuaded him to read out some caramels from a grubby yellow book that stood with a row of other equally grubby volumes on a plank above the fireplace, Dorrie and Marcus explained about all that had happened in Francesco's office.

"So you are keyhands," said Kenzo matter-of-factly as he staggered around in a pair of the strange roller skates with the wheels that looked like miniature bicycle tires, caramel all over his face.

"Well, not really," said Dorrie, her face warming.

"Can we see?" asked Mathilde, her eyes eager.

Slowly Dorrie turned over her hands to show the others her blank fingertips, one now stained with ink. Mathilde whistled. "The real thing."

"Congratulations," said Izel who had silently appeared between Mathilde and Ebba.

Something in her tone made Dorrie felt instantly embarrassed. "It was just an accident."

"That too?" said Izel, pointing at Dorrie's now half-blackened thumbnail.

"Not exactly," said Dorrie, remembering Tiffany's vicious blow. She reached for another caramel, remembering a part of the story that she and Marcus had left out. "Oh, and Francesco pulled this book out of my bag, but I'd never seen it before in

my life. He acted like it was some very big deal that I had it."
Dorrie bit into the soft, sticky cube, allowing a delicate, glistening swoop of it to hang between her fingertips and her teeth.

"I envy you your talent, Sven," said Mathilde.

"I shouldn't do it for you. It just keeps you from practicing so you can do it yourselves."

"I can't read anything out yet!" said Kenzo, hovering over Sven's shoulder while the older apprentice struggled to turn bits of thread and feather into something that, when tied on to a bent pin, might possibly attract a very gullible trout.

Mathilde sighed. "All I seem to be able to read out with any consistency are baked potatoes."

"What was so special about the book?" asked Ebba.

Dorrie hastily swallowed. "Well, someone had cut the shape of a star out of bunch of pages in the middle."

"A secret compartment!" said Kenzo.

"Maybe…" said Dorrie, considering the possibility. She licked her fingers, as something new occurred to her. "You know what else was weird about it? The letters in the title didn't shift and change. I couldn't read them."

Ebba stopped chewing, her eyes wide.

Dorrie pictured Hypatia flipping through the book's pages. "I don't think even Hypatia could read the writing."

"That sounds like Petrarch's alphabet," said Mathilde slowly. "It's the only language I know of that won't auto-translate here."

Marcus reached for another caramel. "You're not going to start pointing at us and screaming 'Foundation!' now, are you?"

"Of course not," said Ebba. "But that's…that's….well, that's unusual."

"I promise," said Dorrie, sorry she'd brought it up. "I'd never seen the book before in my life!"

Ebba pushed back her hair band. "There's hardly anything in the world written in Petrarch's alphabet. It was like his own private language."

Dorrie realized that she'd never thought of the Petrarch in "Petrarch's Library" as even being a real person. "Who is Petrarch anyway?"

"He was here at the Library's beginning," said Mathilde. "One of the first lybrarians. When Petrarch's Library was much smaller, during the Dark History. No one can actually read stuff written in Petrarch's language. The Archivist's been searching for a way to translate it forever."

"The guy's who's into oranges?" and "The really bad singer?" said Dorrie and Marcus simultaneously.

"Oh, you've met him?" said Ebba.

Mathilde shuddered. "He's like a living cobweb. He gives me the creeps."

"He does mumble and mutter a lot," said Ebba, as if sorry to have to admit it. "But he can't help that."

Mathilde sucked noisily on her caramel. "I think he's cracked."

"Well, I'm sure there's some explanation for the book being there," said Ebba.

Marcus snorted. "Yeah, like the director of security stuck it in there himself."

"He wouldn't do that," said Sven, one eye squinting as he threaded a needle.

Ebba turned to Dorrie. "If you get to stay, maybe we can share a room."

Gleeful, Dorrie and Ebba threw their arms around each other. Then Ebba held Dorrie at arm's length. "Either way, we have to find your poor mongoose. He must be so frightened."

"Moe?" said Marcus. "I don't think he even understands that word."

"What's he like?" asked Ebba.

Dorrie racked her brain for something nice to say about the mongoose. "Well, he really makes Rosa happy."

Marcus cut to the chase. "He's a biting, scratching evil nightmare."

"Probably because he's shy," said Ebba with great finality.

"You'd have to meet him to understand," said Marcus.

In high spirits, Dorrie and Marcus ate dinner with the apprentices that evening and then sat on the stone windowsills of the Duc D'Aumale's Reading Room with Mathilde and Saul to watch a group of student lybrarians hold an archery tournament. Ebba, who had errands to run for the fire-and-explosives mistress, said she'd see them later up in the attics. Halfway through the tournament, Sven stuck his long legs through the next window over.

"What took you so long?" said Mathilde. "You missed five bull's-eyes in a row for Lady Marion."

"Callamachus is on the warpath."

"Who's Callamachus?" asked Dorrie.

"Director of reference services," said Mathilde, accidentally dislodging a bit of mortar from the wall with her heel. "Whoops."

It landed on an archer's head. Dorrie, Marcus, Saul, and Sven all quickly pulled their legs back into the room.

Sven looked tentatively down into the archers' courtyard again. "Callamachus made me miss dinner to look all over the Reference Room for some missing page of a book. He wouldn't even tell me what it was. Just that it would be torn on one edge, and that it was very important. He seemed really upset. Kept mumbling about the poor Archivist, and how he's getting too old for his job, and how he didn't want to have to bring it up with Francesco."

Dorrie's high spirits plummeted. Yesterday seemed like a week ago. She had forgotten all about the page Marcus had ripped out of the *History of Histories* book.

Back in the attics, she and Marcus feigned exhaustion and shut themselves away in their bedroom, with just the little kerosene lamp burning for light.

Marcus insisted on pacing in the tiny space with Egeria's left-behind scarf draped around his neck. "I asked Saul what the *History of Histories* was, and he said it's a record of all the deeds of the lybrarians over the last four hundred years! All there, spelled out in black and white. Lybrarian O'Malley rescued this person from a torture chamber. Keyhand Omar foiled a plot to burn down the Sandwich Isles Public Library. Remember I said it all sounded very James Bond?"

Dorrie felt her stomach drop, as though that part of her alone had been thrown off a cliff. "I guess it's not the kind of thing a secret society wants floating around."

"It would be gold for their enemies." Marcus dropped down on his bed.

"They'd know just what the lybrarians had been up to. Their cover would be blown."

"When Callamachus tells Francesco that page is missing, Francesco's just going to get up on his big, fat judgmental horse and assume we took it."

"Yeah, well, we did."

"I know, but it still seems unfair! We didn't take it on purpose. We didn't have nefarious intentions!"

"What are those?"

"Like bad ones. But worse."

"There goes our chance to become apprentices."

"And here comes our second chance at that marooning."

"But Hypatia said..." Dorrie stopped mid-sentence. Hypatia had only said that few maroonings had occurred and those for very good reasons. Dorrie leaped off her bed. "All right, we'll just have to return the page. If we can put it back, maybe Callamachus won't ever tell Francesco."

Marcus eyed Dorrie. "So what's your brilliant plan?"

"Why do I have to come up with the plan?"

"Because you're the one with the idea."

"But that means I've already done half the work!"

"Exactly! You have to follow through."

✳ ✳ ✳

Perhaps the strain of trying to engage in Marcus's argument had exhausted her, but Dorrie fell asleep without meaning to and woke with a sweaty start from a dream that thick, blue-black paint was filling her up from the inside, rising up her legs and into her chest, squeezing out her breath, and carrying with it a tide of pure fear.

Marcus lay fast asleep. Outside the little window, inky darkness still obscured the tangle of buildings outside. She swallowed hard, hoping there was still time. Pushing her covers slowly to one side, she shook Marcus. They'd agreed that they'd return the page in their robes, and if discovered out in the Library, they'd plead the need for a bathroom and no sense of direction.

They'd almost crossed the firelit, deserted Den when Dorrie tripped on a roller skate. They froze, Dorrie shielding the light from the lamp with the furry cuff of her bathrobe. When no doors opened, they slipped out onto the balcony. After three arguments and a bunch of wrong turns, Dorrie and Marcus finally found the Mission Room. It was as deserted as the den, its cheery little fire still throwing shadows around the room.

With Dorrie guarding the door, Marcus slipped toward the window and the funny little tube that had blossomed from the floor there. Dorrie heaved a great sigh of relief when Marcus drew the rolled-up piece of paper out. He stuck it in one of his robe's huge flannel pockets. Looking both ways to make sure the marble hallway was empty, they crept back out of the Mission Room and started for the Reference Room.

They'd only gone a few steps when a door opened somewhere nearby.

"You look terrible," said a man's voice.

Dorrie and Marcus locked eyes and froze.

"Two months undercover as a fasting priestess will do that," said a young woman's voice, as footsteps sounded. "Not my favorite assignment ever."

Dorrie and Marcus slunk back along the corridor in the

opposite direction from the voices, as quickly and silently as they could. They reached a dingy little vestibule bright with electric light, which opened into a room with a tinkling fountain in it to the left and a dark, airless beamed tunnel on the right.

"This way," whispered Dorrie, choosing the cover of the dark tunnel. Along its walls, black smoke rose in malodorous threads from fat candles set in holders. A few yards down, they came to a silent, quivering halt. Dorrie covered her nose with one of her furry cuffs and listened for signs of pursuit but heard nothing. "If we get lost…" Not daring to go back, they pressed forward, relieved at last to emerge into a softly lit carpeted corridor full of dainty furniture and paintings. The sound of distant heavy footsteps made Dorrie whirl in fright.

"There," whispered Marcus, leading them to a set of nearby doors. He flung them open and gave a high-pitched shriek. A bull-like animal the size of a van and the color of red clay filled the space just beyond the doorway. It snorted, and two enormous horns tilted first one way and then another. The creature took a step forward on one of its short, stocky legs, and the room rang with the sound of its enormous hoof hitting the ground. Dorrie thought she heard something crack beneath the carpet. A smell only slightly less repulsive than stagnant pond water filled the room.

"Good cowie, good little cowie," Dorrie cooed desperately if insincerely, as she took a trembling step backward.

The creature tilted its red head at them and snorted forcefully, steam shooting from its nostrils. It took a step in Dorrie's direction.

"Don't call it!" squeaked Marcus.

The animal swung its heavy head toward Marcus.

"Okay, call it, call it!"

The creature began to paw the ground.

"Oh, no," whimpered Dorrie.

As one, she and Marcus slowly grabbed hold of each other and then, "Run!" shouted Marcus.

Bathrobe and dressing gown flapping, Dorrie and Marcus sprinted down the brightly lit carpeted corridor, the creature in hot, thunderous pursuit. Up ahead, Dorrie saw an opening on the left. She felt the ground beneath her shaking and the creature's hot breath on her neck.

With a shout of terror, Dorrie leaped through the opening, hauling Marcus along with her. For a moment, she had the odd sensation of pushing against an invisible barrier and then being pushed from behind. She steeled herself for the impact of the monster cow's horns, but it didn't come. Instead, she collided with a table. Pots of ink, a little vase of flowers, and a rack of scrolls cascaded over the upended table's edges, the clay pots exploding as they hit the tiled floor. There was no door to close.

Covered in spatters of ink, Dorrie spun around to see the

creature skid to a halt in the corridor, its immense nostrils flaring silently. Panting, she and Marcus backed away until a wall made farther retreat impossible. Dorrie trembled as, out in the corridor, in eerie silence, the creature gave one last toss of its head and galloped noiselessly out of sight.

"What was that?" asked Dorrie, her breath still ragged.

Marcus slumped to the floor. "Something that needs to go back into its cave painting." He lifted his head. "Do you hear that?"

Dorrie listened. There was something. Some kind of drumming and maybe a flute. The music seemed to be coming from behind a door hung deep in one of the whitewashed walls. "Now what?"

"That is a kicking rhythm," Marcus said. He hurried to the door and pressed his ear against it. Before Dorrie could stop him, he pulled the door open a crack and then shut it again quickly. He spun to face Dorrie. "There's a toga party going on out there."

"A what?" said Dorrie.

"A toga party. Look for yourself!"

Her heart taking off again like an ambulance, Dorrie dragged herself to the door. Marcus opened it enough for Dorrie to put an eye to the crack. She stepped back and shut the door almost immediately, her eyes wide. She turned to Marcus. "There *is* a toga party going on out there." A prickle worked its way up

Dorrie's neck. She turned slowly to look at the opening they'd come through. It was an archway. She looked up. Tiled dolphins leaped around the top of the walls. They seemed oddly familiar. Stepping over puddles of ink and broken bits of clay pots, Dorrie looked cautiously out into the corridor.

"Where are you going?" asked Marcus.

"I just want to see…" Dorrie's voice trailed off as she stepped through the archway. Above it, between two pictures of a sword crossed with a quill, Dorrie read "Athens, 399 BCE." The water clock trickled.

Dorrie dived back into the little room. "Marcus! We're standing in the Athens Spoke Library. The one we saw Aspasia walk out of." She pointed at the door Marcus had opened. "That's long-, long-, long-time-ago Athens, Greece out there!"

Marcus's eyes danced. "Let's go look around!"

"We can't just 'go look around' ancient Athens," Dorrie chided, seized by a powerful desire to do just that. "We're supposed to be fixing things, not messing them up more!"

"But we may never get this chance again," pleaded Marcus.

A tidal wave of a thought hit Dorrie. She glanced at the archway and then at her fingertips. "We shouldn't be having this chance now. We're Passaic keyhands, not Athens keyhands. How could—" She gasped. Marcus's bathrobe seemed to be moving on its accord. Her eyes bulged. His sleeves were getting shorter, and the hem rising. The whole bathrobe, in fact, was dissolving before Dorrie's eyes. His pocket gave way, and the rolled-up *History of Histories* page tumbled to the floor. A whispery sound jerked Dorrie's attention to her own dressing gown's glamorous fur cuffs. They, too, were disappearing like paper being eaten by flame.

"Full disclosure," said Marcus, diving for the *History of Histories* page. "I'm not wearing anything underneath this robe." Scooping it up, he ran full tilt at the archway, only to bounce backward, like a bird hitting a window. "Ow!" he cried out, slapping the air in front of the archway. His hand stopped dead, making a smacking sound. He tried it again, to the same effect. "I can deal with naked," he shouted, "but I can't deal with looking like a mime!"

Grabbing the remains of her own dressing gown, Dorrie tried to push against the invisible barrier but fell right through into the corridor. Angry, she scrambled to her feet. "Quit fooling around!" she hissed, as Marcus in total silence, continued to make flailing mime motions with his fists. He paid no attention. Furious, Dorrie grabbed hold of one of his arms and hauled him into the corridor.

He clutched at Dorrie. "I couldn't get through. How did you—" He looked down. His bathrobe had almost completely disappeared and so had Dorrie's. Their eyes met for a split second, Marcus holding the rolled-up parchment in front of him like a fig leaf, and then in a blur, Marcus snatched a painting of a bowl full of aggressively green apples off the wall and held it beneath his chin. Dorrie dived behind a floor-length curtain that hung to one side.

Marcus looked sadly down at the painting. "I really liked that bathrobe."

Dorrie stared at the archway. "Marcus, we almost didn't get back out."

"Correction," said Marcus. "*I* almost didn't. *You* got out just fine. You got me out."

Dorrie felt a rush of uncomfortable foreboding. "Oh great, now we're abnormal accidental keyhands." Francesco's face swam before her eyes. "Don't say anything to anyone about this."

Marcus adjusted his painting. "What kind of idiot do you take me for?"

In the distance, they heard a crash as though something very heavy had toppled over.

Dorrie tore the curtain off the wall, and she and Marcus sprinted back to the Apprentice Attics.

Chapter 11
Until Then

PHILLIP CAME TO FETCH Dorrie and Marcus the next afternoon. After all that had happened, he seemed like an old, long-lost friend and Dorrie threw her arms around his generous middle. He seemed his usual perfectly cheerful self, and Dorrie hoped that meant that Callamachus had not yet told Francesco about the missing page. She thought guiltily about having stuffed the page and the borrowed curtain into her duffel bag last night after returning from their failed mission.

Maddeningly, Phillip said nothing about Francesco or Hypatia or what had been decided as he swept them out to the Commons and toward a white building that thrust forward from the interconnecting libraries all around it. Three levels of pillars peppered its facade, and a steady stream of people climbed up and down the stairs that led to three wide entrances.

"That's most of the Library of Celsus from second-century

Anatolia," said Phillip. "It's our main gathering hall, our mail room, and Hypatia has her office there."

Dorrie's pounding heart and racing thoughts made it hard to pay attention to his guided tour. As they ascended the steps, Phillip pointed to a row of marble female figures that flanked the doorways. "Meet Wisdom, Knowledge, Thought, and Virtue." He stopped and looked back out over the vista of the Commons.

"The ancient architect, Vitruvius, advises that all libraries should face east for the benefit of early risers." He looked doubtfully at Marcus. "For the best light, you see." He sighed happily, taking in the mishmash of buildings surrounding the Commons. "And the Celsus always does, no matter how everything else here shifts."

Inside the Celsus, crowds of people swirled around tall banks of cubbyholes that lined the walls of a large hall. Many paused in their conversations or with one hand frozen in a cubbyhole to watch Dorrie and Marcus go by. Dorrie ducked her head. They passed through an immensely tall set of bronze doors and into an echoing room filled with racks of scrolls built into the walls. Curving rows of tables with seats tucked under them faced a podium. Behind the podium, the biggest statue Dorrie had yet seen in Petrarch's Library stood in a raised alcove.

"Say hello to Athena," Phillip said, leading them up three stone steps and around the figure's knees.

In the curved back of the alcove, Phillip led them through a doorway and into a spare, light-filled room. Two windows looked out into a garden. A carpet alive with writhing patterns in blue and gold spread almost to the edges of the room. Hypatia sat on a carpet-covered ottoman behind a low carved table, its delicate legs ending in carved deer hooves. Mistress Wu stood on one side and Francesco on the other. "Please. Sit down," Hypatia said, indicating more ottomans that sat along the walls. Phillip helped Dorrie and Marcus pull them up to Hypatia's desk.

"Best to get right to it," said Hypatia, rolling a beautiful inlaid pen between her fingers. "The Lybrariad feels that it would be unwise at this time to offer you places here as apprentices."

Dorrie, who had not quite settled down onto her ottoman, felt a steely stab of disappointment. She stared at Hypatia, unsure whether to finish sitting or, in the interest of getting on with their banishment, stand up again.

"However," Hypatia continued, "the Lybrariad feels that your proposal to train as apprentices is not entirely without merit." Dorrie stopped breathing and slowly finished lowering herself to the ottoman. "We would like to invite you to stay here until the Midsummer Lybrarians' Conference and Festival, which will be held here in four weeks' time. This will give both the Lybrariad and you and Marcus a chance to get to know each other a little better, before the Lybrariad makes such a momentous decision."

Dorrie felt as if someone had set her heart aflame.

"Lavish!" cried Marcus.

Hypatia tilted her head. "I'm going to assume that was an expression of enthusiasm."

"It was," said Dorrie, as Mistress Wu blew her nose long and hard into her handkerchief, her eyes watery with emotion. "It is!" Looking into Hypatia's calm, trusting eyes, Dorrie felt seized by a powerful urge to tell her everything, to just cough it all up and trust that the Lybrariad would see that coming into possession of the *History of Histories* page and last night's travel into Athens Spoke Library had both been simple accidents. On the verge of speaking, she thought: But what if the Lybrariad sees it all differently and sees us as enemies after all? We'd never even get a chance to prove ourselves. She closed her mouth.

"We chose a period of four weeks," said Hypatia. "Not just so that you can enjoy the Midsummer Festival—I highly recommend the book-cart races, a corking good time—but because that's how long we have until time starts moving again in Passaic."

"Why is that?" asked Marcus.

"Petrarch's Library has its rules. We lybrarians have discovered them slowly along the way. One rule is that when all the keyhands from one wheren are on the Petrarch's Library side of their archway, time essentially stops on the other side of the archway. For about four weeks. Then it slips forward again. You could, of course, get back into Passaic earlier than that—"

"And solve all our problems," muttered Francesco.

"But we'll ask you to promise not to do that," finished Hypatia.

"You simply mustn't!" cried Mistress Wu, as though someone has announced an intention to set her pile of hair ablaze. "If you try to use a new archway too early, you can lock yourself right out."

"We wouldn't!" said Dorrie, who had no intention of leaving Petrarch's Library until someone dragged her out kicking and screaming.

Hypatia gathered her black and gray curls into a loose knot. "While you're here, I'd suggest that you develop a sense of what you'd be getting into, if indeed you became apprentices. Since we're so close to the end of this semester, you might find yourself a bit at sea in the practicums, but you're welcome to attend any of them you wish."

Mistress Wu beamed at Dorrie. "Mistress Mai is teaching a Renaissance blades practicum that may interest you since I assume you already have had some instruction in that area."

Dorrie's felt a nervous thrill run through her. If she could just show the Lybrariad that she had sword skills to offer, then Francesco wouldn't think she was such a waste of a keyhand.

"Like the other apprentices," said Hypatia, "you're also welcome to look for a master or mistress with whom to work."

"Let's see. Master Al-Rahmi doesn't have an apprentice this year," said Mistress Wu, rearranging a pile of quills so that they lay against one another largest to smallest. "He's director of the book preservation department. And there's Mistress Khani. She teaches the patron relations—"

"Plants!" blurted out Marcus. "I'd love to learn about plants."

Dorrie stared at him. "But you said you'd—"

"Rather open my head up with a can opener than go another day without learning something about plants," finished Marcus.

"Is that so?" said Phillip, his eyebrows lifting, as Francesco's eyes rolled almost out of sight.

"Our Egeria just made lybrarian and doesn't yet have an apprentice," enthused Mistress Wu. "She teaches a practicum in foraging. She may be willing."

Marcus looked on the verge of attempting to high-five Mistress Wu.

"One more thing, I think," gritted out Francesco. "Participation in apprentice field trips will be absolutely out of the question."

Madame Wu looked instantly cast down, as if she'd just gotten the news that a meteor had hit her house, but

Hypatia nodded. "Sensible enough." She smiled at Dorrie and Marcus. "Now if you'll excuse us, we have other matters to discuss."

Dorrie followed Marcus through the door in a euphoric daze. At the very worst, she had a month to practice with her sword among the lybrarians and explore Petrarch's Library. And at best, she might be able to convince them to let her become an actual sword-wielding hero. Out of pure joy, she leaped in the air. Landing, she turned her head for one last look into Hypatia's office. Francesco was pulling on one side of his moustache with so much force that Dorrie feared it might come right off in his hand.

✳ ✳ ✳

In the attics, most of the apprentices they'd met were scattered around the den. They sprang to attention upon Dorrie and Marcus's arrival.

"Well?" said Ebba from where she sat writing a letter.

"We're staying," shouted Dorrie. Simultaneously, she and Ebba both felt the need to jump up and down whooping. Envelopes and papers scattered onto the floor from Ebba's lap. "At least for a while," Dorrie said in a rush.

"The Lybrariad is going to think about letting us become apprentices," said Marcus.

Dorrie shyly sat on the arm of a heavy chair. "They're going to decide after the Midsummer Festival."

"It's called the Midsummer Lybrarians' Conference and Festival," said Millie, from where she sat poring over a book of illustrated weaponry on the other side of the room.

Izel blinked in Dorrie's direction. "So Hypatia and Francesco don't think you're a threat to Petrarch's Library?" The little extra emphasis that she put on the word "think" vied with the perfect innocence of her expression.

Dorrie hesitated, thinking about Francesco pulling on his mustache. Mathilde answered for her. "Obviously not, or they'd be out chasing Mongolian gerbils across the steppes for their dinner tonight instead of joining us at the Sharpened Quill."

"I'd like to chase Mongolian gerbils," sighed Ebba.

Mathilde fixed Ebba with a suspicious stare. "Don't even think about reading one of those ugly little things out up here!"

"She's not supposed to read animals out at all," said Millie. "Not after that boa constrictor."

"I was just trying to help scare away the rats!" protested Ebba.

Sven looked up from the fly-fishing book he had his nose in. "That you read out from that Pied Piper story."

Ebba sighed. "They sounded so clever."

"You can read animals out of books," said Dorrie, dumbfounded.

"It's like Sven and Master Phillip with food," said Saul.

"Some people just have a certain knack." He pointed to two leather satchels leaning against the fireplace hearth. "Mistress Lovelace sent those up for you. Basics kits."

Marcus sat down and propped one between his knees. He pulled out a fountain pen, a raincoat, a muffler, a toothbrush, a comb, a bundle of candles, a box of matches, a compass, and some antique-looking clothing.

Dorrie reached cautiously into hers and pulled out the first thing her hand touched. It was a bottle-green dress that looked like it would reach to below Dorrie's knees.

"Oh," said Ebba, sounding pleasantly surprised. "She went modern."

To Dorrie, the dress looked utterly old-fashioned and almost like a coat with its broad lace-trimmed collar, heavy cuffs, and large pockets.

"Be thankful she didn't send a hoop skirt," said Mathilde.

"Gayetty's Medicated Papers?" said Marcus, reading the side of a box he'd just pulled out. "What are these for?"

"I'll give you a hint," said Mathilde. "The Greeks use rocks. The Romans prefer a sponge on a stick, and where, if not when, you're from, people tend to use corncobs or pages from the Sears and Roebuck catalog."

"Toilet paper?" crowed Marcus, pulling a large, rough-looking square of paper from the box. "My God, I can *see* the splinters in it."

"Would you prefer wool soaked in rosewater," said Millie, "or a nice handful of moss, maybe?"

"Why, yes I would," said Marcus, rubbing the sheet of Gayetty's Medicated Paper across his arm.

Millie snapped her book closed, and Dorrie had the distinct feeling that she would have liked it if Marcus's head had been stuck inside.

Dorrie fumbled for a way to change the subject. "So, I'm supposed to find a Mistress Mai and ask her if I can start taking her Renaissance blades practicum."

Millie looked Dorrie up and down, her arms crossed and face stony. "So you know the sword?"

"'Know' is really kind of elastic word, isn't it?" said Marcus.

Dorrie shot him an irritated look. Marcus's lack of faith in her abilities had begun to grate on her nerves. She'd practiced for many, many hours. Not just with Mr. Kornberger and the Academy students, but at home in her bedroom, parrying and thrusting, imagining her opponent's every move. If Moe hadn't escaped and Dorrie had gotten her chance to duel with Tiffany, Marcus would have seen what Dorrie knew she could do.

"So what's your favorite blade?" asked Millie. "Rapier? Broadsword? Cutlass? Swiss dagger?"

"The small sword," said Dorrie promptly, thinking of her own beloved, dull stage-combat sword still tucked in her bag. And because she'd never tried any other kind of blade, beside Tiffany's.

"That's your favorite too," Izel purred to Millie. "Maybe you two can spar sometime."

"Really?" said Dorrie, excitement surging through her.

Millie lifted a sword with a leather-covered tip out of a scabbard that hung off the back of her chair. "Here, catch."

Dorrie just managed to catch the tossed sword by its hilt. Proudly, she held it aloft.

Millie's eyes flicked to Izel's. "We can go down to the Gymnasium and spar right now, if you want."

"I'd love to!" cried Dorrie.

"Um, Dorrie…" began Ebba.

"Let me just get my sword," said Dorrie, hardly hearing Ebba. The prospect of really sparring, not to entertain an audience, but to prepare to face a true villain, made Dorrie's heart pound with pleasure.

In her bedroom, she rummaged in her duffel bag, working to untangle her sword from its nest of sweatshirt sleeves, dirty socks, and candy wrappers. Ebba stuck her head through the door. "Hey, Dorrie," she said quietly. "Millie didn't ask you to spar to be nice. She and Izel are just hoping to make you look bad."

"I'll do fine. I've practiced for years," said Dorrie, finally pulling the sword free. "This is what I'm *meant* to do."

"Are you coming or not?" yelled Millie from out in the den.

"Coming," Dorrie yelled back.

In the Gymnasium, Millie and Dorrie threaded their way along the wall, around lybrarians and students preparing for practice or recovering in states of sweaty exhaustion. Millie found them an open place on the Gymnasium floor.

"You're sure you're experienced enough to do this?" asked Millie.

"Definitely," said Dorrie.

For a fleeting moment, as Millie unsheathed her sword in a swift, practiced motion, Dorrie felt a prick of unease. She shook it off. Recalling Mr. Kornberger's insistence on a salute, Dorrie began to slowly raise her blade. Millie rolled her eyes.

"Don't be cheap, Millie," came a voice from the edge of the Gymnasium. It was the man with the enormous nose that she'd seen fencing so thrillingly when Ebba had first showed her the Gymnasium and then again in Francesco's office. Francesco had called him "Savi." He was lolling on a bench, his face wet with sweat, as if he'd just been working hard. An enormous shaggy-haired man sat on his left and, on his right, a woman with deep wrinkles and a gray knot of hair.

Millie quickly matched Dorrie's gesture. She had a new expression on her face. One that confused Dorrie. One of tentative triumph. "Will you start us, Mistress Mai?" called Millie loudly, her gaze on Dorrie.

Dorrie caught her breath. *Mistress Mai.* The lybrarian teaching the Renaissance blades practicum.

The woman nodded.

"To five, please," said Millie.

With her heart beginning to pound, Dorrie shifted into the en-garde position that Mr. Kornberger had taught her.

"*Allez!*" cried Mistress Mai.

Before Dorrie had even moved, Millie had touched Dorrie's shoulder with the blunted tip of her sword.

"One," said Millie roughly, as Dorrie stared at the spot.

Dorrie shook herself and again took her en-garde position. Over Millie's shoulder, she caught sight of Savi staring at her feet. One of his eyes seemed to have grown and the other to have shrunk in an expression of undisguised horror.

Dorrie glanced quickly at the floor behind her, wondering if she was about to step into something disgusting, but saw nothing. She turned back. Savi made an emphatic separating motion with his hands. Dorrie glanced at Millie and saw that she had her feet spread more widely apart than Dorrie's. Quickly, Dorrie shifted into a wider stance.

"*Allez!*" cried Mistress Mai again. Millie attacked. Dorrie managed to parry once before Millie knocked the blade clean out of Dorrie's hand and touched her on the chest with her own blade.

"Two," said Millie.

Slowly bending down to pick up her blade, Dorrie felt her head whirling. She couldn't understand what was happening. *She knew how to use a sword. Didn't she?*

"*Allez!*" came Mistress Mai's command for the third time.

In an instant, Millie sprang at her. Dorrie met Millie's blows with her own sword any way she could. Clumsily, never quite in time. Meeting them at all and not tripping over her own feet demanded Dorrie's full attention. Clang, clang, clang. Dorrie reached deeper for breath.

"Three," rang out Millie's voice.

Mistress Mai set them going a fourth time. As much as she tried to do something different, Dorrie only found herself stumbling backward in an infuriatingly inescapable circle of Millie's casual design. Dorrie's arm began to burn, growing heavier with every passing second. Millie didn't even look like she was trying! Struggling to keep her sword aloft, her own ragged breath loud in her ears, Dorrie felt that the center of her world was caving in. Something seemed to tear in her chest. *She didn't know anything about sword-fighting!*

Once more, Millie's blade tip found Dorrie's shoulder.

"Four!" Millie came in close. "Fencing you is like fencing a tree," she muttered. "Mistress Mai is never going to let you join her practicum."

Mortified, Dorrie had no breath with which to respond. Sweat poured down her face. Her knees trembled.

The call of "*Allez!*" roused her again. Anger, fueled by humiliation, poured its last energy into Dorrie's arms, and she spent it on her first thrust of their encounter. Millie parried it easily and touched Dorrie lightly for the fifth time.

"Thanks for the bout," murmured Millie. "Glad we all know your level now. Keyhand."

Spent, Dorrie let the tip of her sword fall to the ground and bent over it, her lungs burning with the effort of keeping her in oxygen, her eyes swimming in sweat. The blood pounded in Dorrie's temples. She squeezed her eyes shut on humiliated tears. Dorrie didn't want to recover, didn't want to look up and face the onlookers.

Mistress Mai's voice floated hazily over her head. "Don't feel a bit bad about that effort, child. Millie's been practicing for years."

"You were courageous to try," said the shaggy-haired man.

Dorrie still couldn't make herself straighten. Courage was what you showed when you knew something was going to be scary or hard and you did it anyway. But Dorrie hadn't felt frightened facing Millie. She had thought she knew something. Enough to hold her own with another kid at least, but she hadn't been able to get one touch.

Tiffany's jeers at the Pen and Sword Festival echoed in Dorrie's ears. *Tiffany.* Dorrie's heart seemed to fold down into itself. Tiffany waiting in Passaic for Dorrie to return for their bout. Lavinia had been right. Tiffany was going to destroy her, and Mr. Kornberger was going to pay.

"You'd have to know something to get a touch on her," said Savi. "But you were a nervy sort of a fool to try."

Dorrie forced herself to look up.

"As difficult for me to get a touch on the legendary Savi de Cyrano de Bergerac," said the shaggy-haired man.

Savi de Cyrano de Bergerac. The name tickled at Dorrie's memory.

The shaggy-haired man stood and stretched. "Though you'd think his big, ugly nose would make an easy enough target."

He and Savi burst out laughing.

"Yes," said Savi, "and the prudent recognize a big nose as the mark of a witty, courteous, affable, and generous man."

Dorrie felt in grave danger of breaking down in full-on tears. "Thanks for the help," she said in a strangled voice. Turning on her heel, she looked around wildly for an escape route. A door leading to a courtyard hung ajar. Dorrie headed for it at a run.

Outside, she found a bench set in a clump of bushes, out of sight of the Gymnasium doorway. Huddling there, she felt her tears brim over. Dorrie tried not to make the little sobbing sounds that bring people who want to see if you're all right. *I was meant to do this.* Dorrie mocked her words to Ebba bitterly, every muscle in her body contracting at the humiliating memory of announcing that and then failing so epically.

She wiped her eyes with the back of her arm and stared at her fingertips. How was the Lybrariad ever going to accept her as a real apprentice when she didn't even possess the one skill she'd claimed as her own? She groaned out loud. Whether they did or not, she'd still have to face Tiffany. And her odds of beating her no longer felt like fifty-fifty.

A shadow fell across her knees. Dorrie looked up. Savi stood beside one of the sheltering bushes. Dorrie felt her face warm. She looked down quickly.

"Ah, the duelist from the future," he said, his eyes dancing. "If it's any comfort, I'm sure Millie knew from the moment she saw you wrap your hand around the hilt of your sword that you knew next to nothing."

"Is it that obvious?" cried Dorrie.

"That Millie played the churl to your fool? But, of course."

Dorrie remembered the way Savi's sword had danced the first time she had seen him sparring in the Gymnasium. Oh, to be able to make a sword move like that, she thought fiercely. To face Tiffany with that kind of skill. Suddenly Dorrie didn't care how much more of a fool she looked like. "I'm staying here for four weeks," she shot out breathlessly.

"Yes, I know."

Dorrie licked her lips, feeling desperate and fiercely determined all at once. "Will you let me be your apprentice? Temporarily, I mean? And teach me what you know? I'll work hard!"

"Sacre bleu," Savi swore under his breath. He must have meant it, for Dorrie heard it loud and clear in French. He ran his hand through his hair. He seemed to gather himself. "And do you want to serve as this apprentice to a swordsman or to a lybrarian?"

Dorrie stared back at him. "I...I..." She couldn't make herself say "lybrarian." It didn't feel true.

Savi unsheathed the sword that hung at his side so quickly that Dorrie didn't even have time to flinch. "You have a child's romantic ideas about the sword, I suppose." His eyes looked both hard and sorrowful.

She stood and faced him. "It's...It's...a matter of honor."

"Honor," he scoffed, turning the sword so that sunshine glanced off the blade. "Honor and what else?"

Dorrie poured out the story of the Academy's performance and Tiffany's mockery and the words Tiffany had written on the shirt and her bargain with Dorrie. "So you see? If you taught me even a little, at least I'd have a chance to beat her. I can't let her humiliate Mr. Kornberger like that."

One of Savi's eyes seemed to have developed a twitch. "And this Mr. Kornberger. Is he a big, fat fool?"

"No!" Dorrie cried loyally. "Not really," she said more quietly. "Not underneath."

Savi's shaggy-haired friend strode out into the courtyard with an armload of long poles and propped them up against the wall.

"Well," said Savi, sighting down his sword blade. "I'm afraid this is not the best time for me to take on an apprentice. I've gone seventeen missions back-to-back, and I'm on sabbatical. I have my writing to attend to for a while."

"Love letters," laughed the shaggy-haired man as he laid one of the poles across his knees and began to sand it.

Savi gave him a withering look. "A work of satire. *Voyage to the Moon* needs its finishing touches."

"Please!" begged Dorrie.

"Yes, Savi," said his friend, grinning. "Why not break your perfect record of never taking one on?"

Savi turned back to Dorrie and regarded her for a long moment. "I can teach you for an hour a day, but on one condition. After you vanquish your ill-mannered little nemesis and free yourself from having to wear the abhorrent shirt in question, you will instruct said nemesis that *she* is still entirely free to wear the garment if it so pleases her."

"But why?" Dorrie leaped to her feet. "What she wrote is a lie and mean, and she just wants to hurt Mr. Kornberger!"

"Because I am a lybrarian."

"And because Savi de Cyrano de Bergerac is contrary on principle," added the shaggy-haired man.

Savi ignored him. "If you can agree to that condition, then we'll begin tomorrow."

After a half moment of hesitation, Dorrie nodded so hard she could feel her brain shaking inside her skull.

"Very well. I'll see you here at eight o'clock in the morning."

"Thank you!" called Dorrie, her heart beating wildly as he strode off toward the Gymnasium door. He turned back for a moment. "But only because I was once a fool like you."

Staring at him, doused in sunshine, his nose casting its own shadow, Dorrie suddenly knew exactly where she'd heard the name Cyrano de Bergerac before. *On stage. In New York City with Mr. Kornberger and the Academy students, in a theater hung with balconies and buttery lights.* "Wait, isn't Cyrano de Bergerac a character from a play?" sputtered Dorrie, bewildered.

"That damnable play, again!" Savi shouted, shaking his fist at the sky.

"Oh, come on now, it's a good play," said the shaggy-haired man.

"It's a fiction with my name stuck in it for decoration," declared Savi, a dangerous light in his eye.

"Yes," said his friend, roaring with laughter. "That part about the man's quick temper is definitely off."

Savi's lips twitched. "Touché."

Dorrie gaped at him. "Cyrano de Bergerac was a real person?"

"Still is," Savi replied, removing an imaginary hat from his head and sweeping it before her in a mock bow. "Hercule-Savinien de Cyrano de Bergerac at your service."

A mad elation flushed away Dorrie's recent humiliation.

Cyrano de Bergerac, the legendary swordsman, was a *real* person. A real person who was going to teach her how to use a sword! As he disappeared through the door, he brushed by Millie. In complete silence, Millie's jaw began to work itself around in small circles of ever-increasing speed. Her pale face bloomed pink, which gave way to the speckled light red of a peach and then finally to the deep, angry red of a raw piece of beef.

CHAPTER 12
THE ARCHIVIST

"EBBA!" DORRIE WHISPERED, SHAKING her in the next morning's early light. "Ebba." The burned-down remains of three candles stood on the table at the end of Ebba's bed. An enormous book filled with drawings of mongooses lay open beside her. Ebba yawned and slowly opened her eyes. "I just heard a big bell ring eight times," said Dorrie. "Does that mean eight o'clock? Aren't we supposed to—"

Ebba scrambled out of bed as though she'd been electrocuted. "Yes!"

Dorrie pulled on her new green dress, still confounded by Mathilde's news that women in Petrarch's Library always learned how to wield Renaissance-era blades while wearing dresses. Mathilde had shrugged. "Because that's what women wear out in the Renaissance wherens, and you have to blend in. You can't just stop and change into doublet and hose when you sense a sword fight brewing."

After nearly upending Marcus's bed to get him out of it, Ebba and Dorrie scurried with him to the Commons, where they stopped, panting, knowing they'd need to head in different directions. For the first time, Dorrie took a long look at Marcus's outfit. He wore a pair of close-fitting suede pants whose bottoms disappeared into boots that began a washed-out red at their tops and changed to black halfway down. A short, brown suede jacket, darker than the pants, was double-buttoned snugly across Marcus's middle, and an enormous collar encircled his neck. The generous cuffs of a white shirt stuck just far enough beyond the ends of the jacket's sleeves to be admired.

Marcus gave her a double thumbs-up. "Totally rock 'n' roll, right?"

Dorrie had to admit that on Marcus, the clothes, which had to be from at least the last century, looked somehow like the latest thing.

She arrived at the Gymnasium breathless, her chest heaving, just as Savi appeared through another door, hair hanging loose around his face and a satchel over his shoulder. As he led her along the Gymnasium wall, Dorrie wondered with great excitement what weapon he would start her on. He stopped at a closet. "Here," he said, handing her a bundle of stinking, thickly padded canvas vests, a washboard, and a hunk of slimy-looking soap. Mystified, Dorrie followed him out to one end of the courtyard where they'd spoken the day before. He stopped at a stone-encircled well.

"You can wash them here," said Savi.

Dorrie looked from the well to the pads in her arms. "Oh, I don't mind wearing them dirty."

"You misunderstand, mademoiselle," said Savi, perching himself on a nearby bench. "The main point here is to strengthen your muscles, but the Gymnasium mistress might as well derive some benefit from your efforts."

Leaving her to haul up the water by herself, Savi pulled out an inkwell, a quill, and paper from a satchel. Disappointed, Dorrie dumped the vests on the ground and did what she could with them, wishing mightily for a scrub brush or, better yet, a washing machine. She risked a quick glance at Savi. Was this a test? Was he seeing if she could be patient or thorough or uncomplaining?

She tried to focus on being all these things in turn. He seemed utterly distracted and was not paying the least bit of attention to her. Every once in a while he would sigh violently and scribble furiously with his quill. She glanced at him again. Maybe he was writing out some sword-fighting instructions.

If so, they were very detailed ones. For the next three hours, Dorrie scrubbed and Savi scribbled. When a distant bell tolled noon, Savi finally seemed to come back from wherever he'd been. He gathered his things, packed them back in his satchel, and stretched. "All done with those?"

"Just about," Dorrie said, the last vest dripping in her hands. He pointed to a clothesline.

"Then au revoir, mademoiselle. Just hang those up to dry, and I'll see you tomorrow at eight o'clock. We will practice the art and science of sanding fighting sticks."

✳ ✳ ✳

Though each new day afforded Dorrie the chance to make new discoveries about Petrarch's Library, none were about the sword. A week passed, not in an exciting fever of cutting and thrusting and fancy footwork, but in a sweaty, frustrating blur of cleaning helmets, moving armload after armload of books from a new Ghost Library into the Reference Room for Callamachus to catalog, and running endless errands for Savi. The errands always seemed to involve running at great speed up and down stairways, or jumping on and off bicycles, or clambering up and down the steep, rocky path to the harbor where the water master's boats bobbed.

"If Tiffany wants to settle things with sponges or scrub brushes, I'm all set," Dorrie sighed to Ebba as she enviously watched her friend take aim at a chimney top with her slingshot.

Ebba carried the slingshot with her everywhere. Dorrie had watched her send pebbles flying at pillars and tree knots and once, to Mistress Lovelace's annoyance, at a bell hanging above the spot where the lybrarian sat reading out on the Commons.

Meanwhile, at Marcus's request, Egeria had begun to intersperse her lectures on the edible parts of daylilies and nasturtiums with lessons in the basics of ax-throwing. Jealously, Dorrie watched Marcus hurl his ax into the blindingly pink-striped walls of a forlorn Ghost Library that was unpleasant to spend any time in and had been given over to throwers of the ax for their practice needs. The room held only a tea table, two inhospitable chairs, and a tiny china cabinet full of cracked saucers, broken teacups, and seventeen shabby, well-thumbed volumes that Ursula dismissed with a sniff as novels of the lurid variety. This turned out not to be entirely true.

One day, Dorrie and Ebba came to the little Ghost Library to pick Marcus up on their way to go swimming. They found him sitting against a wall in the otherwise empty room, his ax wedged between his bent legs, the blade embedded in a book that lay open on his knees.

"You know who totally needs Lybrariad intervention?" he said, looking up, his eyes full of indignant fire. "Timotheus of Miletus."

"Okay…" said Dorrie.

"He was just an ancient dude trying to play the music he

wanted to play, experimenting with some new rhythms, and wow, you'd think he'd been eating babies for breakfast." Marcus wrenched the book off the ax, and the heavy weapon clattered to the ground. "They *outlawed* his music and locked him up for months just because some philosopher said his music got people too excited."

"You could tell Mistress Wu about him," said Ebba, sounding doubtful that Timotheus would qualify as an imperiled subject. "She can see if the Lybrariad wants to put him on the mission list."

While Ebba could summon little interest in anything to do with music, Dorrie had found that her friend had a burning passion for turning bits and pieces of metal and wood into useful things. Like Dorrie's father, Ebba loved contrivances. She had apprenticed herself to Hamsa, the director of the field-tech workshop who oversaw the design and construction of all the special equipment used by lybrarians and keyhands on their missions.

Once when Dorrie had visited the workshop, she'd watched Hamsa and Ebba spend an hour digging like happy moles through a bin of potentiometers and a half hour arguing about the relative merits of various kinds of compound cranks. Finally, Dorrie had abandoned them, too bored to stay, even for a good friend's company.

Every day, Dorrie and Ebba checked the traps they'd set for

Moe, who had yet to be glimpsed, though the traps were often emptied of food. When Ebba and Marcus were busy, and Savi had no work for her, Dorrie roller-skated through the endless halls and corridors of Petrarch's Library.

In the chambers farther away from the bustling Commons, Dorrie turned pages of illuminated manuscripts chained to stone walls, pulled dusty printed books off of shelves—one of which turned out to be full of bawdy limericks dictated by Catherine the Great—and heaved big clay tablets from one pile to another. Dorrie reveled in the fact that no one rained horrified objections upon her head when she unrolled papyrus scrolls that would have lived in museum cases at home.

Millie continued to treat Dorrie and Marcus with as much unfriendliness as possible, though Izel filled Dorrie with more mistrust. One crowded evening in the den, Ebba and Dorrie sat on a sofa near the fireplace, finishing off one of Mathilde's freshly read-out baked potatoes, when Dorrie saw Izel pause in her embroidery and gaze at Dorrie's hand. Dorrie glanced at it herself. The thumbnail was now almost entirely black. Izel gave Dorrie one of her flickering smiles and went back to her stitching.

Dorrie picked up *Socrates: A Life* from the back of the couch and went back to trying to figure out why he'd made his fellow Athenians so mad. After a few minutes, Izel spoke, addressing no one in particular. "Is it true that back in the old days, the Founders all had black fingernails or something?"

Dorrie flushed as the apprentices glanced at Izel and at each other, some looking vaguely interested, others perplexed.

"Fingertips," said Sven, without looking up from the tangle of silk fishing line in his lap. "From the ink they used to write with, I guess."

Izel exchanged a look with Millie. "I could have sworn it was fingernails."

Dorrie felt a sudden urge to change the subject. Noticing that Izel wore a band of metal set with a blue-green stone just below her shoulder, just like one she'd seen on Ebba's arm many times. Dorrie pointed to it. "What's with the armbands?"

"All apprentices wear them," snapped Millie. "It's a tradition."

"...You morons!" added Marcus, from where he sat at a table examining his chin for facial hair in a small mirror. "Why does it always sound like you meant to tack 'you morons' on to everything you say to Dorrie and me?"

A few people tittered. Millie glared at Marcus for a brief moment and then busied herself again with repairing the buckle on her baldric.

Dorrie tried for friendliness. "Who makes them?"

Millie stopped fussing with the buckle and gave Dorrie a hard look. "Why would you want to know?"

"...You moron," Marcus tacked on helpfully.

Millie gave him a venomous glance. "So you can run off and have one made?"

Dorrie felt a hot blush redden her face. "No, I—"

"Millie! That's so rude," broke in Ebba.

Millie jumped up and threw her baldric down. "Well, so are they! Pushing in here and trying to jump to the front of the line! Keyhands are supposed to be chosen from the most skilled of the lybrarians."

"We didn't do it on purpose," said Dorrie.

Millie glowered at Dorrie. "If Savi was going to take on an apprentice, it should have been me. I've had my name on his list for a year!"

Dorrie blinked at Millie, glad somehow to think that Millie's main problem with her was that Dorrie had become Savi's very temporary, sort-of apprentice. "If it makes you feel better," said Dorrie, hoping for harmony, "I haven't even touched a sword yet."

Millie only stared at Dorrie as though willing her to explode into flames and stalked into her bedroom, slamming the door behind her.

Millie's hostility turned Dorrie's mind back to the torn *History of Histories* page, which still lay rolled up under a sweatshirt in Dorrie's bag. Right after their meeting with Hypatia, Dorrie had resolved to come up with a new plan to return it to its proper place in the Reference Room, but with Marcus utterly engrossed in pretending to care about plants, and Dorrie busy running errands for Savi, a week had gone by and no plan had been made, let alone executed. But then something happened that made the need to return the *History of Histories* page impossible to ignore.

One morning at breakfast, the Archivist appeared, his hair only slightly less of a wild haystack than it had been the night he had flung oranges at Dorrie and Marcus. His creased, stubbly face looked pale and full of suffering, as head bent low, he served himself a bowl of porridge and took it to a small, unoccupied table in the Sharpened Quill's corner.

"Now he looks cracked *and* miserable," said Mathilde, with some guilt.

Sven glanced around before speaking in a low voice. "Remember when I said Callamachus had me looking for a page torn out of a book? Well, it was a page from one of the *History of Histories* books."

Saul's eyes widened. "That's not good."

Dorrie went still and carefully avoided looking at Marcus.

Sven poured a great cascade of syrup onto his pancakes. "Yeah, and it looks like the Archivist did it. Callamachus found him sleeping in the *History of Histories* cabinet right before he discovered the page was missing. He'd been on his annual orange-reading binge. Now the Archivist can't remember what he did with it. They're both pretty upset."

Dorrie felt a pang of shame.

"Callamachus says if they can't find it soon, he's going to

have to rat out the Archivist to Francesco. He'll probably take his key away and insist on a new younger archivist."

Their conversation was interrupted by the tinkling sound of lybrarians hitting pitchers and mugs and glasses lightly with silverware, which Dorrie now knew signaled the beginning of morning announcements. Those with eyeglasses and monocles on chains swung them through the air where their lenses caught and threw the light from the windows. Talking ebbed away and then ceased altogether.

While Mistress Wu made a breathless speech against heedlessness in the Library, citing many recent cases of overturned furniture and bicycles, Dorrie took another long look at the Archivist—remembering his sad, tuneless singing—and then sought out Marcus's eyes to say silently, "We have to return that page!"

As Marcus nodded ever so slightly, a lybrarian in a blue velvet waistcoat stood. He wore a silk scarf around his neck and an elaborate white wig with curls on the sides of his head and the rest of the hair tied back with a blue ribbon. Pockmarks covered his swarthy, wrinkled face. "It's not too soon to be thinking about the Midsummer Lybrarians' Conference and Festival, which takes place in just a few short weeks. The lybrarian training department is in charge of entertainment, and I will be directing a drama in the Greek style for the occasion. I invite all to audition." He winked boldly at a middle-aged women in a wimple and sat down.

"Who's that?" whispered Dorrie to Mathilde, as another lybrarian began to make an announcement about a shortage of towels in the bathrooms.

"Master Casanova," hissed Mathilde. "He teaches stealth and deception."

"He always writes a Greek tragedy for the festival," Saul explained. "With the chorus and the weird masks, the musicians, the whole deal."

Kenzo checked to make sure the lybrarians weren't listening. "Nobody wants to be in them."

"Why not?" said Marcus, as loud voices argued about the towels.

"He writes them himself," said Mathilde. "And they're well… awful. They're supposed to be tragedies, but you can't watch them or act in them without developing irrepressible hysterics."

Just then, Millie arrived at the apprentice table, looking thoroughly put out. She was dragging Ebba along by one arm, with Izel trailing behind.

"Ebba!" cried Dorrie softly.

"Hi, Dorrie," Ebba said, beaming at Kenzo. Dorrie watched Ebba, speechless, as her friend carefully placed her plate on the empty air beside the table and let go. It landed with a crash on the bench. Mathilde had to dive to save the sausages and peas from bouncing away.

Mistress Wu, in the middle of making an announcement about a missing glockenspiel, cleared her throat.

"That didn't land on the table, did it?" whispered Ebba. She felt for the edge of the bench.

Dorrie stared at her, confused. "Ebba, what's wrong?"

"Temporary blindness," said Ebba cheerfully enough as she climbed carefully over the bench, almost knocking over a water pitcher. "Ursula said it should only last a few hours or so."

Millie slapped her own plate down farther up the table. "She was trying to show that mangy Sardinian pika rat thing how to eat."

Ebba felt for her fork. "You don't have to make it sound so ridiculous. She's not well."

Millie rolled her eyes. "I don't know why the keyhands waste their time bringing you these stupid animals, anyway. So they go extinct. This isn't Noah's ark."

With great dignity, Ebba spoke to a spot where no one was sitting. "It turns out that leafy spurge is a bit toxic to humans."

Mistress Wu had gone on to another topic. "The apprentice field trip to thirteenth-century Korea is today. Apprentices should assemble at the Pyongyang, 1220 CE archway at one-thirty p.m. Please don't keep Haneul waiting. If you haven't already checked out appropriate attire, please see Mistress Lovelace at the circulation desk."

Saul elbowed Marcus. "You don't want to forget that. Try to go into a Spoke Library in clothes that didn't come from that time, and they'll just dissolve."

Dorrie and Marcus exchanged glances. *Well, that explained the disappearing bathrobes.*

As the apprentices began hastily grabbing their satchels and plates and vacating the table in a noisy scrum, Dorrie caught Marcus's eye again, grateful that with the apprentices out of the way for a few hours, it would be easier to talk up in the attics.

Izel put down her water glass and spoke to Ebba in the sugar-laced tone Dorrie had come to hate. "At least you don't have to go on the field trip."

The jostling stopped and a little silence took over the table. Dorrie looked from face to face, confused.

"You do so like to point things out, Izel," said Mathilde, standing.

"She probably ate the spurge on purpose," muttered Millie.

Ebba didn't move.

Mathilde slung her satchel on her back. "Dorrie, will you help Ebba get back up to the attics?"

Dorrie hesitated for the briefest of moments. "Sure. Of course." For once, Dorrie wasn't happy to have Ebba's company.

Upstairs in the attics, Dorrie and Marcus settled Ebba into a chair by the fire, while Dorrie looked hungrily at their bedroom door.

"Do you want anything?" asked Dorrie.

"Yeah," said Ebba. "Throw a cushion at my face."

"Okay," said Marcus picking up a fat red one with vomit-green tassels on its corners.

"What?" Dorrie snatched it from him. "No!"

Ebba waved her arms slowly in front of herself. "I want to see if I can sense it coming."

"Okaaaay," said Dorrie, doubtful about this turning out well for Ebba's nose. "Here it—"

Marcus launched the cushion. It sailed passed Ebba's flailing arms and hit her full in the face. Her head hit the back of the chair.

"Are you all right?" gasped Dorrie.

Ebba rubbed the back of her head and smiled ruefully. "Yes, but I guess I'm still a little spurged."

Dorrie, Marcus, and Ebba broke into laughter. It rose in volume and simmered back down a half dozen times, refusing to die completely until they were out of breath.

"Millie was wrong about the spurge," said Ebba when they could speak again. "I didn't eat it on purpose." She drew her knees up to her chin. "But she and Izel had one thing right—I don't like to go on field trips. I've never gone."

Marcus threw himself lengthwise on a couch. "Why?"

Ebba tugged on one of the pillow's vomitous tassels. "Because just thinking about stepping through an archway into a Spoke Library makes me feel deathly afraid. It's like I can't believe that I'll actually be able to get through the archway. It always seems like I'm just going to slip in between Petrarch's Library time and the other time and then disappear forever into some horrible place. Sometimes it's a cemetery with gaping holes in front of all the tombstones, and sometimes it's a world inhabited only by Punch and Judy puppets."

Dorrie wasn't sure what Punch and Judy puppets were, but since she found puppets creepy in general, she got Ebba's point. "So have you ever left the library?"

Ebba sighed. "No. And every time another apprentice field trip comes around, I can feel all the others waiting to see if I'll be able to do it *this time* and I never can. Then I just feel useless."

Dorrie frowned. "It was mean of Izel to bring up."

"I bet you'll be able to do it someday," said Marcus.

Ebba rested her chin on her knees. "What about you? Are you afraid of anything?"

"Yeah," said Dorrie. "Being marooned in Outer Mongolia."

Ebba giggled into her knees. "But Hypatia told you. That's only happened a few times in the Lybrariad's history and only for very good reasons."

Without thinking, Dorrie said. "Well, now there might be a reason."

Marcus gave her a warning look.

Ebba stared from Marcus to Dorrie. "What do you mean?"

Dorrie hesitated. Ebba had accepted and trusted Dorrie

190

right from the beginning. "There's something Marcus and I have to tell you."

Marcus sat up, his eyes narrowed. "*What* do we have to tell her?"

Dorrie licked her lips. "The day we fell into Petrarch's Library, we ended up in the Reference Room, in that little cage room with the *History of Histories* books."

Dorrie paused. Marcus was silently pounding himself in the forehead with the palm of his hand and repeatedly mouthing "No!" She ignored him and went on. "Marcus and I started to look through one of the books, and then the Archivist kind of exploded from under the table and scared us, and Marcus accidentally ripped out a page. We have the missing *History of Histories* page."

Ebba's unseeing eyes grew large.

Dorrie felt a flutter of panic. "I promise, we had no idea what it was!"

"Why didn't you just take it back to the Reference Room and explain?" asked Ebba. "I mean, it was just an accident. Callamachus might want to dip you in hot tar and roll you around in some feathers, but he'd understand."

Marcus abandoned his attempt to communicate silently. "We sort of forgot it had happened."

"When we found out how bad it would be for an enemy of the Lybrariad to get ahold of a page from the *History of*

Histories," said Dorrie, "we got worried that Francesco would assume we had taken it because we were some kind of horrible Foundation people up to no good."

Ebba nodded slowly. "Oh, that's true. He might see it that way." She waved her hand in front of her face. "Hey, I'm seeing again!"

"We tried to return the page secretly," Dorrie rushed on. "On our second night here, but we got…"—she hesitated, confronted by the choice to tell or not tell Ebba about being chased by the monster cow and inexplicably getting through an archway not their own—"…distracted," she finished.

Marcus snorted.

"I didn't know that the Archivist was being blamed for taking the page," said Dorrie, feeling guilty and wrong-footed about not telling Ebba the whole truth. "Marcus and I were going to try to sneak it back into the Reference Room before Callamachus tells Francesco it's gone."

Ebba tossed Dorrie the ugly pillow and grinned. "I'll help you."

Relieved, Dorrie grinned back at her, and Marcus, to Ebba's seeming consternation, offered her a high five.

"Tonight," said Ebba.

Chapter 13

A Slight Change of Plans

THAT EVENING, DORRIE THOUGHT the apprentices would never go to bed. Marcus hadn't helped by drawing different-colored circles on the floor with chalk and insisting that everyone had to learn how to play Twister. Only Millie had refused, saying she had some reading to do. After that, Mathilde had brought out a jar of popcorn kernels to roast over the fire in a wire basket with a long handle. Just when people finally began to pick up the pieces of their projects and games, and put down their books, the den door opened a crack and Izel slipped inside, home from the evening meteorology practicum.

She hung her emerald-green cloak on a peg. "Did you hear?" She didn't wait for an answer before hurtling on. "The lybrarians have called all three keyhands back from Athens, 399 BCE."

Dorrie spilled some of her popcorn at the mention of the archway she'd gone through.

"Why?" said Ebba.

Izel turned to face them, her eyes bright. "Socrates was found guilty."

There was a general stir in the room, and little gasps and moans.

"Aspasia must feel awful," said Mathilde. "She's been working so hard to sway public opinion."

"She couldn't even get them to change the punishment," said Izel. "The Athenian jury still sentenced him to drink the hemlock."

Watching Izel, Dorrie couldn't help but feel that the apprentice seemed more pleased with the excitement of bearing the news than bothered by its nature.

"But why call them back?" asked Marcus. "Why can't the lybrarians just pour on a little ninja sauce and break him out of wherever they're holding him?"

"Oh, what a brilliant idea," Millie muttered, without looking up from where she sat scratching away with a quill. "We should try that."

Mathilde pulled Sven's fur and leather hat off his head and hurled it so that it caught Millie hard in the chest.

"Hey!" cried Millie.

"So sorry," said Mathilde. "Meant to land it on a hook."

She turned to Marcus. "I think what Millie meant to say was that the Lybrariad would try to help him escape, only Socrates won't allow it. He'd prefer to die and force his accusers to live with their decision, rather than to let them off the hook by escaping and living as a fugitive."

Dorrie shivered. "So, it's a pardon or nothing?" It was hard to imagine a person giving up his life just to make a point.

"I bet that's why the Lybrariad called all the keyhands back in," said Ebba. "To give themselves more time to come up with a last-ditch plan."

"Because time will stop moving in Athens!" blurted out Dorrie, pleased to have remembered something about the Library's rules.

Sven retrieved his hat from the floor. "I bet they're going to try an aversion."

"What's an aversion?" asked Dorrie.

Mathilde laid aside her copy of *The Declaration of the Rights of Women and the Female Citizen.* "It's when the Lybrariad changes something in the past to try to save the life of a person farther along in history."

Millie stopped writing. "You shouldn't be talking to them about stuff like that."

"Is this Petrarch's Library or isn't it?" said Mathilde, with as much force as she could manage, given that she'd just stuffed her mouth full of popcorn.

Millie jammed her quill into a tomato as though both items had recently caused her grave personal injury.

"Don't worry—we'll leave you to your secrets," said Marcus, yawning. "Us Foundation operatives will just head off to bed." Marcus gave Dorrie a pointed look as he swept from the room.

✳ ✳ ✳

Dorrie tiptoed from her room, the rolled-up *History of Histories* page tucked safely inside her satchel. The other apprentices were all asleep in their rooms; they had all shuffled off to bed after Marcus's dramatic exit. Ebba met her and Marcus at the door, an empty cage in hand. If they were caught breaking the apprentice curfew, they intended to use searching for Moe as their excuse.

With Ebba leading them, they managed to evade the few lybrarians they saw and quickly arrived at a little, out-of-the-way stone chamber that adjoined the Reference Room. A pile of musty hay stood in one corner.

Ebba opened one of the doors to the Reference Room a crack and put her eye to it, and then turned back to Dorrie and Marcus, her face glowing. "No one's at the front desk and only the main doors are open. I'll go close and lock them. Dorrie can lock the others, and Marcus, when it's clear, you can put the page on Callamachus' desk. Tuck it in one of his reference books."

Dorrie pulled the scroll out of her satchel and handed it to Marcus. "But make sure it sticks out. Callamachus has to be able to find it."

She and Ebba were just about to slip into the Reference Room when Marcus made a funny, little choking sound.

"What?" said Dorrie, sensing trouble.

Marcus let the paper he'd unrolled spring back into its coil and stared at Dorrie. "We don't have the *History of Histories* page."

Dorrie's blood ran cold. "But you got it from that tube thing in the Mission Room—"

"Yeah, well, the thing I got from the tube thing in the Mission Room is this, and *this* isn't a page from *History of Histories*."

Ebba closed the door. "How do you know?

Marcus glanced at the paper in his hand again. "This writing looks Greek or something before it goes English. I mean, it's a whole different alphabet from ours. The page from *History of Histories* was written in the same alphabet English uses." He passed it to Ebba.

"Then where's the *History of Histories* page?" demanded Dorrie.

"No idea," said Marcus.

"Welcome, valued friends," Ebba read aloud. "If I may quote from" —she hesitated over how to pronounce the next word—"You-bel-us?…in his fine play"—she hesitated again— "Semele: 'Three bowls do I mix for the temperate: One to health, which they empty first, the second to love and pleasure, the third to sleep.'"

Dorrie shook her head with frustration. "It's just some kind of letter or speech or something." She looked at the page over Ebba's shoulder. As Marcus had described, unfamiliar letters seemed to dance before her eyes for a slice of a second before the figures shifted and twisted so that she saw English written with its familiar ABCs.

Marcus tapped his lips with one finger, looking off into a cobwebby corner. "Uhhhhh. Dorrie, you don't think that maybe after we got..."—he cleared his throat— "*distracted* when we were trying to return the *History of Histories* page the first time and I dropped it, I might have maybe possibly picked up a different rolled-up piece of paper off the floor? I mean, *remember,* there were a lot of scrolls on the floor."

A Technicolor vision of the stampeding monster cow, the upturned table, the spattering inks, and the cascading scrolls on the other side of the Athens archway flashed before Dorrie's eyes. "You didn't check that you had the right one after you dropped it?"

"I refuse to feel guilty," said Marcus. "My bathrobe was melting!"

"*What!*" said Ebba.

Dorrie looked with alarm at Ebba. If Dorrie told her about going through the Athens archway, would Ebba then feel duty-bound to tell the Lybrariad? Dorrie gazed into Ebba's warm brown eyes. Ebba had trusted Dorrie with her fears about the field trips, and she'd taken Dorrie's word that she and Marcus hadn't meant to rip out the *History of Histories* page.

Dorrie came to a decision. Surely she could trust someone who shared her fear of puppets. She took a deep breath, her heart pounding. "Ebba, there's something else we have to tell you." She sank into the musty pile of hay. "The night we tried to return the page, we sort of accidentally went through the ancient Athens archway."

Ebba eyes bulged. "But that's impossible! You're not Athens keyhands!"

"I...I...know," stammered Dorrie. "We don't understand why it happened. We didn't mean to, I promise!" Dorrie watched Ebba's eyes flick to Dorrie's thumbnail. "You have to believe us!" For a moment she was back in the hallway looking over her shoulder as the enormous, steaming creature bore down on them. "I know this is going to be hard to believe, but we got chased through the archway by this monster cow thing."

Ebba took a step backward. "A monster cow?"

"I know it sounds crazy," cried Dorrie.

"But it's true," said Marcus. "It almost flattened us."

"I just saw an opening," said Dorrie, "and we jumped through."

"Our clothes started falling apart—"

"Oh, yeah, that will happen," said Ebba in a soft, distant voice.

A realization hit Dorrie hard. "If we did drop the *History of Histories* page in Athens, then we *have* put the Lybrariad in danger." She jumped up. "That page is full of the names of lybrarians and dates of rescues and the locations of Spoke Libraries." Her stomach roiled. "We've got to get it back!"

Ebba seemed to come back to her senses. She sprinted back through the Library's labyrinth with Dorrie and Marcus pelting after her, making little effort at silence.

Skidding to a stop in front of the Athens archway, Dorrie caught her breath. The floor of the little room had been thoroughly cleaned. The potsherds and scrolls had all been picked up, the furniture righted, and the ink mopped away. "Someone's cleaned everything up!"

"Always a mistake," panted Marcus, expressing a long-held belief.

Dorrie was about to plunge through the archway and search through the scrolls that now neatly filled the rack, when Ebba grabbed her arm. "Wait! You can't!"

"I can!" cried Dorrie. "I did it before."

Ebba shook her head. "No. I mean the lybrarians wouldn't want you to." She pointed to the calendar etched in the stone to the right of the archway. In the month marked Gamelion, the number 18 glowed white. "Remember, the Lybrariad called all the keyhands back. So they'd have time to try to think of a way to get Socrates pardoned. If you go through the archway, time will speed up again."

The memory of Izel's news flooded back through Dorrie's brain. She took a step backward, unsure.

Ebba stared at the rack on the table. "It would take hours to go through all those scrolls."

"And what if you can't get back out again?" said Marcus. "I couldn't last time. Also, unless the clothes you're wearing were made in ancient Athens, which I highly doubt, they're going to melt. We're already in trouble for the bathrobe and the dressing gown."

Dorrie looked down at the green dress Mistress Lovelace had sent up in her satchel.

"This is all my fault," said Ebba softly.

Dorrie felt punched. She supposed she understood how Ebba could feel that way. Maybe if she hadn't been so quick to befriend Dorrie and Marcus, then…

Ebba covered her face with her hands. "I never should have read Roger out of that book."

Dorrie wondered if Petrarch Library's instant translation was failing her. "Who's Roger?"

Ebba collected herself. "He's an aurochs," she said reverently. "He's not a monster. Really, he's not!" She looked from Dorrie to Marcus and back again. "It's just I think he's lonely. That's why he wanders! He probably just wanted you to pet him."

"You read that monster cow thing out of a book?" said Marcus, clearly staggered.

"I know I shouldn't have," whispered Ebba, pushing back her headband. "But it worked with the boa constrictor and the rats, and the last of his kind gets killed in 1627 in Poland, and they're such magnificent creatures. I couldn't bear to think of them going away forever." She stared morosely through the archway. "I'm so sorry. I guess we have to tell Hypatia what happened."

Dorrie swallowed hard. "But what if then the Lybrariad doesn't want Marcus and me here anymore? Things are going so well."

"Yeah. Let's not get all hasty about telling anyone anything." Marcus brought his thumb and finger together so that they almost touched. "I'm this close to getting Egeria to go out on a date with me."

"Is that all you care about?" cried Dorrie.

"No, but it's one thing," said Marcus.

Dorrie looked at the scrolls again. "We have to think of the Lybrariad. I guess we can't just leave the page out there and not tell them."

"Wait!" A grin spread over Marcus's face. "Why can't we? Just for a little while. Time's more or less stopped out there for now, right? The *History of Histories* page is sitting up there in the rack, completely safe until the keyhands decide to go back."

Together Marcus, Ebba, and Dorrie stared at the rack. A comet of hope ricocheted around inside Dorrie's rib cage.

"I guess that's true," said Ebba uneasily.

"In the meantime we can think of a foolproof plan to get it back," said Marcus.

The sound of whistling wafted down the corridor. Dorrie, Marcus, and Ebba all froze as Mr. Gormly came walking around a corner, balancing the end of a billy club on his outstretched flattened palm. Seeing the apprentices, he lost his concentration, and the billy club fell to the ground with an echoing clatter.

"Mr. Gormly," Dorrie managed to get out.

Mr. Gormly stowed the billy club under his arm. He scratched his head. "I suppose I have to ask you what you're doing wandering around at this time of night."

"Nothing bad," said Dorrie, her throat tight.

"Of course not. I'm sorry to even have to ask a fine gentleman and two fine ladies such a question."

"Dorrie thought she heard our lost mongoose outside the Apprentice Attics," said Marcus. "We were trying to track him down."

Ebba slowly lifted the cage they'd brought along.

Mr. Gormly scratched at the stubble on his chin with the end of his billy club. Dorrie could hear her own heart beating.

"I'm supposed to, you know, let Francesco know if I see you

out in the corridors after curfew." Mr. Gormly looked carefully up and down the corridor. "Just go on back to your rooms now, and there'll be no need for me to say anything."

Dorrie and Ebba beamed with relieved gratitude, while Marcus looked at Mr. Gormly with pitying amazement that the man could possibly believe they were telling the truth.

"Thank you, Mr. Gormly," said Dorrie. "We'll get right back to our room. You won't regret this."

Chapter 14
Tragedy and Comedy

The next morning, Marcus, Ebba, and Dorrie skipped breakfast. Instead, Ebba brought them to the distant Ghost Library where she'd been keeping the aurochs. It had been a small monastery chamber and only boasted one wooden chest full of books, but it connected to a grown-over walled garden with a stream running through it. Dorrie noticed with no small fear that the aurochs had broken the original latch on the wooden plank door that led from a dust-choked corridor to his quarters. In its place, Ebba had bolted on a massive wooden leg that she had sawn off a table from the corridor.

"Impressively sneaky," said Marcus, lifting up the edge of the moldering brocade cloth that covered the vandalized table. Ebba had replaced the table leg with seventeen volumes of the *Encyclopedia Britannica*.

Marcus refused to enter the aurochs' quarters until Ebba had lured Roger out into the sunlit garden with an apple plucked from a high branch of the lone skeletal tree that still grew there. She came back in, shutting the door to the garden behind her, and joined them on a splintery window seat.

"Isn't he amazing," sighed Ebba, handing them each an apple, as they watched the massive creature paw at the ground.

"Yeah, amazing," said Dorrie weakly. "Like a volcano is amazing."

"He wouldn't hurt a fly," crooned Ebba. "Would you, Roger?"

Roger charged the remains of a scarecrow grown over with vines.

"That is no Roger," pronounced Marcus. "Maybe Vlad or Ghengis or Igor, but definitely not a Roger."

"He's how I really got that temporary blindness," said Ebba. "I nibbled some of the leafy spurge with him so he wouldn't feel so alone."

"Oh, that makes sense," said Marcus.

Dorrie bit into her apple. "It makes a kind of sense."

Ebba beamed at her. "You'd do the same for Moe, if he was feeling lonely, right?"

Dorrie thought of the earthworms and raw eggs and dead birds they'd been using to bait the traps for the mongoose. "Uh, well, the things he eats are a little more disgusting. The real question is, how are we going to get that *History of Histories* page back?"

Marcus tossed his apple up in the air and caught it. "As soon as we hear that the Lybrariad has its Socrates plan together, Ebba and I guard the hallway outside the Athens archway while you go in, find the right scroll, and bring it back out. Boom."

Dorrie rolled her eyes. "What are we going to do about clothes? If we wear our own, it'll be the bathrobes all over again."

Ebba stopped nibbling her apple. "We could—"

"—leave an extra set of clothes for Dorrie outside the archway," said Marcus lifting his fist high. "Boom."

Dorrie reared back. "I'm not going to stand there naked looking for the right scroll. What if some Athenian walked in on me?"

Ebba tossed her apple core through the window. "We could—"

"—barricade the door into Athens with the encyclopedias that Ebba didn't use to prop up the table. Boom!"

"Stop saying 'boom!'" shouted Dorrie. "Stop saying anything!"

"I didn't say 'anything,'" said Marcus. "I said, 'Barricade the door...'"

Dorrie felt a vein in her forehead pounding. "Marcus!"

"I think we'd better all go in," said Ebba.

There was finally silence.

"You?" said Dorrie. "But you never—"

Ebba shrugged slightly, as though she'd been through a hundred archways. "Did you see how many scrolls are in that rack?"

Dorrie nodded, full of gratitude.

"We'll have to pick a time when the lybrarians are at a staff meeting or something," said Marcus.

"We can check out Athenian clothes from the circulation desk." Ebba climbed off the window seat. "I've got to get to my escape and concealment practicum now. I guess I'd better pay special attention. Let's meet at the Celsus before lunch, and we can figure out more."

✳ ✳ ✳

A half hour later, Dorrie found herself carefully polishing scimitar blades while Savi pored over his pages and scritched and scratched with his pen. "I once saw the play *Cyrano de Bergerac*," Dorrie found herself saying, emboldened to interrupt him by sheer boredom.

"And I," Savi said, turning a page, "have, thankfully, never seen or read it."

Dorrie looked at him with amazement. "But it's about you! How can you resist? And it's good. It's really good!"

Savi lifted one eyebrow, which Dorrie took as an invitation to continue. "In the play, Cyrano de Bergerac has"—Dorrie paused, feeling as though she were about to grab a cobra—"a largish nose."

Savi raised his head. "I'm excruciatingly familiar with that aspect of the story."

"Well, anyway," Dorrie went on, trying to tear her eyes away from Savi's real-life proboscis, "he's clever and brave and in love with this very smart woman named Roxane, but he thinks that if he tells her he loves her, she'll reject him because he's, er, um, ugly." She gulped, adding hurriedly, "I mean, he just thinks he's ugly. In the play."

Savi raised his eyebrow again, higher this time.

Dorrie licked her lips and picked up another scimitar to polish. "But there's this other guy—Christian—who's sort of perfect on the outside. You know, like one of those statues around here, only he's, I don't know, not a quick thinker. A brave soldier and stuff, but not very good with words. He tells Cyrano that he's in love with a woman, and it turns out to be the same woman that Cyrano is in love with."

Dorrie rubbed the dagger's blade carefully, enjoying the break in the monotony. "So Cyrano has this crazy idea. He'll write love letters to Roxane for Christian. That way he gets to express his love to Roxane, but he won't have to worry that she'll reject him."

She checked out of the corner of her eye to make sure Savi hadn't drawn his sword. He hadn't. "Okay, and here's where it goes out of control. Christian says he wants to, you know, stand on his own two feet and tell Roxane how he feels about her in his own words. So he stands under her balcony and just starts to fail epically in the beautiful-words department.

Roxane has totally fallen in love with the writer of the letters she's been getting. So she keeps begging Christian to impress her with his fancy poetry, but all he can say over and over again is something like: 'Wow, you're beautiful. I sure love you.'"

Dorrie took a breath and looked over at Savi. His pen had stopped moving. He actually seemed to be listening. She hurried on. "Okay, so Roxane is totally disappointed, but then Cyrano feels sorry for Christian and starts telling him what to say from behind this bush, and Roxane falls madly in love with Christian and—"

Savi gave a little bark of laughter. "A talking bush. Yes, that's about what I need at the moment."

"Why?"

Savi spoke in the quietest voice Dorrie had ever heard him use. "I myself have things to say to a…woman, and I fear that I may have trouble in the task."

"Trouble?" Dorrie repeated, imagining Savi facing a dozen swordsmen intent on keeping him away from the woman. "What kind of trouble?"

"Trouble saying what I want to say."

Dorrie stared at him, her mouth opening wide. "You mean like Christian?"

"I'm nothing like that idiot," said Savi. "I can write the poetry." He looked furtively around, as though to make sure no one was listening, and dropped his voice again. "I just can't recite it. I've slipped twenty missives beneath the beautiful M's door in the dead of night, and now I've received a request to show myself and speak in the flesh, but when I try to deliver words in that fashion, my wits flee, and I can remember nothing."

Dorrie goggled at him, unable to take in the idea that Savi could be defeated by any task.

Savi looked appraisingly at Dorrie, his mouth twitching with recovered good humor. "Something like you with a sword, perhaps." He stood and stretched. "I suppose it's time to stop cleaning scimitars for the day, and move on to learning how to do something useful with one, or with a rapier at least." He strode off toward the Gymnasium door.

Dorrie leaped to her feet, blades clattering to the ground, her arms and legs flying in all directions.

"I'm sure I don't need to tell you not to leave the scimitars there," called Savi over his shoulder. "And if you ever let them go bouncing all over the cobblestones like that again, you'll probably be banned from the Gymnasium."

Dorrie scrambled to pick them up, her heart beating with dizzy anticipation. Finally, she was going to cross swords with Cyrano de Bergerac. Fifteen minutes later, Dorrie found herself standing across from Savi, holding a rapier aloft. She'd been doing so for at least three minutes, without him saying or doing anything. The muscles in her arm burned. She was embarrassed that the rapier shook in her trembling hand.

"En garde?" said Dorrie tentatively, unsure what else to do.

"That's very sporting of you," said Savi, his own rapier held out, steady and relaxed. "But people who want to kill you do not tend to warn you of their intentions, by calling out an 'en garde.'"

Savi took a step forward without moving his rapier. Dorrie didn't move.

"And now you're dead," said Savi.

Dorrie blinked at him.

"The most dependable way to keep the pointy end of a weapon from being stuck into you is to move away from it." Savi quickly stepped forward. "Dead, again," he barked before Dorrie could even lift her foot. "It's no good stepping backward *after* I've stepped toward you!" said Savi. Dorrie nodded vigorously.

"You must sense my movement before I make it. You must step backward before I even fully intend to step forward." Dorrie began to sweat profusely. She strained to feel when he would take another step. The sounds and smells of the Gymnasium bounced around them. Again Savi stepped forward. Again she stepped backward. A thrill ran through her.

"Again," said Savi.

For the next hour, Dorrie and Savi circled the Gymnasium like an oddly disjointed pair of dancers, Dorrie trying only to step backward before Savi had stepped forward and to contain her wild, mad happiness.

As Dorrie finally lowered her rapier, her arm aching, she saw Francesco striding along the Gymnasium wall, heading straight for them. Her heart faltered. *The page has been found missing,* pounded the words in her head. *They know we did it.*

Her hands began to sweat so much that she lost her grip on the rapier and it clattered to the ground.

"Savi," called Francesco, coming to a halt, his hand tight on the hilt of his sheathed sword. "I need to speak with you."

Francesco gave Dorrie a hard look as she fumbled with the rapier on the floor. "Outside, perhaps."

"You may go to lunch," said Savi with a nod to Dorrie.

The two men strode out into the courtyard. As she hung her rapier on the wall, Dorrie could hear Francesco's tightly controlled voice through the partially open door. "It's about Kash."

Dorrie watched a fierce wariness creep into Savi's face.

Francesco cleared his throat briefly. "When last we heard from him, he'd made contact with someone who claimed to know both the history of Petrarch's Library and the Foundation. That person said he knew of a serious threat to Petrarch's Library."

"I know that," burst out Savi roughly. "What's happened?"

For a charged moment, Francesco kept silent.

"Perhaps nothing," said Francesco, his jaw twitching. "But Kash missed his intelligence rendezvous with our field lybrarian in Thebes."

"How long ago?" Savi demanded.

"Several days."

"And you didn't tell me!"

Dorrie had never heard Savi sound so angry.

"I'm telling you now as a courtesy because you and Kash are close. I've already sent Tameri out to make inquiries."

"Inquiries?" Savi almost spat. "We should have a full team out there. I should be out there!"

Dorrie risked a peep through the door.

"Don't get above yourself, Cyrano de Bergerac," said Francesco. "Kash won't thank us if we come galloping into a delicate situation. We'll wait. I've considered the approach carefully."

"You'll excuse me if I think your approach not quite adequate," said Cyrano, his eyes flashing.

Dorrie didn't dare move as Francesco's face went rigid. "Don't let that be the last thing you think," he said coldly. Francesco and Savi stared hard at one another for a moment.

"My apologies," said Savi, his mouth hardly moving.

Francesco turned on his heel and Dorrie, not daring to think what he'd do if he found her there listening, fled across the Gymnasium and out another door.

As arranged, just before lunch, Dorrie met Ebba on the stairs of the Celsus. Nearby, Marcus was nodding with violent enthusiasm as Egeria pointed out something on a leaf she'd handed to him. He seemed to Dorrie to be shaking his hair out of his eyes with more style and more often than strictly necessary. Not watching where she was going, Dorrie almost bumped into Millie coming the opposite way.

"He's wasting his time," said Millie, acid mixed in with the words. "She's madly in love with someone else."

An urgent need to defend Marcus vied with Dorrie's own contempt for his ridiculous panting. She went with loyalty. "He's just very interested in plants."

"I bet," said Millie, marching away.

Dorrie was glad Millie didn't see Marcus, the moment Egeria walked away, toss the leaf she'd given him over his shoulder as though it were a particularly disgusting used tissue.

Inside the Celsus, Dorrie, Marcus, and Ebba headed for the mailboxes. Dorrie had been amazed earlier in the week when Ebba had pointed out a pigeonhole in the vast wall of pigeonholes saying, "You have a mailbox now too." Beneath it, a little brass plate read, "Dorothea Barnes."

"No one knows how the Library does it," Ebba had said. "Whenever someone new comes into the library, a new pigeonhole squeezes itself into place here, and a new nameplate appears." Dorrie had felt grateful to the Library for not engraving the brass plate with "Chewbacca."

Dorrie peered into her mailbox, not expecting much. "Hey, look! I've got something!" Excited, Dorrie pulled the thing out. It was a printed postcard. In bold typeset italics across the top were the words "Petrarch's Library Circulation Desk."

Two printed paragraphs followed with some blank spaces filled in by a neat hand. Dorrie read them out loud. "The dressing gown numbered C-DG 23.7 was checked out June 13, 421 PLE. (Petrarch's Library Era). It is now subject to a fine of 15 minutes of labor for the department of circulation for each day of further possession. *Your borrowing privileges are hereby suspended.*"

"Oh, not here too!" cried Dorrie, stamping her foot.

Marcus dug in his mailbox and pulled out a postcard of his own. He picked up where Dorrie had left off. "On the date of June 22, 421 PLE, if not previously returned, the bathrobe will be sent for by messenger, and the cost in time of obtaining it collected in addition to the fine *accruing to the date of the recovery* of the dressing gown, which cost and fine must be paid *to make your card good for future use. All fines must be paid in full by the date of the recovery.*"

Dorrie stared at the bottom of the card. It was simply signed: "Mistress Lovelace." She glanced back up at Marcus and Ebba, and said softly. "Well, so much for just checking out some Athenian bell bottoms or togas or whatever the ancient Greeks wore." She shook her head, remembering that the past was also the present here. "Wear."

"Chitons," whispered Ebba. "That's what they wear." She glanced around. "Don't worry, I don't have anything due. I'll just have to get out three." She pinched her lips together. "Though I'm not sure how I'm going to explain why I need them exactly."

The distant sound of shattering glass from out on the Commons made them all jump. A look of puzzlement and then dread crossed Ebba's face as shouts and shrieks rent the air. She sprinted for the doors. Confounded, Dorrie and Marcus followed. They got outside just in time to see Roger plunge onto the Commons from an alley between two buildings, dragging what looked like the contents of an entire garage along with him. Lengths of rope, and a tangle of bridles and fishing rods, and a smashed crate hung from his immense body. He thundered toward the Celsus, a long blond wig hanging from one horn, and a trellis full of grapes on the other.

Lybrarians and apprentices dived and leaped out of his way. Dorrie watched Izel scramble up a tree with the speed and agility of a squirrel.

"No! Don't move. Stop screaming!" Ebba called, as with a great tearing of turf, Roger changed direction and headed toward Mistress Wu, who, chest heaving and crossbow at the ready, had charged onto the Commons.

Dorrie gasped as Ebba launched herself off the stairs and between the aurochs and the lybrarian.

Roger just about sat down on his haunches to stop, sending the wig flying from his horns.

"Easy, boy," crooned Ebba in her low singsong voice, edging toward the aurochs. "You're just scared. Aren't you, Roger?"

Mistress Wu pulled back on the crossbow, setting it. "Ebba, I don't want to even guess where that monstrosity came from, but don't go a step closer."

From all around the Commons, lybrarians were drawing up in a circle.

"He won't hurt me," said Ebba, holding out her hand. Roger's gargantuan lips rummaged over her palm. "Poor thing."

Dorrie felt for her satchel and unbuckled its strap. "Here," she called softly to Ebba, tossing it to her.

Ebba gently looped it around Roger's neck at the only spot it would fit, right behind his ears. He sighed peacefully.

Mistress Wu lowered her crossbow. There wasn't enough handkerchief in the world to mop the sweat off her face. "Is everyone quite all right?"

"I could have been killed by that foul cow!" shrieked Izel from up in her arboreal refuge, her eyes snapping.

Ebba discreetly rubbed at something gooey and green on her arm. "He's very clean, actually."

Mistress Wu took a long, steadying breath. "Ebba, did you

read that colossus out?" Dorrie thought she looked both utterly betrayed and magnificently impressed.

"I'm sorry," whispered Ebba, patting Roger's manhole-cover-sized face.

"Put him away wherever it is you've been keeping him," said Mistress Wu, sounding certain that Ebba herself would soon be facing a marooning, "and make sure he stays there. We'll need to speak to Hypatia."

"Not to mention Mistress Lovelace," murmured another lybrarian, as the director of circulation emerged onto the Commons.

Mistress Wu blanched momentarily and then shooed at Dorrie and Marcus. "Well, go on to lunch."

"Sorry," mouthed Ebba to Dorrie, before she slowly turned to face Mistress Lovelace. Walking toward the Sharpened Quill, Dorrie sighed. "Something tells me Ebba's not going to be able to borrow anything from the circulation desk for a while, either."

✳ ✳ ✳

Inside, the Sharpened Quill, the apprentices' table was crowded.

"How's foraging with Egeria going?" asked Mathilde, after Dorrie and Marcus had sat down with their lunches.

"Ask me anything about cat mallow. Anything," said

Marcus, shoving an enormous spoonful of some sort of stew in his mouth.

Anxious about Ebba's fate, Dorrie craned her neck to look out across the Commons through one of the Sharpened Quill's diamond-paned windows, but Ebba and Roger and most of the lybrarians had disappeared from view. Only Mistress Wu and Mistress Lovelace remained.

Saul squeezed onto the bench between Kenzo and Mathilde. He laid a piece of paper and a fountain pen on the table. "Okay," he said brightly. "I'm supposed to find eleven actors to be in Master Casanova's Greek tragedy." He looked around the table hopefully. "Who's in?"

"I'd rather have the meat eaten off my toe bones by a rabid dog," said Mathilde, taking a delicate bite of her stew.

Looking away from the window, Dorrie noticed that everyone else had suddenly become very busy making small adjustments to the positions of their napkins and plates.

"C'mon, please," Saul begged. "He's not going to let me rest until I've got actors."

"What's it like apprenticing with him?" asked Marcus. Dorrie thought she heard a note of longing in his question.

"He's great on the stealth and deception stuff, but you don't want to be stuck with him right before the Midsummer Festival."

Mathilde passed a plate of bread and cheese to Dorrie. "Last year, Master Casanova's two dogs were in the tragedy. They played goats."

Dorrie took a piece of cheese absently, her eyes back on the window. Mistress Wu was flinging her arms around in gestures of horror while Mistress Lovelace, with great deliberation, wrote in a small black book.

Mathilde's next words jerked Dorrie's attention away from the window. "During the play's big finale, one of the dogs relieved himself on one of Mistress Lovelace's best Greek chitons. You can imagine how well that went over."

An idea caught hold of Dorrie. As the apprentices argued loudly over which of Casanova's plays had been the worst, Dorrie kicked Marcus sharply under the table.

"What was that for?" Marcus demanded.

"I have an idea."

"Yeah, well now I have a dent in my leg!"

"It's about returning the *thing*," Dorrie said meaningfully.

Marcus blinked at her. "Do you not know how to tap someone on the shoulder?"

"Okay. I'm sorry," Dorrie whispered, trying not to roll her eyes. "Master Casanova's doing an ancient-Greek-style play. Master Casanova's play uses clothing from Athens for costumes! Master Casanova needs actors!"

Before Marcus could stop her, Dorrie put one hand in the air. "I'll be in it!"

"You will?" said Saul, looking gratefully at her from beneath his dark lashes.

"And so will Marcus."

"Nooo!" howled Marcus.

Dorrie kicked him under the table again.

"There is nooo way I'd miss an opportunity like that," said Marcus, glaring at Dorrie as she scribbled down their names on Saul's list. She added Ebba's for good measure, hoping Ebba would forgive her.

Most of the apprentices looked at Dorrie and Marcus in amazement, but Millie crossed her arms, her eyes full of suspicion.

"Really?" said Mathilde.

"Yeah," said Millie. "Why would you want to do that?"

"Don't scare them off," said Saul, sweeping his gaze along the benchfuls of apprentices, and blinking his thick-lashed eyelids. "Now who else is in?"

"If I said yes, would you promise to read *A Vindication of the Rights of Women*?" said Mathilde, holding a piece of bread and cheese a few inches from her mouth in a considering fashion.

"Done," said Saul, touching his silver armband as if that sealed the deal.

Mathilde bit her lip and then finally shook her head. "Sorry. Not even for that pleasure."

Chapter 15
Bliss and Bleakness

Mistress Lovelace's moving pen had spelled trouble for Ebba. Her borrowing privileges had indeed been suspended, and she was now expected to spend a good portion of every day into the foreseeable future washing and ironing clothes for Mistress Lovelace, and repairing all the objects that Roger had broken. She'd also been summoned to a Lybrariad staff meeting to discuss Roger's fate. Francesco had argued for the aurochs' immediate butchering on the grounds that he was a menace to the community.

Ebba had argued that the solution was to read out just one more aurochs to keep Roger company. The Lybrariad staff present had not shared her view of the elegance of that solution and forbade her to read out any more animals, period, of any size. In the end, Mistress Wu, her eyes brimming over with tears, had brokered a compromise. Ebba had until the Midsummer

Lybrarians' Conference to turn Roger into a model, useful citizen of Petrarch's Library, or Francesco would have his way.

Despite missing Ebba's company while she worked and the ongoing worry about the safety of the *History of Histories* page (Dorrie checked the Athens archway every morning and evening, not trusting the Library grapevine or Izel to let her know when the lybrarians had decided on what to do about Socrates), Dorrie's next week bordered on the blissful.

Ursula and Phillip hosted a "Get to Know the Twenty-First Century" party for Dorrie and Marcus at Ursula's little stone cottage off the department of human repair and preservation. A good number of lybrarians and residents had attended, and Dorrie marveled at the fact that they all wanted to talk to her. Mr. Gormly howled with laughter at the mention of plug-in air fresheners, and Ebba's mother had a hundred questions about skateboards.

Dorrie felt a little mean telling them about the Internet and computers and the fact that you didn't have to go to a library to find a lot of kinds of information anymore. Some did indeed look stricken at the news, and one older man had to be helped to a chair, but most of the lybrarians seemed more intrigued than horrified, full of questions about what it all meant for the future flow of information and libraries that neither Dorrie nor Marcus could really answer.

And then, one evening, lounging by the fire with the other

apprentices in the attics after a swim in the frigid sea, Dorrie heard a knock on the door. More than a few people glanced up from their mugs of cocoa and their books and projects to look beseechingly at Ebba, who happened to be sitting closest to the door.

She sighed, pushed a woolly blanket off her legs, and padded to the door in her slippers. "I guess I'd better go check on Roger again anyway."

Yawning, she lifted the latch. Dorrie, her nose already stuck again between the pages of *Kidnapped*, heard a joyful shriek. She raised her head. There in the doorway stood Mr. Gormly, grinning, a cage under his arm containing a leaping, chittering Moe.

For Rosa's sake, Dorrie felt a surge of relief that lasted for all of the ten minutes it took Moe to bite her twice. A much bigger surge of relief filled her when Ebba, certain that the mongoose could alleviate Roger's loneliness, begged to take over Moe's care in return for Dorrie allowing the mongoose to sleep in Roger's quarters.

But best of all, Savi continued to teach her the sword, working on her footwork, her grip, and her first parries and thrusts. He swore often and passionately in French whenever she did something Mr. Kornberger would have loved.

During one practice session, Savi hung his rapier back on the Gymnasium wall earlier than usual. "We'll have to cut practice short today. My sabbatical is over, and I have research to do for the Lybrariad's next mission in Paris."

The word "mission" worked an instant, electrifying magic on Dorrie. "What kind of mission?"

Savi picked up his satchel. "To spring a manuscript from its prison."

"What kind of manuscript?" Dorrie demanded, tantalized.

"The kind that from a prison needs to be sprung." He strode toward one of the Gymnasium's many doors.

"No, really!" she pleaded.

Savi stopped in the doorway. "The Lybrariad has recently become aware that in the early 1590s in Germany, a manuscript by one Cornelius Loos was confiscated by the Bishop of Trier before it could be printed. It offended the good bishop, you see, for the manuscript protested the witch hunts taking place under the bishop's leadership and made quite clear their cruel absurdity. The Lybrariad intends to find it if it still exists." He made to leave again.

"To give it back to Cornelius Loos?"

Savi's fingers drummed on the doorjamb. "No. He died in prison before we were aware of his predicament. The Lybrariad wants to see the manuscript published as intended. The way history runs now, witch hunts continue deep into the 1700s. Perhaps if Cornelius Loos's manuscript sees the light, they'll end that much more quickly."

Dorrie flashed on the birthmark that stretched across Ursula's eye and the story she'd heard from Phillip about how the people in her village had tried to burn her as a witch in part because the birthmark looked like a cat. A book that could stop a person from being set on fire felt like the strangest and most powerful magic. "Can I help you?" Dorrie blurted out.

"I don't know. Can you?" said Savi in a prickly voice.

"Please! I mean, aren't I supposed to help you with your work?" Not knowing where she was getting the courage to beg, Dorrie waited, tense, for his answer.

Savi drummed his fingers on the doorjamb again, as if considering. "Very well, mademoiselle."

From that day forward, Dorrie spent part of every day toiling alongside Savi in his research, looking for whatever he requested in books and files in a dozen different chambers of Petrarch's Library, finding out all they could about what might have become of Cornelius Loos's manuscript.

Once, when Savi had asked her to read aloud a list of private libraries he'd written out on a piece of paper, Dorrie had gotten a good way into one of his poems before she realized her mistake. "'Since we must all become slaves to beauty,'" she'd read with increasing confusion, "'would it not be better to lose our freedom in chains of gold, than chains of hemp or iron?'"

"That's not it," Savi had snapped.

Dorrie had stopped abruptly and scrambled to find the right piece of paper while Savi, replacing a book on a shelf, went red. A little while after Dorrie had read from the proper piece of paper and gone on to another task, she had looked sidelong at Savi and gathered her courage.

"You could get a friend to do what the Cyrano from the play did. You know, stand behind a bush and sort of remind you what to say."

Savi's face stiffened with pride. "And be mocked forever after!"

Dorrie was surprised that Savi, a master swordsman and a keyhand of the Lybrariad, could care about that so much. But she understood how it hurt to be mocked. "I…I wish I could do it for you."

Savi smiled, his good humor stealing back. "Your nose isn't nearly impressive enough for the role." He scratched something with a flourish on a fresh piece of paper. "But the good news is that I believe I now know where to find Cornelius Loos's manuscript." His eyes gleamed as he crammed the piece of paper into his satchel. "I must be off." He rushed toward the door, and then stopped, spinning around. "I thank you for your help, mademoiselle."

✳✳✳

The next day, Dorrie, Marcus, and Ebba all got notices in their mailboxes announcing that the first play rehearsal was to take place after dinner.

"Is this really necessary?" grouched Marcus that evening

as Ebba led them to the Old Field, the spot Casanova had specified for the rehearsal. It lay low and to one side of the architectural tangle, a good trek from the Commons. "I mean, I could be soaking trumpet-flower seeds right now, which I would hate, but at least Egeria would check on me every once in a while." He gave Dorrie a put-upon look. "I still say you should just deal with a few minutes of nakedness."

"For the last time, I'm not going naked," cried Dorrie.

"Fine," said Marcus. "But as soon as we get the page back, I'm quitting the play."

"You can't do that," said Ebba, horrified. "Not if we said we'd do it. Master Casanova will be counting on us."

The Old Field was a barren piece of pebbly ground where only saw grass grew. Ebba led them to where a fire blazed inside a low circle made of rough stones. A little way behind the fire stood the mouth of a shallow cave, set in a dark, jagged rock face.

Watching the flames leaping, Dorrie thought of a question. "How come Petrarch's Library is full of fires, but I never see any piles of logs?"

Ebba shrugged. "If a library arrives with a fire or a candle or a torch or something burning, it just keeps right on burning, but the candles don't get any shorter, and the wood never seems to go to ashes. Some of them have been burning for almost four hundred years."

"I love this place!" said Marcus.

"Ah, good, fresh talent," Master Casanova said, turning away from a very elderly lybrarian with a monocle that kept falling out. Master Casanova flung the loose end of a brilliantly yellow scarf around his neck. On either side of him, his two little terriers jumped up and down like furry Super Balls. "Down, Sophocles! Down, Euripedes!" Casanova bellowed. He stared intently at Ebba, and then Dorrie and Marcus in turn. "You," he said, pointing at Marcus. "You will read for the part of the hero, Iakchos."

"Total typecasting," said Marcus.

"Yes," said Callamachus. "You're the only male person here under fifty."

"Is this hero an Athenian?"

"What?" asked Casanova.

Out of Casanova's sight, Dorrie jumped up and down, and shook her head violently back and forth.

Marcus paid her no attention. "I only like to play Athenians."

Dorrie dropped her face in her hands.

"I assure you," said Casanova, thrusting a sheaf of papers at Marcus. "He's an Athenian's Athenian."

Master Casanova sized up Dorrie. "Can you act?" he demanded, throwing his arm up and out forcefully to one side so that the papers in his hand trembled.

One of the dogs gave a sharp bark.

"Yes," said Dorrie, glad to be on familiar ground. "Mostly I've played pirates."

"Pirates?" said the old man, obviously appalled. "What authentic writer of tragedies would insult an audience with the presence of a pirate?"

"Well, usually the plays were more pretend sword fights than real tragedies," stammered Dorrie.

"Oh, I think you could call them tragedies," Marcus put in.

Casanova took in a deep, slow breath. It took him some time. He seemed to be carefully keeping track of all the air entering each of his individual lung sacs. "When I ask, 'Can you act,' I mean, have you ever donned a mask in a proper Greek tragedy?"

"Not exactly," said Dorrie.

Master Casanova lifted his eyes to the heavens. "Oh, Zeus, bring me *actors*!" He thwacked a sheaf of papers against Ebba's chest. "Here. You shall read for the part of the devastated Parthian Queen, our heroine."

"What? No." said Ebba firmly, handing back the script. "How about a part in the chorus?"

Master Casanova ignored her words and swung one of Ebba's hands high in the air. "My Parthian Queen!"

Dorrie looked into Ebba's stricken face and tried to radiate deep apology.

Casanova chose that moment to turn back to Dorrie.

"Chorus," he pronounced, handing her a script and turning quickly away.

Just then Millie marched into their midst, with Izel sidling along beside her.

"Millie!" Dorrie stammered. "What are you doing here?"

Millie shook her bangs out of her face and stared hard at Dorrie. "I guess the same thing you are."

"…You morons," Marcus offered up solicitously.

Millie glared at him as Master Casanova took a step backward and a sidelong look at Millie. "In you, I sense the natural energy of a powerful goddess complete with destructive tendencies."

"Goddess?" repeated Millie, her eyes wary now.

Master Casanova took in Izel. "And her wily maidservant." He put on a falsetto voice. "'Artemis, Artemis, where art thou?'"

"Chorus?" muttered Dorrie to Ebba. "What about me screams out 'chorus'?"

Casanova clapped his hands together. "Now, I'm thinking of playing a good deal of the action in the cave. It's not traditional, but with the echoes and a few torches, I think the effect will set the hairs on people's heads standing straight up."

"And Millie—Millie screams out 'goddess'?" added Dorrie. She had to firmly remind herself that the whole point of being in the play was just to get the costumes. She leafed through the script, growing more and more alarmed. Mathilde hadn't been kidding. Even Dorrie knew that a story needed a beginning, a middle, and an end. The script seemed to be all middle, with the hero mostly giving long, long speeches.

"He makes Mr. Kornberger look like Shakespeare," hissed Marcus.

"We did try to warn you," whispered Ebba.

"A true Greek tragedy," trumpeted Master Casanova, "has episodes wherein the characters interact, and passions are aroused by a swirl of circumstance and fate." His voice rose higher. "Heroes and villains take actions." His arms flailed. "Death and misery, ingratitude and the bitter curds of envy rain down upon the hero. Between the episodes, the chorus will gossip cruelly about what has just transpired and—"

Marcus raised his hand. "Excuse me, but when do we get our costumes?"

"Your costumes?"

"Yes, I'd like to get my costume as soon as possible. I really want to start living the life of my character in, uh, my imagination. All the time. I'm sort of a Method actor."

Casanova looked puzzled and then pleased. "You mean not just at rehearsal?"

"Exactly!" said Marcus. "All the time. I want to live the life of an Athenian. I want to wear a chiton and eat a lot of grapes, maybe do a little geometry with a stick in some sand. I want to really *become* Icky-Tongue, I mean Taco-most, I mean…" He flipped through his script.

"Iakchos!" cried Casanova.

"Yes!" cried Marcus with the same fever pitch of excitement.

"A splendid idea! I'll have costumes for everyone by tomorrow morning. But you must promise to tell me more about this 'Method acting.'"

Dorrie felt a great wave of appreciation for Marcus.

A few evenings later, Athenian chitons stowed in their room, Ebba and Dorrie checked the Athens archway again to make sure nothing had changed. Marcus felt like he had already done enough good in the world, having both managed to get the costumes *and* talk Casanova into making some changes to the script that definitely seemed to make it less bad, though Dorrie felt that the Greek tragedy now read suspiciously like an ancient version of *Star Wars*. And even though the spring practicums were almost at an end, Marcus had begun to attend Casanova's on stealth and deception.

"He's not much of a playwright," Marcus told them as they met up near the Commons afterward. "But that man can lie convincingly! I have so much to learn."

They were on their way to play croquet with the other apprentices, but from the moment they arrived, Dorrie felt a strange reluctance on the part of everyone but Mathilde and Saul and Kenzo to meet her eyes.

"Why's everyone acting weird?" murmured Dorrie to Mathilde as they stood waiting for their turns near the same wicket.

Mathilde rolled her eyes. "Just ignore them and carry on."

Her words did not reassure Dorrie. "Ignore what? What's going on?"

Mathilde took a deep, reluctant breath as though she'd rather not say. "Izel's been telling anyone who'll listen that Millie told her that she overheard Francesco telling Callamachus that 'persons unknown' have been asking about Kash in Thebes, and that a couple of them supposedly had blackened fingernails."

Dorrie's heart began to bang wildly. She reflexively tucked her thumb with its ugly black nail inside her curled fingers.

"Is that all?" choked out Dorrie, in a stab at humor.

Mathilde sighed.

Dorrie's hands began to sweat. "There's more?"

"Izel said that Callamachus said that these two historians, Sima Quian and Strabo, now mention people called 'Blacknails' in their writings, and he seemed concerned."

Dorrie felt paralyzed with sick dread.

"Look," said Mathilde briskly, catching Dorrie's eye, "Izel's just trying to stir up trouble. Whatever is or isn't going on with people making questionable fingernail fashion choices in China, you know you have nothing to do with Kash disappearing, right? You took a blow to the hand."

Dorrie nodded dumbly.

"So, just act like it!"

Despite Mathilde's bracing words, Dorrie could only think of fleeing to the solitude of her own room. "I think I left Moe's cage unlocked," she managed to choke out.

Instead of heading toward the Apprentice Attics, she walked with stormy steps toward the Gymnasium. She forced herself to stare at her thumbnail. It was entirely black. A sick chill crept through her. *Was she serving the Foundation in some way without even realizing it?* She thought of the *History of Histories* page she'd lost. *That had been a pure accident. Hadn't it?* She shivered and pushed on the black thumbnail. It caused no pain, but blood pounded in her temples.

What if there was something in her that really was rotten, that would be at home with the Foundation? That was everything a lybrarian wouldn't be? She thought back to her interrupted sword fight with Tiffany. Maybe, despite all she'd told herself, her nail hadn't actually blackened because of that one blow from Tiffany's sword, but because of something Dorrie had done or thought.

She cast backward to the moment when Tiffany had made fun of her for pretending too well, too eagerly. Dorrie's breath became ragged, remembering how intensely she'd wanted to shut Tiffany up and make her take back her words, how she'd demanded that Tiffany not wear the insulting T-shirt. Maybe she was truly more of a natural Foundation operative than a keyhand of the Lybrariad.

She slipped into the Gymnasium, which was almost entirely empty. Not even the idea of practicing with a sword seemed appealing at the moment. She ached to feel her mother's hand on her back, hear her father making noise in his workshop. Her fear fed an overwhelming urge to be back in Great-Aunt Alice's house drinking cocoa with Miranda and her parents in the kitchen.

Holding back hot tears, Dorrie slipped into the Roman bath. It was empty. At her feet lay the gently splashing pool, and high above her head, the cracked ceiling gave way to the hole. A rough wooden stairway had been constructed from the edge of the pool to a platform below the "not-a-real-archway." Her way home. The lump in her throat grew unbearably large as she gazed up into the Passaic Public Library. It seemed to call to her.

"May I help you find something?" said a harsh voice behind her.

Dorrie jumped and then spun around. She found herself looking into Francesco's deeply cragged face.

His one visible eye searched her own thoroughly. "Or have you already found exactly what you were looking for?"

Dorrie swallowed hard. "I…I…I wasn't looking for anything."

Francesco continued to stare at her for a long moment. "Hypatia has decided to trust you," said Francesco. "I haven't.

Put one toe over the line, compromise the Library's work in any way, and I will find out about it."

Dorrie felt cold to the bone. Did he know that she and Marcus had been to Athens? Did he know about the missing *History of Histories* page? She made a little sound in the back of her throat and nodded vigorously.

Without another word, Francesco stretched out his arm toward the door to the Gymnasium. Dorrie scuttled toward it, grateful that he didn't follow her.

In the Apprentice Attics, Dorrie threw herself on her bed and let the sobbing come.

CHAPTER 16
THE STAR BOOK

O VER THE NEXT FEW days, Dorrie felt the full brunt of the effect of Izel's rumors. Whispers and averted eyes seemed to greet her at the mailboxes, in the Gymnasium, in the Sharpened Quill, and out on the Commons. Marcus didn't seem the least bit fazed, but then again, he wasn't the one walking around with the suspicious nail.

It didn't help that she'd received a note from Savi telling her he'd be out of Petrarch's Library for several days and to go on with her practicing without him. Despite Mathilde, Saul, and Kenzo's unchanged behavior, Dorrie found excuses to eat as few meals as possible in the Sharpened Quill, where the whispering and pointing and double takes from the other apprentices, and even some of the lybrarians, made eating a misery.

It was a relief when, one morning at the mailboxes, Dorrie received an invitation from Ursula to have lunch at her stone cottage, which always felt like a welcoming place. Dorrie had just reached into her mailbox to pull out an item—another overdue notice from Mistress Lovelace—when she heard the swish of silk behind her.

"How are you getting on?" said a quiet voice.

Dorrie whirled to see Hypatia reaching into her own message box.

"F–f–fine," stammered Dorrie, feeling a warm flush creeping up her neck and somehow immediately making her conscious of every lie she'd ever told in her life.

"Everyone treating you well, I hope," said Hypatia, a questioning smile on her lips.

Dorrie nodded silently, absolutely sure for a fleeting second that she should have told Hypatia about her accidental trip to Athens and the missing *History of Histories* page a long time ago, but finding it impossible to tell her now.

After eyeing Dorrie for a moment longer, Hypatia patted the satchel she carried. "I believe I'm carrying something that belongs to you." She reached inside and pulled out the book with the stars cut out of it. Dorrie stared at it dumbly.

Hypatia held it out to her. "Thank you for letting us look it over. The Archivist wasn't able to make use of it as a translating tool, unfortunately, but the handwriting is Petrarch's."

"But it's not mine," said Dorrie, a tremble in her voice. "I told you."

A small smile played on Hypatia's lips. "Well, let's just say that it's more yours than ours, since it came from Passaic."

"Did it?" said Dorrie, more sharply than she meant to, longing to throw off some of the blame and suspicion she felt had been heaped on her by Francesco and Millie and Izel from the moment she'd come to Petrarch's Library.

"It did," said Hypatia, her eyes calm. "I believe that as firmly as I believe you had never before seen this book until Francesco pulled it out of your bag."

At Hypatia's words, Dorrie's eyes pricked with the threat of relieved tears. The director glanced out of one of the tall, open doors. "Midsummer is drawing near. No matter the decision made about your future with the Lybrariad, we'll all need to venture back out into Passaic with caution. Especially given the unusual, not to mention damp, circumstances of your arrival."

She leafed through the red book's pages. "Knowledge of where the book might have come from could be of great use in understanding our position. Give it some thought, will you?" She held the book out to Dorrie again. "And do come out for croquet tonight. It's payback time for Mistress Lovelace, and I intend to do the winning whacking."

"Th–thank you," stammered Dorrie, taking the book.

With a pleasant nod, Hypatia turned, her blue silk tunic making a whispering sound. She disappeared into the Council Chamber.

At lunchtime, Dorrie brought the book with her to Ursula's cottage.

"I don't know how much more enthusiasm for the wonders of calyx variation I can fake!" groaned Marcus, putting his head down on the round table he and Ebba and Dorrie had just pulled chairs up around. Wooden bowls filled with herbs, and a stone mortar and pestle jumped at the force of his dejection.

"So stop pretending," said Dorrie, lifting her legs as a golden chicken stepped through the doorway that led out to a little grassy area planted with one of Egeria's medicinal gardens, and headed pecking for Dorrie's feet.

"Never," vowed Marcus into the tabletop. He hauled himself upright again. "But it's so hard to focus on tricks for identifying spotted dead nettle when I could be helping Master Casanova make a batch of invisible ink."

Ebba gave Moe a bit of the boiled egg she was eating. For all the meals he'd missed, Moe chittered with as much energy as usual. Already, Ebba had him sliding around her neck and happily curling up in her arms as though he'd never clawed a human in his life. A dull thud made them look out the window. Phillip, squatting alongside one of Ursula's goats, lunged for a rolling bucket and stuck it under the goat again. As he reached for the goat's udder, she twitched her tail, and Phillip drew back as though the udder had just burst into flames.

Dorrie smiled. "He doesn't look comfortable with the whole milking thing."

"*He* doesn't look comfortable?" said Ebba. "Look at the poor goat!"

Just then, Ursula swung through a door in the back of the room. She put a jar of jam and a warm loaf of bread on the table. As Marcus pounced on the loaf, the goat gave an angry bleat, and Phillip swore lustily. In another moment, Phillip was chasing the goat round and round the yard.

"I think I'd better help Phillip," sighed Ursula. "Though he hates to admit it, he was more born to the manor than to the barn."

Left alone with Ebba and Marcus, Dorrie pulled the book out of her satchel and laid it on the table.

Ebba's eyes widened. "Is that the star book?"

Dorrie nodded. "Hypatia gave it back to me."

"Why?" said Marcus, trying to look suspicious while cramming his mouth full of bread and jam. A feat, Dorrie decided, that was hard to pull off.

Dorrie told them about her conversation with Hypatia.

"So," said Ebba, when Dorrie had finished. "Do you have any ideas?"

"It could have been anyone," said Dorrie, reaching for what was left of the bread. "We were at the Pen and Sword Festival for hours. There were tons of people. Anyone could have stuck it in."

"Maybe it was a mistake," said Ebba. "Maybe your bag looked like someone else's."

"But what if it was on purpose?" said Dorrie.

"What random person sticks a random book in some random bag on purpose?" said Marcus, eating a glob of jam off the knife.

"But what if it wasn't a random person?" said Dorrie. "What if it was someone we know? Or someone who meant to do it?" All at once, she had a vivid vision of Miranda sitting at the kitchen table the morning they'd left Passaic. She looked sharply at her brother. "Marcus, remember Miranda said she put *The Three Musketeers* in my bag? What if she only thought she did? What if *she* put the star book in there?" Dorrie felt a little sick. "What if she took it from someone in our house?"

"She does enjoy her petty-toddler-criminal hobby," said Marcus thoughtfully, dropping the knife back in the jam.

Dorrie chewed on her fingernail. "And she's always taking stuff from Great-Aunt Alice's room."

Marcus snorted. "She takes stuff from everybody's rooms."

"Who's Great-Aunt Alice?" asked Ebba.

"She lives with us, or I guess it's more like we live with her," said Dorrie, thinking about how little she knew about her great-aunt, really.

Marcus tilted back in his chair. "Uh, you do know that

Great-Aunt Alice was a librarian before she was an anthropologist, don't you? Like a million years ago."

"What?" screeched Dorrie.

"Yeah. For like five minutes. Dad told me that her father got really mad when she gave it up. He wanted her to run the Passaic Public Library, since he'd built it and started it and stuff, but she refused and ran off with some airplane pilot."

Dorrie looked at her brother in amazement. "I never knew that."

They watched Phillip step in the bucket of milk he'd managed to coax out of the goat.

Marcus searched the tabletop for crumbs. "Don't you ever ask Dad random questions that you know he'll be all psyched that you're asking, right after he's asked you to do a chore?"

"What? No," Dorrie answered, confused.

Marcus shook his head. "Oh, Sister, Sister, I'm not sure I should be giving away my proven work-avoidance techniques for free."

Dorrie looked at him blankly.

Marcus rolled his eyes. "Dad'll go on and on and on with his answer until he completely forgets he ever asked you to do anything. The most you have to do is help him along with an additional question now and then, as though you're really interested in what he's saying, and you're golden."

"You actually think those things out ahead of time," said Ebba, awed.

"I am a planner," said Marcus.

Dorrie was only half listening. Since they'd begun to talk about Great-Aunt Alice, a vague memory had been trying to take definite shape. She gasped and grabbed hold of Ebba with one hand and Marcus with the other. "What if Great-Aunt Alice has been trying to find Petrarch's Library?" Just the thought of such a possibility filled Dorrie with a dazzling sense of gloriousness.

Marcus stared at her with big eyes. "And what if my name is really Swisscheese McCranklespanx?"

Dorrie ignored him. "I heard Great-Aunt Alice talking to Amanda right before the Pen and Sword Festival. They didn't know I was listening." She didn't feel it necessary to explain about her panicked stint in the wicker basket. "They were talking about waiting for something important to happen. They never said what, but Great-Aunt Alice was disappointed and said she didn't believe it was going to happen, and Amanda seemed excited and tried to convince her that it would." She looked back and forth from Marcus to Ebba with shining eyes. "What if they were waiting for Petrarch's Library to connect with the Passaic Public Library?"

"Did either of them mention a library?" asked Ebba.

Dorrie strained to remember. "Not exactly."

Marcus unpeeled Dorrie's fingers from his arm. "They could have been wondering if N'Sync was going to record a comeback album." He brought the front legs of his chair down with a crash. "And have you thought about this? Maybe Great-Aunt Alice is some kind of rogue ex-librarian working for that new version of the Foundation that Francesco's so worried about."

"Marcus!" protested Dorrie. "Don't say that! Why are you saying that?"

"Because I'm kidding."

"I swear, she's not!" cried Dorrie to Ebba. "The Foundation wanted to control the flow of information, and who got to know what. Great-Aunt Alice wouldn't like their ways at all."

"Now who's kidding?" snorted Marcus. "She loves to control stuff."

"Well, it sounds like lots of people could have put the book in your bag," said Ebba, scratching Moe under the chin. "But definitely tell Hypatia what you remembered. Maybe the Lybrariad can talk to your great-aunt."

A thought struck Dorrie. While she was sure that if Great-Aunt Alice had been looking for Petrarch's Library, it was as a friend, she had no proof. Telling the Lybrariad about Great-Aunt Alice might make them even more suspicious of Dorrie and Marcus. Dorrie nodded vaguely at Ebba. She'd tell Hypatia soon, Dorrie resolved. Once the *History of Histories* page was back where it belonged.

CHAPTER 17

AT THE PORTE DE NESLE

INALLY, AFTER THREE LONG days, Savi returned. His mind seemed elsewhere as he watched Dorrie practice, coming back only to chastise her. "You look like a monkey poking a stick into a termite mound. If you're going to hold a sword, then hold it! Do you think your enemy will wait and write a poem while you pick up your sword if it falls?" When Dorrie stopped for a moment, exhausted, Savi drummed his fingers on the bench he sat on.

"The time for you to face your little unmannerly nemesis fast approaches. I know that you have received a good deal of excellent, perhaps inspired, instruction in the art of the sword." He picked up his own rapier. "I'd like to see some proof of that by watching you go one minute with me without dropping it. *Allez!*"

Dorrie cried out with gleeful pride when she'd managed the feat.

"There," said Savi, as Dorrie worked to get her breath back. "I'd say your chances of beating her, though still dismal, are now infinitesimally greater." He fiddled with the hilt of his rapier. "I understand that there's an apprentice field trip to Geneva this afternoon, and that you won't be going."

Dorrie colored. "Francesco won't let us."

"Meet me at the Paris, 1643 CE archway at noon." He strode away.

Her heart beating fast, Dorrie got to the Paris, 1643 CE archway early. It stood in an intolerably hot, low-ceilinged little room. The brick back side of some other Library chamber blocked the room's one window, and the only light came from the archway. Dorrie gently touched the black and gold clock that stood on its stone ledge. Its face, painted with Roman numerals, sat beneath the arm of a sculpted woman in a long dress reclining on a bench. Her other arm held open a book on her knee.

Savi arrived at the appointed time. His wavy dark hair looked carefully brushed. A great broad-brimmed, feathered hat cast a shadow on his face. An embroidered blue cloak hung over one of his shoulders, and he carried a dress made out of an immense amount of flowered fabric.

"What's that for?" asked Dorrie.

"You can't walk around the streets of Paris in that," said Savi, looking out across and down his nose at Dorrie's late-nineteenth-century dress.

Dorrie's heart began to race.

"If you're still willing, I would like to take you up on your offer of assistance in the little matter of my poetry."

"You would?" Excitement seized Dorrie at the thought of walking into the France of centuries ago. "Of course I will, but what will Francesco—"

"No need for him to know," said Savi. "I'll wait in the hallway while you change."

With trembling hands, Dorrie pulled on the seventeenth-century dress. The skirt dragged on the ground, and the stiff sleeves entirely covered her hands. She rolled them up and gathered up a wad of material in each hand so that she could walk without tripping.

Savi sniffed when he returned. "Perhaps a stable boy's outfit would have been better. Well, come on! Are you waiting for me to throw down my cloak for you to walk upon?"

"Of course not," Dorrie said. She held up her skirts with as much dignity as she could muster and joined Savi in front of the archway. Beyond it lay an airy little hall, the polished wood of tables and floor and bookshelves reflecting back sunshine from two tall windows.

"We're going into Gabriel Naude's private library." Savi caught her in a piercing gaze. "One must never let go of the keyhand when going through an archway, or you will dissolve into an unrecognizable puddle formerly known as Dorothea. Do you understand?"

Dorrie nodded quickly, all the while thinking back with horror to when she'd hauled Marcus through the Athens archway. She hadn't taken any special care at all. It had been dumb luck that they'd held on to each other and she hadn't killed him.

Savi took firm hold of Dorrie's hand.

"Wait!" said Dorrie.

Savi looked at her impatiently.

"Will I be able to understand you out there?"

"The more instant translation of a language your ears have done inside Petrarch's Library, the better you can understand that language outside Petrarch's Library. I've shouted an immense number of corrections at you in the past weeks. You'll be fine."

As they stepped through the archway, Dorrie felt as she had going into and out of Athens, a force first pushing against her and then pulling her forward. Emerging on the other side, she experienced a powerful head-spinning exhilaration. When they'd gone to Athens, there had been no time to soak in that fantastical reality. Now, her feet seemed to tingle where her shoes met Gabriel Naude's floor.

They descended a narrow set of stairs into a vestibule. Dorrie's heart began to pound as Savi laid his hand on the knob of the door that led out into France.

"Are you ready, then?" said Savi, an expression of understanding on his face. Dorrie nodded. Outside, she blinked in awe. A narrow, cobbled street ran in front of Gabriel Naude's door. Horses and carts and crowds of people moved in both directions in noisy confusion.

Staring at the houses and the hats and the cobblestones and the raggedy children shouting and running after a wagonload of apples, Dorrie felt her senses pulsing. She sniffed tentatively. The air seemed full of ten kinds of rotten, mixed with the sweetness of flowers and the salt of sweat.

Savi drew in an enormous breath. "Yes. Paris has a way of crawling up one's nose." They stepped down into the street. "Do not get lost, mademoiselle. For that, Francesco would not forgive me."

With that, he set off at a brisk pace down a crooked street. Being careful to stay in his wake, Dorrie let her head swivel hungrily around as they turned into another crooked, crowded street full of signs hanging over doors, and then along a broad river and then up a set of stone stairs and into a grander avenue where fewer people shouted and jostled. In an alley to one side of a forbidding-looking house, Savi paused before a little iron gate.

"My Madeleine made arrangements to have the gate left unlocked."

He pushed it open, and they found themselves on a flag-stone path that wound among some birch trees and gave out on a great swath of lawn. Taking a deep breath and straighten-ing his hat, Savi hurried toward the lawn. At its edge, a bush not being conveniently located, he installed Dorrie behind a pile of steaming garbage and hurriedly handed her a copy of his poem. "The words have already flown from my head."

Dorrie looked over the page. "If you get stuck, I'll whisper the next words." She smiled at him shyly. "You can do it."

He closed his eyes for a moment, turned, and then called softly toward a balcony that hung from a solid-looking three-story stone house. "Madeleine."

Dorrie eyes watered as an invisible cloud of noxious vapors from the garbage pile enveloped her.

When Madeleine appeared, or at least the small bit of her forehead not obscured by a lacy fan of immense proportions, Savi's face flushed the red of a dark wine. He did not greet Madeleine but stood stock-still in stiff, panicked silence. The moment stretched painfully until Madeleine finally shifted her fan so that Dorrie could see her face for a moment, framed in cascades of red-gold hair. Her plump lips were drawn together in an annoyed pout. Dorrie glanced wildly down at her papers, wondering if she should begin. She glanced back at Savi's frozen face and whispered, "Since."

"Since!" cried Savi, the word exploding from his mouth with the force of a popping champagne cork.

"We must all become slaves to beauty," hissed Dorrie.

"We must all become slaves to beauty," repeated Savi, gulping visibly halfway through the sentence.

Dorrie took another breath. It seemed that Savi couldn't even bring himself to look at Madeline. "Would it not be better to lose our freedom in chains of gold, than chains of hemp or iron?"

Savi repeated the line without gulping between any of the words, but said "lions" instead of "iron" which Dorrie thought ruined the whole sense of the thing, but she didn't have time to dwell on it. "All I desire…"

"All I desire…" said Savi, throwing out an arm too late for his gesture to be interpreted as having anything to do with his words.

"Is that in wandering at liberty amongst those little labyrinths of gold you have for hair," Dorrie found herself saying in tandem with Savi.

"I should soon lose myself there," Savi finished by himself, looking triumphant. But the look faded in a moment. His lips rummaged about, making desperate preparatory motions but nothing came.

"Monsieur!" hissed a voice from the iron gate they'd passed through. Dorrie glanced around and saw a boy about Kenzo's age in stained clothing, his hands around the bars of the gate.

She turned back to the page she held. "And all that I wish for," Dorrie began again in a whisper, but Savi was already off.

"Is never to recover my freedom once lost," he nearly shouted. Dorrie looked anxiously at Madeline to see if the mangled sentence had made an impression on her. She looked neither particularly confused or particularly comprehending, but a movement in a window to her right caught Dorrie's eyes. A man who could have been Madeline's brother stood there looking with affectionate amusement at Savi.

"If you would but promise me," Savi continued clearly, his hands locked in an imploring clasp, "that my life will not last longer—"

"Monsieur," hissed the voice again from the iron gate.

Savi whirled in a towering temper and gnashed his teeth at the boy. "This is a difficult enough endeavor without the contributions of an urchin chorus!"

"But you are needed," said the boy. "Monsieur Naude sent me." Savi's face seemed to electrify with attention. "There is an ambush forming somewhere on the Quai Conti for Udo Gurren."

Savi's eyes flashed. "Back through the gate," he ordered Dorrie. "And do exactly as I tell you."

Leaving the boy, they dashed through one street after the next, until Dorrie's lungs burned and a stabbing stitch developed in her side. The heavy skirt dragged. Dorrie forced her sweat-blurred eyes to focus only on Savi's back. An alley let them out onto a broad expanse of cobbles that overlooked the river. Savi skidded to a stop near a heavy building, its front wall lined with market stalls and wagons, where crowds of people milled about, buying and selling. Great, round towers soared upward on either side of the building.

"He would have—" Savi began. He broke off his sentence, unsheathing his sword. Where the footpath of a nearby bridge met the broad quay on which they stood, two much smaller stone towers marked the connection. Against them, a motley assortment of men lounged. On second look, Dorrie realized that each held a club or a heavy stick or a blade or a knife, and they appeared anything but relaxed.

Slowly, Savi's eyes traveled up the highest of the building's towers and then focused on the gate embedded in the building's center. Dorrie watched him pale and just as quickly recover his color. "The Porte de Nesle it is, then," he murmured.

In another moment, Savi had thrust Dorrie behind an unattended wagon heaped high with hay not far from the gate. "Do. Not. Move." At that moment, a lone figure in dusty black clothing came into view from between the two bridge towers, carrying a sack over one shoulder, his head bent.

"Udo!" Savi shouted, too late to warn the figure. One of the lounging men had sprung to attention. He sent Udo staggering forward with a blow to his back. Another leaped on him, knife flashing in the sun. In the next moment, Savi had traveled the breadth of the quay. His sword aloft in one hand, he shouldered the man with the knife sideways and pulled Udo up from where he'd fallen on the cobbles.

"Look out!" Dorrie shouted, as the horde of other armed men swarmed toward Savi. Dorrie felt terrifying dread. So many!

Thrusting Udo behind him, Savi engaged the first of his attackers and sent one man's sword flying. It bounced and grated against the cobbles. With a leer, the man lunged for Savi with a knife he pulled out of his belt. Savi jumped backward, pushing the dazed Udo along with him.

"I wouldn't," said Savi, backing up farther, his sword extended, "unless you want to pay full price."

Two other men joined the man with the knife, one with a long rusty blade and the other with an ugly club. The man with the knife lunged again and this time shrieked, dropping the knife as Savi's blade flew through the air, slicing open the man's arm. Dorrie felt as though she might faint as Savi sent the other two whirling away with painful-looking slashes across their buttocks. Shoppers and stall-keepers shouted and milled, trying to get away from the flashing blades.

As another wave of attackers drove Savi farther back toward the gate, he thrust Udo into the wedge of open space between the hay wagon and the tower wall. Udo fell to his knees, his hand against his neck. Dorrie tried to catch him. As Savi drove forward again out of sight, Dorrie and Udo fell together in a tangle. A sheaf of papers bound with a wide strap of leather slid from the sack. Dorrie gasped, catching sight of two words in large, looping script: "Cornelius Loos." She looked at Udo.

Though he wasn't bleeding much, he seemed dazed. She snatched the bundle of papers from the ground in a panic and jammed it inside the hay wagon.

Now Savi and his attackers came into view again. He was crossing blades with two swordsmen at once. Dorrie scrambled to her feet as a man with a long, thick pole caught Savi with a blow on the side of his head. He staggered but didn't fall. Dorrie felt a surge of pure rage. She longed to drive them all back and away from Savi, but she had nothing to fight with, nothing to hurl but hay, and Savi had told her to stay put. In that moment, Dorrie realized that if Savi's attackers drove him back any farther, they would be able to reach her and Udo.

"Under, under," she cried to Udo, pointing beneath the wagon. Together, they scrambled between the heavy wooden wheels. Peering out through the wheel's spokes, Dorrie stifled another cry as one of Savi's attacker's strokes hit Savi, ghastly and hard and unforgiving. Dorrie saw Savi grimace. To Dorrie's horror, a red stain bloomed on his side. She stared at it, paralyzed.

With a snarl and all in a blur, Savi switched sword hands, parried another attack, and then thrust hard. Savi's attacker fell, his head hitting the cobbles with a thud and his blade clattering to the ground beside the hay wagon. Dorrie broke out of her trance and pounced on the hilt of the sword, dragging it beneath the wagon. The forest of shifting, shuffling legs showed her that three or four attackers were still pressing Savi.

Fighting the skirt she wore, Dorrie pulled the heavy sword back. "Don't drop it!" she ordered herself through clenched teeth. "Don't drop it!" With a grunt, she thrust the blade forward toward one of the attacker's legs as hard as she could. She closed her eyes at the last minute, but the point of the sword must have found its mark, because she felt resistance and then heard a scream. Her stomach turned violently.

She opened her eyes again to see that Savi had reversed the press and was moving his attackers backward again. Panting, Dorrie pulled back the sword. This time she forced herself to keep her eyes open and aimed for a man's calf just above his heavy boot. She heard another howl.

Suddenly there were fewer legs. She heard a crash of steel against wood and saw a club go spinning across the cobbles. Only Savi's legs and one other pair now danced before her eyes. She didn't dare thrust again. They were moving too fast and too close together. And then suddenly they were moving apart and a man tumbled to the cobbles. Savi slid down behind the wagon, his back against the wall, breathing in great hoarse rasps.

Dorrie hurled herself toward him. "Savi!" she cried out as he closed his eyes. He had gone still and deathly pale. Kneeling, she hovered over him, afraid to touch him, afraid to let him alone, afraid to make a noise, afraid of the sudden silence on the quay, afraid the way she'd never been in her life. "Don't die," she whimpered, trying not to look at the red stain spreading along his side.

The sound of running footsteps coming closer filled her ears. With a fierce growl, she lifted her sword.

A man in a dark cloak appeared around the end of the wagon. "Friend," he said, lifting his empty hands at the sight of Dorrie's quivering sword.

Savi took a long, shuddering breath and opened his eyes. "What took you so long, Gabriel?"

Back in Petrarch's Library, Dorrie sat alone before the crackling fire in Ursula's cottage, waiting for a chance to talk to Savi after Ursula finished attending to his wounds. Dorrie stirred the contents of a black kettle round and round in mechanical circles. Ursula had given her the job to stop her pacing back and forth in front of the door to the room full of beds where Ursula tended her patients.

Dorrie's thoughts turned along with the spoon. She saw Udo Gurren sprawled, knife at his throat on the cobbles. She saw the thugs creeping in from all directions toward Savi, the stain of blood spreading along his side. She felt again the fear that had almost paralyzed her below the wagon. People had been willing to hurt other people to keep Loos's manuscript a secret. Udo had risked his life to bring the manuscript out of its hiding place, and Savi had risked his life to save that man and to keep the manuscript from being destroyed or hidden again.

Dorrie had seen the danger that mere words could put a person in. She had seen what the Lybrariad's work meant to those they protected. Savi had made a difference. He had stopped something horrible from happening to Udo, and perhaps now a hundred or twenty or even five fewer people would be accused of witchcraft and made to suffer like Ursula, or die. A time-traveling lybrarian's job was exciting, yes, but scary and so dangerous. Dorrie shivered, thinking about what a world without a Lybrariad might look like.

Finally, Ursula let Dorrie in to see Savi. Ursula took a closer look at Dorrie's torn dress and dirt-smeared face. "So she—"

"Admirably if…unconventionally," said Savi, wincing as he stood. "I thank you, apprentice. For everything you did today."

Dorrie's breath caught. She almost glanced behind her to see if someone else was standing there. Savi had called her "apprentice." Her heart swelled with pride. "I don't think I've really been paying attention to what the Lybrariad's trying to do," Dorrie said all in a rush. "I've just been thinking about— I've just been thinking about what I could get out of staying here. You know, sticking up for Mr. Kornberger a little, but mostly thinking about how cool it would be to learn how to sword-fight and go to other times."

"And now?"

Dorrie bit her lip. "Remember when you asked me if I wanted to apprentice to a swordsman or a lybrarian?"

"Yes."

Dorrie met Savi's gaze. "I want to apprentice to a lybrarian."

Savi was silent a moment and then smiled ever so slightly. "Well, for now, go get cleaned up."

She turned to leave.

"And don't forget to give me back the dress. A hundred swordsmen I'd gladly face, but not Mistress Lovelace empty-handed."

Chapter 18
The Midsummer Lybrarians' Conference and Festival

WORD SPREAD ABOUT DORRIE'S actions with Savi at the Porte de Nesle. Francesco had been furious that Savi had taken Dorrie out of Petrarch's Library, but since neither Francesco nor Hypatia had told Savi that he couldn't do such a thing, Francesco had to content himself with blustering.

The apprentices, however, spent hours reading out a feast's worth of caramels, hot chocolate, rice pudding, baklava, and sweet custard breads to spread out on a table in the den. Sven and Saul put Dorrie up on a chair with a bedsheet cloak and a garland of olive leaves on her head, while Mathilde read out a limerick she'd written to document forever Dorrie's adventure.

The lybrarians seem to have more smiles for her in general, and Phillip gave her a bear hug out on the Commons, saying, "I knew you belonged here!" No longer did Dorrie have to hear Millie mentally tack "…you morons" onto anything meant for Dorrie's ears, because Millie now refused to speak to Dorrie at all. Even at Master Casanova's rehearsals, Millie carefully avoided even looking at Dorrie as if determined to balance out, with pointed oblivion, all the attention that Dorrie had been getting.

Between all the smiles and pats on the back and the undying honor of Mathilde's limerick, Dorrie felt an occasional twinge. The page from *History of Histories* still lay in Athens. Would the lybrarians and apprentices treat her with so much goodwill and acceptance if they knew that she was responsible for it being there? She shook off the worry—nothing could be done until the lybrarians reopened the Athens archway anyway.

Soon Dorrie's exploits were set aside as a topic, and all the talk at the apprentices' table shifted to the upcoming Midsummer Lybrarians' Conference. Keyhands and lybrarians from all the wherens would soon be descending on Petrarch's Library for three days of sport, entertainment, celebration, and meetings. They'd compete in the Lybrarian Games, which supposedly featured just as fierce competition in timed scroll-shelving and book-cart racing, as in rappelling and dagger-throwing, and Casanova would present his play, which actually seemed to be coming along quite well.

Dorrie was looking forward to the conference with both excitement and dread, for when the last event had concluded, it would be time for the Lybrariad to make its decision about her and Marcus. While Dorrie ached to see the rest of her family and Passaic, she wanted to return to them as a true apprentice of the Lybrariad, not just someone who had had a wonderful adventure that was over.

Her experience in Paris had filled her with fresh energy for her sword-fighting lessons. No longer did she spend her time daydreaming about the Passaic Academy students cheering her on as she conquered Tiffany Tolliver. Instead, she saw herself fighting side by side with Cyrano de Bergerac to free people like Cornelius Loos from their prisons. Preferably before they died in them.

The first day of the Midsummer Festival finally arrived. Getting through the Library's most central rooms and corridors was now difficult, choked as they were with people arriving from every corner of the world and from fifty different centuries. Every handcart had been pressed into use and loaded with boxy suitcases, cloth sacks, carpetbags, leather satchels, baskets, and heavy-looking wooden trunks.

People called out to one another and stopped in inconvenient clumps to chat. All day long, in her travels through the Library, Dorrie had to dodge this way and that, her head in constant danger of being stove in by heavy luggage toted on visitors' shoulders.

In the Gymnasium that early evening, Dorrie and Savi had

just finished a lesson when the distant sound of tambourine and drum erupted. A merry bout of fiddling followed. Over at the Villa de Papyri, the Opening Day Party had begun.

Savi hung up their swords. "Your parry, though still dreadful in many ways, now has a little something to it."

A thrill ran down Dorrie's spine. It was the closest thing to a compliment that Savi had ever paid her. Dorrie hid her grin and went into one of the changing rooms. Pulling the wadded-up pirate costume that she'd worn to the Pen and Sword Festival out of her satchel, she sighed.

Almost everyone at tonight's party would be wearing fun clothes from whichever era and place tickled their imaginations. Checked out from the circulation desk with Mistress Lovelace's blessings. Still unable to produce their overdue dressing gown and bathrobe, Dorrie and Marcus hadn't dared approach her. They'd decided to attend the party in their Passaic clothes, as a pirate and a twenty-first-century teenage sleepwalker.

Out in the Gymnasium, Dorrie could hear Savi reciting his latest epistle to Madeleine. When Dorrie emerged, Savi abruptly stopped speaking. He wore his regular clothing, but set off by his best cape and hat.

Dorrie hitched her satchel onto her shoulder. "The party already sounds crowded!"

"Oh, it'll be packed," said Savi. Dorrie watched him fold the papers he held into a small square. He carefully stowed them in a red cloth pouch that hung from a thin braid of leather around his waist. "Lots of visiting field lybrarians."

Dorrie picked up Savi's feathered hat from a bench and handed it to him. Savi settled it on his head.

"So you're going to go through with it on your own?" asked Dorrie.

Savi brushed at his sleeve. "How can I not when you've set me such an example? When day after day you are willing to boldly present yourself to me with such a severe paucity of skill in the art of the sword that I tremble for you?" He bestowed the tiniest of smiles upon Dorrie. "If you can do that, than surely I can stand in front of…Madeleine all by myself"—here he paused—"whether I make a hash of it or not."

Dorrie didn't try to stop her grin.

"But first," he said, holding out his arm. "The party."

At the Villa de Papyri, they emerged into an open area enclosed on three sides by long, low grand-looking buildings, each with a half-dozen doors opening onto covered walkways. A glinting pool of clear water rippled in the center of the space. It was much cleaner looking and more spacious than the bath beside the Gymnasium and open to the sky. Candles floated in the pool, and reflections of their tiny flames danced in the water. Someone had hung Chinese lanterns all along the covered walkways that ran along the surrounding buildings. The thrum of conversation and laughter mixed with the music filled the air.

"As I said in *Areopagitica*," Dorrie heard a loud voice pronounce. "He who destroys a good book kills reason itself."

The tall speaker was addressing Phillip, who was leaning against a pillar as though hoping its atoms would rearrange themselves and allow him to disappear inside it.

"If I may add to that thought, Mr. Milton!" said a very short man beside the tall one. "The opinion compelled to silence may be the opinion that describes a truth."

Phillip suddenly noticed Savi and Dorrie and waved frantically to them. "Oh! Savi!" he called out with clear desperation.

Dorrie began to wave back, but Savi held her arm down.

"Just walk along. No need to engage," Savi said in a singsong voice, steering Dorrie past Phillip and the strangers.

"Oh, Savi!" called Phillip again, more loudly.

Dorrie glanced back.

"Well, don't look right at them!" growled Savi, glaring at Dorrie as if she'd used his sleeve to blow her nose.

"I think he needs us!" Dorrie protested.

Phillip was looking pleadingly at them and making desperate gestures with his finger across his throat, as the men surrounding him droned on with their conversation.

Savi sighed. "I am about to officially pay Phillip back for any favors rendered in the past or future!" He spun on his heel and headed for Phillip, Dorrie trailing in his wake.

A third stranger with a bushy beard was speaking. "New

opinions are always suspected and usually opposed, without any other reason but—"

"Many pardons, gentlemen," Savi interrupted loudly, striding through the living fence the conversationalists had made around Phillip. "Tedious keyhand business." He bowed and then spun on his heel again. Phillip gave a passable impression of disappointment and followed Savi out of their midst.

"Beware the Johns!" Phillip warned. He shook his head as if to clear his ears. "Otherwise known as the Titans of Free Expression. Not that I don't love what they have to say."

"Over and over again, and they hardly go far enough," said Savi.

"Who are the Titans of Free Expression?" asked Dorrie, looking back at the huddled threesome.

"John Milton, John Locke, and John Stuart Mill," said Phillip. "Look them up sometime." He rocked up on his toes. "Now where is Ursula? I'd just convinced her to dance when they cornered me."

Dorrie scanned the crowd. People sat and stood in little clusters on the pool's patio, or eased through the crowds with plates full of dolmas and tall glasses of white beer or pomegranate punch. Others danced at the far end of the pool where the musicians sent the bright, stinging music into the air. Dorrie shivered with pleasure.

"I don't see Ursula," said Savi, his lip curling. "But there's Mr. Gormly, using every talent he possesses at the buffet table."

"You really are terrible to him, you know," said Phillip amiably.

As they watched, Francesco marched up to Mr. Gormly, tore the plate he was filling out of his hands, and pointed to the spot on the patio that Dorrie supposed he was supposed to be patrolling.

"I feel sorry for him," said Dorrie. "He doesn't even like the job. Really. He's told me so."

A little way down the patio surrounding the pool of water, Dorrie caught sight of a group of female apprentices clustered around Saul, their giggles curling and twisting around him. Saul looked earnestly confused.

"There's Ursula!" Dorrie shouted, pointing. Beyond where Saul leaned, at one end of the pool, iron gates opened into a large garden. Ursula was being led around a fountain on the back of the aurochs by Ebba.

Dorrie watched proudly. "Hasn't Ebba done a good job training Roger? And you should see what she's done with Moe."

"Excuse me," said Phillip, moving off into the crowd. "If Ursula can ride that beast, she can certainly give dancing with me a go!"

"Hi!" shouted Marcus from behind Dorrie, his head bobbing to the rhythms of the music. He held a cup of pomegranate juice in each hand.

Dorrie reached for one.

"Get your own," said Marcus, taking a sip out of each cup.

Dorrie pulled one out of his grasp.

Marcus looked around them, satisfied. "Lybrarians gone wild."

Dorrie grinned. "I can't see Mr. Scuggans enjoying this." She tried the punch. It was tart and sweet and delicious.

For the next two hours, Dorrie and Ebba danced with the other apprentices, rode the aurochs, and tried everything on the buffet table. Dorrie had only been forced to endure three minutes of Millie's company when they stood waiting to have their glasses refilled with pomegranate punch at the same time. Izel stood with Millie, wearing a long, sky-blue velvet dress. "It's from nineteenth-century Venice," Izel had said, looking at Dorrie's stained and tattered "pirate" outfit with a wrinkled nose.

She had lifted her foot slightly to show Dorrie the soft suede ankle boot she wore. It was the color of milk. "These were last worn by Caroline Bonaparte, Queen of Naples." Dorrie wasn't sorry when Moe experienced a relapse and, snarling, leaped from Ebba's shoulder onto Izel's head, ruining her painstakingly arranged hair.

Later, as Dorrie watched some of the visiting field lybrarians perform acrobatics on ropes strung across the pool, Savi sidled by. "I'm off," he said.

"Good luck," whispered Dorrie.

When the performance ended, Ebba went to get them more mince tarts, and Dorrie sought out a quiet patch of patio. She eased herself back in a woven rush chair, the scent of jasmine in her nose. Her heart stretched satisfyingly at the turn her life had taken. This was her world now too, as much as Passaic was. And she'd proven her worth and dedication to the Library at least a bit. They had to let her stay on.

Hypatia stood nearby, talking with a few lybrarians Dorrie didn't know. The light from a nearby torch illuminated the scars on Hypatia's face as she laughed at something one of the other lybrarians had said. Dorrie wondered, not for the first time, how exactly Hypatia had gotten those scars. A splashing attracted her attention. Kenzo, Saul, Mathilde, and a few people Dorrie didn't know stood in the pool, a blanket suspended between them. She giggled as an older woman, wearing an enormous flowery bonnet, threw herself onto the blanket.

Ebba returned with the mince tarts and Marcus. "Dorrie!" she hissed, squeezing in beside her on the chair. "Izel says that Aspasia and the other Athens keyhands are going back in first thing in the morning. They're going to hold this um...um.... symposium thing where people sit around and talk about an idea. They're going to invite all the big decision-makers in Athens to debate Socrates' situation and try to argue their way to a pardon."

Dorrie's mouth had gone dry five words into Ebba's announcement.

"It's going to happen tomorrow! In the Athens Spoke Library," said Ebba. "Well, not in it. It's too small, but in the house on the other side of it."

Dread stole through Dorrie. Though she wanted things to go well for Socrates, a part of her had been hoping that the need to act would somehow be put off indefinitely. "We've got to go in right after Aspasia goes in. We've got to be ready. Early. With our costumes on."

"Yes!" said Marcus, with great enthusiasm "We'll just get down there at dawn and totally *lurk*."

Dorrie and Ebba stared at him.

"What? I enjoy lurking. It's one of the twelve core skills in Casanova's stealth and deception curriculum."

Ebba bit her lip. "I don't know. Maybe we should forget our plan and just tell the lybrarians what happened."

"Why?" cried Dorrie, stunned.

"Yeah, why?" echoed Marcus.

"Because," said Ebba, fiddling with the edge of the mince tart, "the lybrarians trust you now. I'm sure of it. And the fact that you can get through other archways is amazing." She looked at Dorrie, her eyes bright. "I don't think they'd hold what happened against you. It was an accident. They could help us get back the *History of Histories* page."

She glanced at Dorrie's thumbnail. "And it is strange that your thumbnail hasn't healed after all this time."

"What, now *you* think I had something to do with Kash disappearing!"

"Of course not!" Ebba said, looking hurt. "But it's unusual. And what you can do is unusual. Maybe the two things are connected?"

"I don't see why they should be," Dorrie said mulishly. "That sounds completely random."

Ebba looked disappointed in her. "Maybe if the lybrarians knew about both things, they could figure out if there was a connection."

"And figure out that they don't want me here!" said Dorrie.

"Yeah," said Marcus. "I say we just keep Dorrie's little abnormalities to ourselves for now. I mean, the lybrarians have enough to worry about with Kash still missing and Socrates about to check out for good."

Ebba looked dubious about Marcus's concern for the Lybrariad's peace of mind.

His words had grated on Dorrie. She threw her mince tart into his lap. "Stop talking about them like they're just characters in a story or something! They're real people!"

"Okay, for reals?" said Marcus, leaning forward and holding the tip of his index finger and thumb so that they almost touched. "I'm this close to Egeria begging me to kiss her. I can feel it! We can't risk getting kicked out now!"

"That's not important to anyone but you!" said Dorrie angrily. The moment the words were out of her mouth, she flushed with the realization that she might as well have been talking to herself. She couldn't bring herself to look Ebba in the eye, and instead looked out at the crowd by the pool in time to watch Phillip throw his head back and laugh in his big way at something Mistress Lovelace had said.

She thought of the sword-fighting lesson she'd had with Savi that evening. She thought of collapsing with laughter playing Twister with Ebba and the other apprentices up in the attics; she thought of Paris. Dorrie forced herself to look back into Ebba's eyes. "I don't want to lose all this. I want to keep training. I want to be accepted as a real apprentice. I don't want to seem like some freak threat to the Lybrariad when I know I'm not! I want to belong here."

Ebba shrugged. "I think if you want to belong here, then you belong here."

"Not according to Francesco." Dorrie grabbed Ebba's hand. "I promise. As soon as we get the page safely back, I'll tell Hypatia about getting through the archway, okay?"

Early the next morning, before anyone else was stirring, Dorrie, Ebba, and Marcus donned their chitons and tip-toed into the den. "If anyone asks," whispered Dorrie, "we just say—"

Someone knocked firmly on the den door.

Dorrie, Marcus, and Ebba froze, looking at each other with wild eyes. The knocking came again. For a furious moment, they discussed in sign language the possible costs and benefits of diving back into their rooms, simply waiting for the knocker to get tired and walk away, which might happen only *after* other apprentices had been awoken, or answering the door. In the end, Dorrie found herself being propelled toward the door by Marcus and then abandoned there as he and Ebba dived around the back side of the fireplace.

Dorrie lifted the door's latch, her heart hammering. *Had Francesco come to march her off in chains? Had the lybrarians decided that Dorrie and Marcus would have to leave right away?* The knocking ceased. Dorrie slowly swung the door open.

Mistress Lovelace stood outside the den door, in front of a bicycle hung with two enormous wicker hampers. Her glasses and pearls gleamed.

Dorrie gaped at her.

"Good morning, Dorothea," Mistress Lovelace said pleasantly.

Dorrie shook her head. "Uh. Good morning."

Mistress Lovelace consulted a little black book in her hands, and then looked back up at Dorrie with cordial calm. "I've come for items C-DG 23.7 and C-DG 23.7."

Dorrie looked at her blankly.

"A dressing gown and a bathrobe?" said Mistress Lovelace helpfully. "Checked out from the circulation desk on your behalf by Phillippus Aureolus Theophrastus Bombastus von Hohenheim? I've come to collect them."

"Oh, right," said Dorrie, flashing on the moment the garments in question had begun to disintegrate. She cleared her throat. "I'm sorry. We've...uh...misplaced them."

Mistress Lovelace adjusted her glasses slightly. "Both?"

"Temporarily," Dorrie added hastily.

Mistress Lovelace consulted her little black notebook again. "I'm sorry but if you can't now return those items to the circulation desk, they must be considered permanently lost." Her tone was irreproachably amicable and firm as stone. "We'll need to add the value of those items to your fine, naturally."

"All right," stammered Dorrie, thinking that she and Ebba and Marcus were losing time.

"As I'm sure you know, the fine must be paid in full by the close of day."

"But, but we don't have any money," said Dorrie.

Mistress Lovelace drew a card from between the pages of her notebook. Dorrie recognized it right away as a copy of the many overdue notices she'd been sent. She read it out loud:

"The dressing gown numbered C-DG 23.7 was checked out from the circulation desk on your card and is now subject to a fine of fifteen minutes of labor behind the circulation desk for each day of further detention. If, after thirty days, the item is not returned, the dressing gown must be sent for by messenger, and the cost in time of obtaining it collected in addition to the fine *accruing to the date of the recovery* of the dressing gown, which cost and fine must be paid *to make your card good for future use*."

Mistress Lovelace tucked the notebook away. "Each of you owes a fine of seven hours and twenty minutes. We begin fine work at six a.m. promptly on the day of collection."

"What time is it now?" asked Dorrie.

Mistress Lovelace consulted a little silver watch around her wrist. "It's 5:51." She mounted her bicycle.

Dorrie grasped for a way out. But what could she say? *Sorry, not a good day for this. We're busy waiting for a chance to sneak into ancient Athens?* "But…but the Lybrarian Games are this afternoon," she stuttered instead. She looked down at her chiton. "And we have a rehearsal for Master Casanova's play this morning!"

"I'm afraid there's nothing that can be done about the rehearsal," said Mistress Lovelace, her voice supremely level. "But if you begin right away, it's just possible that you won't miss the quill-sharpening competition. One of my favorites."

Exactly nine minutes later, Dorrie found herself pushing an iron the size and approximate weight of a cinder
block over a pair of pantaloons in the vast warren of rooms
behind the circulation desk. Beads of her sweat kept falling
and hissing on the iron. An enormous basket of washed,
dried, and badly wrinkled clothing sat nearby waiting for
her attentions.

One of Mistress Lovelace's assistants walked by with a box
full of wallets of wildly different designs. "Mind you don't let
that iron run too long, or you'll start scorching things. You
have to turn it off now and then to cool it down."

Dorrie nodded, too breathless to acknowledge the assistant's
advice in any other way. The assistant pushed through the curtains that led out to the circulation desk itself. Elsewhere in
the rooms full of storage bins and clothing racks, Marcus sat
sewing missing buttons on vests. They'd left Ebba to patrol
the Athens archway with Moe until Dorrie and Marcus could
get free, keeping an eye on the rack of scrolls and tabs on the
Athens keyhands. The plan was to tell anyone who passed that
Moe had gone missing in the area. Mathilde had also been
roused by Mistress Lovelace for her own crimes against free
circulation and stood nearby, arranging coins and paper money
from various wherens into neat packets.

Dorrie stopped ironing, her fingers suddenly cold, as she
recognized Francesco's voice on the other side of the curtains.

281

"I'll need three tube dresses, two collars, six pairs of palm-fiber sandals, two loincloths, two kilts, six cloaks—"

Dorrie listened carefully for words like "History of Histories" or "Athens" or "instantaneous marooning."

"Make that three loincloths," barked Francesco. "And hurry."

Mistress Lovelace's assistant swished back through the curtains. Dorrie pushed the iron back and forth again vigorously, hoping the woman wouldn't notice the unfortunate scorch mark Dorrie had just made.

"Francesco!" called another voice she recognized. It was Savi! His voice sounded tight and worried. "So Kash has been captured! When were you going to tell me?"

Dorrie's heart seemed to stop for a moment. She met Mathilde's eyes. Mathilde shook her head, holding up her hands. Dorrie crept closer to the curtains and peered through the gap to one side.

"We only just got the news via messenger," said Francesco, his face grim.

Savi grabbed hold of the counter. "I want to be part of the rescue mission, of course."

Francesco looked down at a list he held. "You may sit in on the mission meeting, but you'll stay here."

Savi's eyes burned with cold fire. An uncomfortable silence took hold around the circulation desk. The few other borrowers who'd come to return costumes they'd worn at last night's party eased away from Francesco and Savi.

"Kash is my friend," said Savi, his words sharp as glass. "It's my job to help get him back."

Francesco fixed Savi with a hard look. "You are over-involved and your judgment of late has proven supremely underwhelming." Dorrie's breath caught, sure he meant Savi's decision to take her to France. Francesco turned to the enormous box of goods that Mistress Lovelace's assistant had placed on the counter in front of him. "I don't want any mistakes made."

Now, Dorrie's face burned for Savi. A mask seemed to descend over Savi's face. He lowered his voice. "Francesco, I beg you."

"Enough!" said Francesco. "Do your duty here, and don't dishonor your friendship with Kash farther with any more heedless actions."

Savi went perfectly still. Dorrie had the distinct feeling that Savi might at any moment interpret "doing his duty" to mean running Francesco through with his sword.

Instead, he simply bowed slightly. "I shall, indeed, do my duty."

"I'm glad you're finally being sensible," said Francesco stiffly. "Tameri should reach Petrarch's Library this afternoon. We'll get the whole story from her then. We'll hold the emergency mission meeting after that."

He shouldered past Savi and out of the Circulation Room.
"Indeed, I shall," said Savi softly.

Chapter 19

Athens

When Mistress Lovelace finally released them, Marcus insisted that they walk, not run, through the deserted corridors. "Stealth and Deception 101. People notice you if you walk quickly or slowly. And they definitely notice sprinters. Oh, and notice how I'm not whispering?" he continued, looking horribly self-satisfied in Dorrie's opinion. "Whispering only attracts attention."

They saw Moe before they saw Ebba. He was sitting on a tattered sofa near the Athens archway. A generous helping of gold fringe obscured the sofa's legs. Ebba eased herself out from underneath it and brushed herself off, her face full of worry. "I've been watching all day, and no one's touched the scroll rack, but look."

She pointed to the archway's calendar. Under the month Gamelion, the number 19 blazed brightly. "Time's moved forward! The keyhands must have gone in *yesterday* morning. Izel must have gotten the story wrong! Anything could have happened yesterday."

"We should go right now," whispered Dorrie. "Just about everybody's out on the Commons watching the Lybrarian Games."

"I think we've talked about the whispering," said Marcus.

Ebba stared at the archway, as though into the maw of a great heartless shark, her breath shallow and loud.

Dorrie patted her chiton, where she'd tucked in the scroll that belonged in Athens, and took a deep breath. She took hold of one of Ebba's cold, trembling hands and reached for one of Marcus's warmer ones. "*Don't let go when we're going through. It's an instant-death kind of thing.*"

"Good to know," Marcus said, squeezing Dorrie's hand hard.

"Wait," hissed Ebba, as Marcus and Dorrie were about to step through. She took one last look up and down the corridor, and then nodded.

Taking a deep breath, Dorrie stepped through the archway. Just like the first time, she felt the familiar resistance and then pull. Ebba's hand seemed to be crushing her own. When they were well clear of the archway, Dorrie slowly let go of their hands.

A wild happiness shined in Ebba's face. "I did it!" She spun round to face the archway. "I did it."

Marcus went to the wooden door and put his ear to the crack. "There's music playing again."

Dorrie and Ebba began to pull scrolls out of the rack, unfurling and glancing over them with furious speed.

The sound of strumming and the thin, reedy sound of flutes suddenly became much louder. Dorrie turned. Marcus had opened the door a crack and stood, tapping one foot and moving his head back and forth like a chicken.

"What are you doing?" Dorrie demanded, picking up another scroll. "Help us look!"

"What?" said Marcus absently, his face pressed to the crack.

"The page!" hissed Dorrie.

"Right!" Marcus reluctantly joined them at the table. For what seemed like a half an hour, they unfurled and scanned, unfurled and scanned, jumping at every noise from the other side of the door.

As the number of unexamined scrolls diminished, Dorrie grew increasingly anxious. "What if it's not here?"

Marcus unfurled a particularly long scroll, written over in red letters.

As Dorrie stared at the vivid red ink of the letters, a hideous thought occurred to her. Her gaze raked over the remaining scrolls. "None of these have ink splatters on them."

Ebba stopped mid-roll-up. "Yeah, so?"

"When we crashed into the table, some of the scrolls fell

into the spilled ink," said Dorrie, a note of barely contained panic in her voice. "I remember seeing them on the floor, soaking the ink up." She looked back at the scroll rack. "Whoever cleaned up didn't put the ink-stained ones back!" Slithery eels seemed to be practicing figure eights in her stomach. "What if the page has been thrown away?" She said it louder than she meant to.

Almost immediately, the door in the whitewashed wall was shouldered open by a woman with three chins and a mountain of sweaty hair. Dorrie quailed.

The woman shifted the tray of food she had balanced on an arm and got a better grip on the two enormous pitchers that she held, one in each hand. She nodded with the particular satisfaction of the predictably disappointed. "'The hirelings are coming,' the steward says. 'They'll be here any minute,' he says. 'I hired you plenty of help,' he says." She eyed them up and down. "How long have you been hiding out in here, eh? Think you're clever, do you? Charging the master good money, while you shirk in his library?"

She paused for an asthmatic breath. "I could get better service out of a pack of alley cats." The sweaty flesh hanging from the underside of her arms shook as she held out the tray and the pitchers. "Well, don't just stare at me! Take these out to the symposium guests." She thrust the pitchers at Dorrie and Marcus and the tray at Ebba, and pushed them all along through the door. They soon found themselves in an open courtyard filled with talking and laughing people.

A wizened old man with eyes like milky marbles stepped into their path. "About time!" he said impatiently, herding them toward another door. "The master wants to make a toast." Just inside the doorway, Dorrie, Marcus, and Ebba stopped, uncertain.

"Have you lost your senses? Move on!" the old man cried. "They can't have a toast without wine." On the other side of the doorway, crowds of men filled a long room. They stood in clusters and reclined on couches. The air hummed loudly with their conversation. "You come with me," said the old man, taking the second wine jug from Marcus. "I need some chairs moved." Marcus looked back at Dorrie and Ebba helplessly as the old man dragged him away by the arm.

Dorrie huddled close to Ebba, the enormous clay vessel in her trembling arms becoming heavier by the moment. "What should we do?"

"Stay together!" hissed Ebba, her wide dark eyes sucking in the details of the room with the power of two of the hungrier black holes in the universe.. "And hope we don't run into any of the lybrarians." A man with drooping eyes snapped his fingers at her. When she didn't move, he snapped them again more insistently. Slowly, Ebba held her laden tray out to him. He rummaged for the grapes he wanted and stuffed them all in his mouth, talking to another man all the while.

"He didn't even say thank you," said Ebba, as they forced themselves to move forward through the crowd in the direction Marcus had gone. "And no women here, of course. Typical ancient Athenian deal. Mathilde told me all about it."

Another man brayed at Ebba. "Olives! Over here!" Ebba gave Dorrie a pinched, helpless look and eased toward him with the tray. Dorrie was about to follow her when a man held out a black and red bowl with two little handles under her nose. She froze, staring at him blankly, until he jiggled the bowl. "Some wine if you please."

Dorrie slowly lifted her pitcher, glancing wildly around for Marcus. He was standing next to the cluster of musicians, head bouncing to the drummer's rhythms. "I don't believe him!" she murmured.

"Any time, girl," said the man. Dorrie tipped the pitcher up over his bowl, and before she could tip it back, an overflowing slosh of red wine poured onto the man's hand and the floor.

"You dunce!" said the man, passing the bowl to his other hand and shaking his arm. She tried to look as apologetic as possible.

Dorrie heaved the jug of wine into a more secure bear hug and hurried off in search of Ebba. Coming around a group of men, she almost dropped it. Not far away stood a long-boned man with a purple cloak over his chiton, holding his hand up for attention. It was one of the other Athenian keyhands, Leandros. She dived behind the fronds of a potted plant.

"Oh Mercury! I entreat you! Get our host on with his speech!" groaned a man sitting on a couch nearby. "And on with this blasted symposium." He had a great globe of a forehead and a thick, black curling beard. "Socrates wants to be free to call the sun the moon and the moon the sun. And I say—prattle away! But laws are laws and he must be willing to take the consequences."

Marcus appeared beside her. "Nice guy, that drummer. We traded a few rhythms."

"You are impossible!" hissed Dorrie. She pulled him closer. "One of the Athenian keyhands is out there!"

Ebba sidled up beside them. "I hope there's a really nice room for women in this place," she said, "and men better be serving the grapes. What do we do now?"

Dorrie pointed Leandros out to her and checked to make sure no one was listening. "If the *History of Histories* page did get thrown away, maybe the trash is still around here somewhere." She turned to Ebba. "I don't suppose Mathilde happened to mention what ancient Athenians do with their trash?"

Marcus tapped his foot to the music. "Well, I know it eventually gets dumped in a big pile about a mile outside of town."

Dorrie's hopes shriveled. "How do you know that?"

"Oh, I had to come up with an equivalent of the trash-compactor scene in *Star Wars* for Casanova's play, so I asked him what the ancient Greeks did with their garbage."

Dorrie dropped her face into her hands. "No, no, no, no, no."

"But maybe no one's taken it there yet," said Ebba, putting her tray down on a handy table.

Dorrie raised her head. "At home, we put trash out on the curb. By the street. Near the front door." She pushed the wine jug into Marcus's arms. "Here. Just keep serving people so that old guy doesn't come looking for us. And stay out of sight of Leandros. We'll be right back."

In silent agreement, Dorrie and Ebba ducked and slipped their way back into the courtyard, just in time to watch a man with an enormous stomach waddle into it through a wide opening.

"That sort of looks like a street out there, doesn't it?" said Ebba, her voice giddy with new sensation, her eyes on the opening in the mud-colored brick courtyard wall. Dorrie nodded. Shoulder to shoulder with Ebba, she made her leaden legs move forward, her heart crashing about at the thought of moving even farther away from the safety of Petrarch's Library.

At the opening, they stood aside as three men entered laughing boisterously, and then ducked through. They found themselves in a narrow, crooked street lined for the most part with more two-story brick buildings, roofed with heavy-looking tiles. Great clay vessels stood against the walls beside various doorways, and a thin stream of dirty-looking water wended its way down the street's middle.

A mound of rubbish lay in front of the building across the street and in front of another building beside it. A strong wind carried the scent of rot and plugged-up toilets. Against the near wall, a few yards away from the entrance to the courtyard they'd exited, Dorrie caught sight of a half-circle of mud mixed with straw. A few bits of broken pottery and pomegranate peels poked out here and there.

"Oh, no," whispered Dorrie, running over to the spot. "If this was the trash, someone's already taken it."

"Look," said Ebba moving a bit of the straw with her foot. A piece of papery material lay in the mess. Just as Dorrie reached for it, the foul wind sent it flipping and flopping down the street.

Dorrie and Ebba dashed after it, their sandals making slapping noises on the dirt. As they approached a corner, the wind died. "Hah!" shouted Dorrie, leaping, stretching out her leg, intent on coming down with her foot on the runaway piece of papyrus. Instead, she found herself crashing with great force into a person just turning the corner.

She felt trapped and entangled for a moment before the person threw her off and she landed hard on her side. Something hard and shiny bounced into Dorrie's lap. It was a little, stoppered silver bottle. Dorrie stared at it, blinking, frightened of it somehow. For a moment, she had the inside-out feeling that the little bottle *knew* her.

The man snatched the bottle up as Ebba pounced on the piece of paper. Dorrie staggered to her feet. "I'm sorry," she exclaimed. The tall man, his hair silvery, said nothing but regarded her with an air of withering accusation. Like everyone else Dorrie had so far seen in Athens, he wore a chiton, but he also wore a wide belt and an extra piece of cloth over one shoulder.

In the dusk, his nails glowed clean and ghostly white, as though he never had to do anything with his hands except perhaps wave them through the air. He walked on, followed by a cadaverous man, his stringy hair blowing in the wind, carrying an enormous lizard wearing a jeweled collar.

Dorrie shuddered and took firm hold of Ebba's arm, in case she had any ideas about chasing after the men and trying to pet the crocodile thing. They scuttled back toward the house, trembling. At the entryway, breathing hard, they huddled and hurriedly smoothed out the piece of paper. Ebba read aloud. "Almonds, grape leaves, salted pork, anchovies...It's just a shopping list." Dorrie felt like weeping. "We have to get back and tell Hypatia what's happened."

Dorrie and Ebba dashed through the courtyard and then plunged back into the crowded inner room to fetch Marcus. Something felt different. The music had become faster and wilder and louder. The old man was looking with great antagonism at the musicians. Some guests had stuck their fingers in their ears, while others had begun to dance wildly. The man who'd complained about the symposium looked positively wrathful. As Dorrie watched, he marched over to one of the drums and gave it a mighty kick. The musicians' playing came to a dissonant halt.

"Let that be the last anyone ever has to hear of Timotheus."

The drummer that Marcus had been talking to leaped to his feet. He had bits of leather and cloth braided into some of his long locks. "That's my best drum! How dare you?"

"How dare you inspire this company to ill-bred wildness with your uncivilized rhythms!" raged the drum-kicker.

"The only thing wrong with the rhythms is that they're ones you haven't heard before," said Timotheus. "You old goat."

At that, the "old goat" launched himself at Timotheus, and they fell crashing into the other musicians. A great shouting and jangling rose up as the other musicians fell upon Timotheus' attacker, and still more guests came to the aid of the man who'd kicked the drum. Seeing Marcus, Dorrie grabbed hold of him, and together with Ebba, they ducked and dived their way through the crowd toward the door—to the accompanying sound of breaking crockery and angry shouting—and then out into the courtyard.

Marcus looked back at the mayhem. "You don't think that's the Timotheus of Miletus, that I read about in that book, do you? Because if it is… then I just…uh-oh."

Dorrie ducked as a wine bowl went sailing overhead.

They piled into the little library room and Ebba slammed

the door behind them. Not even bothering to check and see if the corridor was empty, Dorrie sprang for the archway, with the others in tow. They landed in a tangle on the corridor's carpet. From his perch on the tattered couch, Moe greeted them with a luxurious yawn and turned over, all docile sweetness, his paws in the air. Ebba scooped him up.

"Anybody could be reading that page right now." Dorrie scrambled to her feet and began to sprint down the corridor. Hypatia has to know the page is really gone."

Dorrie sped up, summoning her courage. Telling Hypatia what she'd done would be much harder than facing any sword-wielding villain she could imagine. She flashed on her old problems in Passaic. They looked so tiny. A brother who was going to make her late for the Pen and Sword Festival? A sister who had poured a little bit of dirty water into Dorrie's orange juice out of…a little silver bottle. Dorrie skidded to a halt, the others ploughing into her. "Now what," demanded Marcus.

Dorrie sucked in her breath. The bottle that had fallen into her lap in Athens was the twin of Miranda's. But where had Miranda found hers? Dorrie had never seen it before. It had been such a crazy rush of a morning, with Mr. Scuggans calling and books falling and her boot missing and the doorbell ringing.

A bolt of lightning seemed to fly right through Dorrie's chest. She stared at her thumbnail.

"Dorrie, what is it?" said Ebba. "What's wrong?"

"That man we saw on the street out in Athens. I've seen him before. In Passaic. He came to see Great-Aunt Alice." Dorrie remembered now the way his gray hair seemed to absorb the sunlight and that he'd worn gloves on that warm June morning. Mr. Biggs he'd called himself. A feeling of horror stole cold and jagged through Dorrie. She shivered and closed her eyes, notions of past, present, and future sliding over each other, pieces of a puzzle grabbing at other pieces.

"How?" said Marcus, staring at Dorrie. "He'd have to time-travel, and only the lybrarians..." His words trailed off, leaving an awful silence.

"If he is time-traveling," whispered Ebba, "is he a friend or an enemy, or someone who doesn't even know about Petrarch's Library?"

"I don't know, but he wasn't very nice," said Dorrie. She pictured the man again as he snatched the silver bottle from her lap. His fingernails had looked odd. Not pinkish, but white. A dull perfect white. The white of chalk or paint or.... "And I think he was wearing nail polish." She turned frightened eyes on Marcus, feeling utterly sick now. "Great-Aunt Alice couldn't be working against the Lybrariad, could she?"

Marcus shrugged. "I don't think she hated being a librarian *that* much."

Without another word, Dorrie spun and resumed her sprint towards Hypatia and the Celsus, her legs moving faster than she ever thought they could. "We have to tell Hypatia. About everything! Before something terrible happens."

Inside the main hall of the Celsus, neat stacks of paper lay on the tabletops in preparation for the next day's scheduled Keyhand Council meeting. When they reached Hypatia's office, chests heaving, Dorrie could hear voices rising and falling from inside. Feeling sick, she forced herself to travel the last few steps to the door, Marcus and Ebba beside her. She raised her hand to knock but hesitated as she heard Hypatia's voice. "You're absolutely sure about what you saw, Mr. Gormly?"

"Yes," Dorrie heard Mr. Gormly say. "They went through the Athens archway. At first I thought they must have had been with one of the keyhands, so I just went about my business, but then I got to thinking that it just didn't make sense, and with things as they are, I ought to say something."

Dorrie's heart sank. She gave Marcus and Ebba a despairing look.

"How much more proof do you need that Dorothea and Marcus Barnes are mixed up in something dangerous to the Lybrariad?" barked Francesco. "The people who trailed Kash were asking everyone they came in contact with about a small gray star. Just the size that would fit in that book of the girl's."

Dorrie inhaled sharply.

"We shouldn't have trusted them," said Francesco.

"You never did," Dorrie heard Savi say. "But some of us still do. Being mixed up in something dangerous to the Lybrariad is not the same as intending us harm."

Francesco went on. "The people who captured Kash had black nails. Callamachus tells me several historians now mention 'Blacknails' in their books. Millie tells me that Ms. Barnes's thumbnail is black as night and has been since the day she arrived."

The grim satisfaction in Francesco's voice began to turn Dorrie's fear into outrage.

Dorrie knocked hard on the door. Heavy footsteps sounded, and Francesco jerked it open. Hypatia sat behind her desk. Mr. Gormly stood to one side of it and Savi to the other. Even in her shame, Dorrie couldn't help but feel a stab of betrayal as she glanced at Mr. Gormly.

Dorrie forced herself to walk through the doorway, Ebba and Marcus at her heels. "I did go through the archway," said Dorrie, finding Hypatia's eyes and then Savi's. "Mr. Gormly is right. That's what I came to tell you."

A tense silence filled the room. From the window, Dorrie could hear the shouts and cheers of the crowds watching the stone-tablet relay races. On Ebba's shoulder, Moe dug around in her hair, chittering.

Hypatia slowly tapped one finger gently on her desk. "May I see your hand?"

Slowly, Dorrie extended it toward Hypatia. Hypatia turned it over gently so that the thumbnail showed. "It looks as though the aurochs stepped on it."

"I...I thought I bashed it sword-fighting."

Hypatia pressed gently at the base of Dorrie's nail. "Does that hurt?"

"No," whispered Dorrie, wishing it did.

Hypatia released Dorrie's hand. "Did you realize before today that you could pass through the Athens archway?"

Sick shame rolled through Dorrie, mixing its stickiness with the anger. "Yes," she finally said, her voice a near-whisper. "It's what I came to tell you about."

"Oh, ho, *now* she wants to tell us about it," said Francesco, his eyes icy. "After she's been caught red-handed."

"Dorrie didn't even know that Mr. Gormly had seen us," said Marcus.

Ebba turned pleading eyes on Hypatia. "Dorrie came to tell you about it because she wanted you to know!"

Hypatia leaned back in her chair. "Please don't shout, Ebba."

"And return to the attics, at once," added Francesco furiously.

"No," said Hypatia. "I think we'd better hear from all three of them."

"We can start," said Francesco, "by having a very detailed discussion about what exactly you were doing in Athens."

It was an awful conversation. Dorrie told them everything. About Marcus accidentally tearing out the page from the *History of Histories* book, about accidentally stumbling into Athens and dropping the page there, about trying to get it back and failing. She told them about how she'd been afraid to tell the truth at first out of fear of being marooned, and then because she wanted to train in the sword, and finally because she'd wanted so badly to be a part of Petrarch's Library. About how Ebba had encouraged her to tell the Lybrariad and how Dorrie hadn't wanted to jeopardize her chances of becoming a real apprentice.

Dorrie's insistence that she cared about the Lybrariad and was beyond sorry about putting it in danger sounded hollow even in her own ears. Savi insisted to Hypatia that he could vouch for Dorrie's best intentions, while Francesco accused her of outright lying about them.

"I know what I did was wrong, but I *wasn't* lying to hurt anyone," Dorrie said, her chest tight with heartsickness, her eyes trained on Savi.

Listening, Hypatia's calm eyes had neither excused nor accused Dorrie and Marcus, but they seemed to contain deep disappointment. How terribly it had burned Dorrie to tell them about seeing Mr. Biggs and his disguised nails in Athens, and the fact that he had been in the Barnes' own home as a guest of her Great-Aunt Alice.

"Well, we know at least that the aunt is definitely working against us," said Francesco. "We cannot afford to keep the question of the loyalty of these two young interlopers open."

"We must, until and unless we can't," said Savi.

Francesco looked at his pocket watch. "Kash's search team leaves in just a few minutes. I must go."

Savi's jaw tightened.

Francesco leaned on Hypatia's desk and fixed her with his one good eye. "We have about forty-five minutes left to exercise…all of our options, if you know what I mean. After that we no longer will be able control the situation. I beg you, think of the Lybrariad's security."

"I'll need to gather as many keyhands as I can on this short notice," said Hypatia. "We'll need a formal decision."

She turned to Dorrie. "I'd like you and Marcus and Ebba to go to your rooms as quickly as possible, get cleaned up and changed—your own clothes will do—then come back here. Bring the star book, please."

Dorrie could feel her heart sinking, down, down, like an anchor into a bottomless sea.

Only Savi, mouthing, "It'll be all right," kept that anchor from pulling her completely under.

Francesco pushed himself off Hypatia's desk, his triumphant eyes on Dorrie. He smoothed his moustache. "Mr. Gormly can escort them." He strode out the door.

Savi's sword hand twitched, his eyes ablaze. He took a step forward as if he meant to hurry after Francesco and then looked back at Dorrie. He seemed to come to a difficult decision and turned his back on Francesco. "I'll go ring the emergency bell."

CHAPTER 20
SEEING STARS

WALKING THROUGH THE DESERTED library, Dorrie shot Mr. Gormly an angry look.

Mr. Gormly looked sheepish. He scratched his head. "I know what you're thinking, but don't look at me that way. I told 'em about that funny business for your own good. Best to have it all out in the open. You could get hurt going out on your own like that. Hypatia will stand by you."

Dorrie stared straight ahead and said nothing. Mr. Gormly led them through the Gymnasium and into the room that contained the Roman bath. Dorrie looked up at the hole that led back into the Passaic Public Library. The flickering blue light around its edge seemed to be flashing out a message: "Game Over. Game Over. Game Over." It seemed to overpower the gas lamp's warm glow. Again, Dorrie saw them pushing the wall at the back of the mop closet and discovering the little secret room for the first time. The dust-covered furniture, the little paintings, the books, and the strange floor with its network of lines connecting circles and triangles and—Dorrie stopped short, her throat almost closing as she remembered. *And one star. In the middle of the room. The dust around it brushed away.*

"Wait!" she called out to the others, a few steps ahead. "That star! The one the people who captured Kash were looking for? I think I might know where it is!"

The others stared at her, mouths open.

"I think it was stuck in the floor of the little room!" she cried, pointing at the hole. "Before it exploded."

Mr. Gormly's eyes went wide. His eyes darted around the Gymnasium. "Is this some kind of trick?"

"No. We've got to go back to Hypatia's office and tell her!"

Mr. Gormly rubbed his chin, looking troubled. "It's a long way back. If you're right, I hate to think of it sitting out there on its own when we could just snatch it back for the Lybrariad."

"Let's get it," cried Marcus.

Ebba's eyes widened. "But we promised Hypatia!"

Dorrie's heart pounded. If they could get the star back, perhaps it would tip the balance in favor of Dorrie and Marcus getting to become apprentices, after all. "I'll just stick my head through and see if I can reach it!"

Mr. Gormly looked around it. "I guess it'd be safe enough with me here."

Dorrie and Mr. Gormly quickly climbed the stairs. Dorrie took a deep breath and reached toward the hole with one fingertip. It felt hot but passable. Suddenly, Dorrie felt herself grabbed from behind. Something hard and cold pressed was against the side of her neck. In another moment, Mr. Gormly's hand had covered her mouth. He spun her to face Marcus and Ebba where halfway up the stairs they stood gaping with raw, uncomprehending fear.

"Now," said Mr. Gormly, smiling wolfishly. "Sorry to be so boorish about this, but I think I'd like that star for myself. Not to mention a horse to gallop away on."

"Let her go!" shouted Marcus, bounding farther up the stairs with Ebba behind him, Moe clinging to her shoulder. They only stopped when Dorrie cried out as Mr. Gormly pressed the cold knife harder against her neck. Marcus's eyes found Dorrie's. His fists curled and uncurled, his face full of fear and rage.

"If you try to hinder me in any way, I assure you that I'm more than willing to cut Dorrie's pretty little neck and use you to get to Passaic, so no attempts at heroics."

"Help!" Dorrie shouted with all her might.

Mr. Gormly shook her like a rag doll. "And definitely no more of that." He thrust his chin at Marcus. "You first. I need all the Passaic keyhands." Marcus's jaw worked wildly as he slowly made his way to the hole. "Don't worry," said Mr.

Gormly. "We'll be simply the best of friends on the other side. You'll see."

"Why should they believe that?" cried Ebba, edging up another stair.

"Don't come any closer," said Mr. Gormly, shoving at Ebba with a foot. With an angry hiss, Moe leaped from her shoulder at Mr. Gormly's face. Mr. Gormly roared and batted at Moe, sending him flying through the air.

"Moe!" shouted Ebba, hurling herself at the rough banister with outstretched arms as the mongoose sailed over it. He plummeted into the water, landing with a splash.

"Move!" growled Mr. Gormly, pressing Marcus and Dorrie forward.

"You better not hurt Dorrie, or I'll kill you!" Marcus shouted, as, wincing at the heat, he backed up the rest of the stairs and into the little five-sided room.

Mr. Gormly grinned at Dorrie. "Your turn, missy!"

She and Ebba turned petrified eyes on one another, and then unable to think of what else to do, Dorrie began to climb. The hole felt unbearably hot, like scalding bathwater. She hurried through into the Passaic Public Library, feeling half boiled alive, with Mr. Gormly hanging tight to her arm.

Without letting go of Dorrie, Mr. Gormly began to sweep his feet this way and that across the ruined floor of the little gaslit room, sending the broken bits of parquet clattering.

Suddenly, he crowed and kicked at something in a mound of debris. It was a thick, little five-armed gray star. When he let go of Dorrie to snatch it up, she dived for the protection of Marcus's arms. Mr. Gormly didn't try to stop her. Instead, he began to plant loud enthusiastic kisses on the star. In between kisses he praised himself. "Oh, you clever, clever man! You canny, cunning, artful, wonderful dodger!"

Suddenly, Dorrie wanted to know very badly what Mr. Gormly knew that they didn't. "What is it?" she blurted out.

"This?" Mr. Gormly said, clasping the star against his chest and grinning so that there really wasn't any face left on either end of his smile. "This?" he repeated, holding the star out on his palm. It shined dully as though made of pencil lead.

Something chilly and unpleasant slithered through Dorrie. As she had suspected, the star was indeed the same shape and size as the space cut out in the book she'd brought from Passaic.

"This is my future, my front-row ticket, my place at the table of my choosing," crowed Mr. Gormly. "This is butlers, and a carriage and eight, and a sea of champagne. This, my little friends, is additional and staggering proof of the bottomless fountain of my intelligence."

During his speech, Dorrie had begun to edge toward the hole, pulling Marcus along with her. They needed help. They had to stop him. If they could just get back down the stairs with a head start.

"I have what I want, and you're no worse for the wear. I told you we'd be the best of friends on this side," sang Mr. Gormly as he did a little jig. "It's about time I got to visit a new village. Three years in Petrarch's Library were three years too many."

"Now!" Dorrie shouted. Holding tightly to one another, Dorrie and Marcus tried to sprint down the stairs, but only succeeded in falling into a tangled heap. Dorrie felt hard floor beneath her knees. She was resting on an invisible barrier. Far below, she could see Ebba racing along the edge of the bath. With a cry, Dorrie tried to reach toward her, only to bash her knuckles on what felt like rough, invisible stone.

"Oh, good," said Mr. Gormly, watching Dorrie cradle her hand. "I was worried your special little power might be a problem." He yawned and tucked his dagger into his belt alongside his sword. "Use a new archway while it's too warm and fresh, and you'll lock yourself right out of Petrarch's Library." He tapped his head. "A little nugget of knowledge you pick up doing internal security."

Dorrie stared at him with a burning, desperate hatred as she remembered the words of caution that Mistress Wu had shared about that so many weeks ago.

"Now thankfully, you won't be able to return," He looked around the little room, his gaze stopping on the door to the mop closet. "And of course, without you, no one inside Petrarch's Library can get out. So that's that."

"That's that!" shouted Marcus, sounding outraged. "They're going to think we're traitors and ran away or something!"

"Well, to be fair, I think they already do think you're traitors," said Mr. Gormly, stepping over a pile of broken bits of wood.

"I was going to kiss Egeria after the play!" Marcus roared.

"Wasn't going to happen, chappy," said Mr. Gormly. "Look on the bright side. I won't have a bunch of barmy lybrarians chasing around after me as I search for my perfect customer."

"Perfect customer for what?" said Dorrie, already knowing the answer.

Mr. Gormly smiled and held the little star up in the palm of his hand. "It's sure to be horribly tricky to make, full of many difficult-to-find ingredients, and wonderfully powerful. I'm betting someone will give me the prettiest of pennies for it. Maybe that friend of your auntie's. That Mr. Biggs fellow."

"Why would he want it?" cried Dorrie.

Mr. Gormly rolled his eyes disbelievingly. "Why would he—? Put the pieces together, girl. You set it on the ground and, pop, there's a rabbit hole into the heart of Petrarch's Library. That should make someone very giddy with desire, which will make this—" He cuddled the star close. "Nearly priceless!"

"You'd just *give* it to him?" Dorrie sputtered.

"Well, only if he paid a sufficiently exorbitant amount of money for it," said Mr. Gormly.

"After the lybrarians saved you!" Dorrie cried.

"Well, it's not like they *meant* to," said Mr. Gormly indignantly. "I just happened to be in the right place at the right time. Though I admit it was nice to get away from the rats."

"Rats are a thousand percent nicer than you," said Marcus.

"Anyway," said Mr. Gormly. "I'll be off now. Take a little look around, see the sights, taste the vittles, squeeze the wenches. Thank you again for holding open the door."

Marcus blocked the door to the mop closet, outraged, his fists curled. "What if we try to stop you?"

"Well, I wouldn't recommend trying to get in my way by yourselves," said Mr. Gormly in a friendly voice, his hand brushing against the knife in his belt. "You can try telling someone I abducted you at knifepoint from the hidden lair of a tribe of warrior librarians and see what that gets you." Mr. Gormly pushed Marcus to one side and swung the door to the mop closet wide open.

Dorrie felt like weeping. "You can't sell that star! You can't! In the wrong hands it could destroy everything the lybrarians have created. The world could go back to being a place you wouldn't even want to live in!"

Suddenly, they all heard someone unlocking the staff-room door on the other side of the mop closet. Dorrie and Marcus froze.

"Suit yourself," Mr. Gormly said placidly. "Must run." He

patted his breeches. "I feel the need for a new set of clothes coming on."

He stepped through the doorway into the mop closet and collided with Amanda, who was hurrying into the closet from the staff room.

"Oh!" she said, her mouth hanging open in surprise.

"Oh!" Mr. Gormly said in his wolfish way. Without another word, he swung her down into an embrace, kissed her full on the lips, and plucked the key she held out of her hand. "I'm an adaptable sort," he said, setting the speechless Amanda back on her feet and making for the exit.

Dorrie and Marcus crowded into the mop closet as Mr. Gormly disappeared through the staff-room door.

"We've got to stop him!" Dorrie said, stumbling over buckets and cans of paint. "He's going to destroy the Lybrariad!"

"The what?" said Amanda, as Dorrie ran for the door.

"Lybrarians from all over the place, all over time!" said Marcus, grabbing a plunger and leaping after her. "Seriously dangerous, endangered lybrarians."

"But good dangerous," added Dorrie.

"Petrarch's Library!" cried Amanda, clasping her hands together. "Is it real?"

"Yes!" said Dorrie. "And that guy who kissed you has this star thing—it's like a key to the lybrarians' hideout—and he's going to sell it to the lybrarians' enemies!"

Amanda paled, her eyes growing large. "We have to stop him. We have to get that star back."

In that moment, the truth about Great-Aunt Alice came crashing in on Dorrie. "Oh, no!" she cried. "Great-Aunt Alice wasn't working with Mr. Biggs." She tugged on the doorknob furiously. "Mr. Biggs came looking for Great-Aunt Alice because he thought she had the star!" she kicked at the door. "He's locked it!"

As Amanda pulled a ring of keys out of her pocket, Dorrie heard a familiar whispery sound. She looked down at her chiton and then at Marcus's. They were disappearing.

Marcus dived for the coatrack, and tossed Dorrie a trench coat. For a moment he vacillated between an enormous down parka and the eye-popping flowered raincoat. He took the parka.

"You have to warn Great-Aunt Alice!" cried Dorrie, as Amanda unlocked the door. "We'll find the star!"

Marcus yanked the door open, and they burst through it pell-mell.

Dorrie dodged something hairy on the floor. A moment later, Mr. Scuggans burst out from between two bookcases with a great, bald expanse visible on the top of his head and a flapping poster wrapped around his middle. "Where will a book take you today?" it proclaimed in rainbow letters. Dorrie and Marcus skidded to a stop. The parts of Mr. Scuggans that Dorrie could see didn't have a stitch of clothing on them.

"Help! Police!" he shouted, disappearing down another aisle.

"Mr. Gormly," murmured Dorrie fiercely, running for the door. Her mind reeled. Outside, the Pen and Sword Festival was still going strong. She and Marcus ran to the railing of the library's porch and, breathing hard, looked up and down the street.

"There!" Dorrie shouted, pointing into the park. Wearing Mr. Scuggans's khakis and yellow button-down shirt, Mr. Gormly was turning a water fountain off and on, looking delighted. Dorrie and Marcus scrambled down the steps in pursuit. A large herd of people in monk's robe costumes followed and obscured him from view.

Marcus surveyed the crowds in the park. "You will never find a more wretched hive of scum and villainy."

"Stop *Star Wars*-ing!" snapped Dorrie. "This is serious."

"That's how I *do* serious," said Marcus.

The traffic stopped, and Dorrie caught a glimpse of Mr. Kornberger at the wheel of the bookmobile. He waved happily as she and Marcus shot across the street.

Inside the park, Dorrie saw Mr. Gormly sauntering toward a tent. "There he is!"

Dorrie and Marcus plunged into the crowd. Beyond where the blacksmith banged mightily on a piece of armor, Mr. Gormly paused at a tent displaying slingshots, pouches, and leather shoes with upturned toes. Dorrie and Marcus watched him trail his fingers along a table and then disappear down the little alley between two tents.

Putting on a burst of speed, Dorrie found her path blocked by a pudgy man hung with cameras, his hands full of steaming turkey legs. Dodging him, she caught one of the blacksmith's iron racks with her foot. Hoes and shovels and a collection of blades clattered to the ground.

"Sorry," Dorrie called back over her shoulder as she and Marcus reached the tents between which Mr. Gormly had disappeared.

Breathing hard, they squeezed through, and poked their heads around the back of a tent. Mr. Gormly was strolling away along a hedge as though he didn't have a care in the world. He stopped and carefully slipped the star into a pouch, hung it around his neck, and tucked it inside his shirt.

"He just stole that pouch!" whispered Dorrie.

"What can we do besides follow him?" said Marcus. "He's got a knife and a sword!"

"Sacre bleu!" spat Dorrie. She didn't think they were going to be able to *talk* Mr. Gormly into giving up the star.

"Keep an eye on him. I'll be right back!" called Dorrie, sprinting back the way they'd come.

The little crowd around the blacksmith's area had begun to melt away, and the blacksmith had picked up all the things that Dorrie had accidentally knocked over. As Dorrie watched, the blacksmith stepped over to a nearby tent full of looms. Dorrie's fingers twitched. She'd be borrowing, not stealing. A trench coat had its uses.

Two minutes later, Dorrie plunked herself down beside Marcus and pulled something vaguely rapier-like out from inside her trench coat. "Here," she said, holding an orange-sized iron ball out to Marcus.

"What am I supposed to do with that?" complained Marcus, his hair limp with sweat, the voluminous parka half-way unzipped. "I'm an ax-thrower."

"I didn't see any axes!"

"I don't think you even looked," sniffed Marcus, finally taking the iron ball.

"Where is he?"

Marcus pointed to the open part of the park, where crowds had gathered around the enormous circle of straw bales. Mr. Gormly had stopped beneath an immense oak tree that stood between two bales on the far side of the circle. All his attention seemed focused on a plump woman with a garland of flowers in her curly brown hair.

"Oh, isn't he the player," said Marcus. He turned to Dorrie. "So what's the plan?"

"We grab the pouch from him?" said Dorrie uncertainly.

"I like it," said Marcus. "Bold. No irritating details to remember."

"Do you have a better one?" snapped Dorrie.

"We get closer to him, and *then* we grab the pouch."

Dorrie hefted the sword. "We should come at him from different directions."

"Fine," said Marcus, shoving the iron ball experimentally into the rubbery bottom of the plunger. It stuck there.

At that moment a loud cheer went up all around them. From opposite sides of the circle, two groups of fully costumed medieval battle reenactors entered the circle carrying shields, foam-covered swords, and foam-covered battle-axes.

"The Melee!" said Dorrie, remembering how little time had passed in Passaic. "They're just about to start the Melee."

"We've been looking all over for you!" said a voice behind Dorrie, as a man with a horn walked to the center of the field.

Dorrie spun around to see Lavinia and Rosa running toward her.

"Rosa! Lavinia!" Dorrie said, pleased and shocked somehow to see them standing there.

Rosa's face was bunched with worry. "Did you find him?"

"Who?" said Dorrie, craning her neck to keep Mr. Gormly in sight.

"Moe!" said Rosa.

Dorrie's brain creaked backward through all the days spent in the Library, their fall through the hole, and all the way back to the moment when Moe had gotten loose in the park. Of course. Moe. To Rosa, Dorrie and Marcus and Moe had only been gone a few minutes. "Uh, he's…he's in the library," said Dorrie, catching Marcus's eye. "It's a long story, but he's… safe." She stood on tiptoe, looking over their heads.

"Tiffany said if you don't come back in two minutes, then you've forfeited, and she's still coming after you for her points," panted Lavinia.

"Uh-huh…" said Dorrie absently, creeping to the right to get a better view of Mr. Gormly. Marcus, Lavinia, and Rosa trailed after her.

"Don't you care?" Lavinia's puzzlement seemed to give way to irritation. "And why are you wearing those coats? And why is Marcus carrying a plunger?" she asked as Dorrie peered between a man and a woman bouncing fussy babies in their arms. "And uh, Dorrie? Tiffany is heading this way!"

Lavinia's speech, which Dorrie until this point had heard as simple noise, suddenly became words with meaning. Dorrie's head snapped around. She sucked in her breath. Swords at the ready, Tiffany and her two friends were standing on a straw bale, examining the crowd, midway along the circle between where Dorrie stood and Mr. Gormly lounged against the tree.

Dorrie swallowed hard.

"Hey!" said Justin, jogging into their midst, panting. "Any sign of Moe?" He caught sight of Marcus's parka. "Dude. It's seventy-five degrees out."

"I uh, chill easily," said Marcus. He elbowed Dorrie in the ribs. Mr. Gormly looked as though he was saying good-bye to the woman with the flowers in her hair.

Dorrie spun to face the Academy students. "Look, forget Tiffany."

Justin's mouth fell open. "But what about the T-shirt?"

"Forget the T-shirt," cried Dorrie. "We've got bigger problems." She pointed out Mr. Gormly. "See that man? He stole something. Something really important. And a whole lot of people might get really hurt if we don't get it back."

Justin, Lavinia, and Rosa stared at her bug-eyed.

Dorrie licked her lips. "Mr. Kornberger would want us to go after him!"

"But he does have a real knife and a real sword," said Marcus. "So don't get too close to him."

"Um, I think he's getting closer to us," said Justin.

Dorrie spun to see Mr. Gormly sauntering across the circle.

"And I think Tiffany just noticed you," said Lavinia.

Dorrie shifted her gaze to find Tiffany glowering at her in a purely predatory fashion. Dorrie's attention snapped back to Mr. Gormly as the man with the horn sounded a short blast. Mr. Gormly jerked his sword upwards as the two costumed teams of reenactors surged toward him, swords aloft. He disappeared in their colorful cloud.

"C'mon!" said Dorrie. "Before he hurts someone!" She

lifted her borrowed blade, jumped the nearest straw bale, and ran forward with the rest of Mr. Kornberger's students into the swirling mob of foam-wielding warriors. "Try to keep people away from him!" She pushed and shoved her way through the crowd, desperate to glimpse Mr. Gormly again.

Finally getting through to clear ground, she saw him put a great gouge in a foam-covered shield and was about to sprint toward him when Tiffany Tolliver jumped in front of her. "I want my points, geek girl," snarled Tiffany. "So I can see you wear that T-shirt fair and square."

"I don't have time for this," said Dorrie, craning her neck to keep Mr. Gormly in sight.

Tiffany lunged at Dorrie, sword extended. Without stopping to think, Dorrie parried it to one side. For a split second, Tiffany looked shocked before going on the attack again. Once more, Dorrie parried and then tried to sprint past Tiffany, but Tiffany, with a roar of rage, blocked her path, crossing swords with Dorrie so that their hilts clattered together. "You're not going anywhere."

Dorrie tried to dodge around Tiffany in the other direction, but the bigger girl gave her a mighty push backward and lunged again. Furiously they lunged and blocked, thrust and parried. Dorrie deflected Tiffany's attacks one after another, her blade dancing, and her feet alive and shifting the way Savi had taught her. Salty sweat trickled onto her lips, as she glanced desperately in Mr. Gormly's direction. He seemed to have figured out that the "warriors" around him were anything but and had cleared a wide circle around himself, laughing.

Frustration set Dorrie's blood on fire. Desperate to be done with Tiffany, Dorrie went on the attack, touching Tiffany twice on the shoulder, and then on her arm, and then "There! Now can we be done?"

Tiffany's face reddened, her eyes narrowing with fury. She sliced at Dorrie's arm, narrowly missing it. Dorrie sifted through the strategies Savi had taught her. When Tiffany lunged at her again, Dorrie let her sword blade slide against Tiffany's until their hilts banged together again, the blades trembling against one another, their faces inches apart.

"I said I don't have time for this," Dorrie panted.

Savi had made Dorrie practice her exit strategy from a moment like this over and over. She hoped it worked now. She hooked her foot around Tiffany's ankle and, with all her might, pushed against Tiffany's sword while pulling her leg out from under her. Tiffany fell to the ground, bellowing. A sprinkling of applause came from the spectators. Shocked that the move had worked, Dorrie remembered her promise to Savi. "And you can do whatever you want with that T-shirt," wheezed Dorrie. In another instant, she was running as hard as she could toward Mr. Gormly. She planted herself in front of him in a fighting stance.

"Don't be an idiot," he said, grinning.

Dorrie took a step toward him. In a flash, he'd kicked her blade to one side. She only barely held on to the hilt as the tip hit the ground, twisting her wrist painfully.

"I'm warning you. I have no scruples." With practiced fluidity, he pulled his short sword from his belt.

"Yes," said Dorrie, as she stepped warily around him, "but you don't want to make yourself obvious by killing anyone, either."

On other side of the circle, the Melee's raging combatants swirled, hacking at one another with loud shouts. Dorrie caught a glimpse of Marcus running along the edge of the mob.

Dorrie engaged Mr. Gormly in earnest, hoping for a chance to pull the pouch from his neck. He swung hard at her legs with his sword. Dorrie only just had time to leap out of the way. The crowd cheered. She thrust forward as she landed off balance, meeting his blade with hers, as he swung again for her legs. The force of the blow sent tremors down her arm.

Dorrie's confidence fled. Mr. Gormly knew far more about sword-fighting than Tiffany. All Dorrie could do was to try to stay just out of his reach and hope for an opportunity to grab the pouch. The tip of Mr. Gormly's blade caught her in the shoulder and scratched deeply into her skin through the trench coat. She cried out in shocked pain.

"Had enough, little madcap?" said Mr. Gormly.

Anger flooded Dorrie. She had trusted Mr. Gormly. She

had defended him against other people's insults. "No," she said, her lungs heaving.

"Your choice."

Dorrie raised her sword again and then went slack-jawed. Out of sight of Mr. Gormly and led by Marcus brandishing his plunger, the shouting, seething scrum of red-faced, foam-wielding warriors was heading straight for them.

Dorrie took three giant steps backward, and just as Mr. Gormly began to look vaguely inquisitive as to why, the mob simply ran over him. As the scrum stampeded on, leaving Mr. Gormly facedown and dazed in the dust, the crowd roared its approval. In a flash, Dorrie was at Mr. Gormly's side, pulling the pouch string over his head, terrified at every second that he'd grab her. It finally came loose and she bolted after Marcus and his legion of Kornbergers.

"Home, Marcus!" she shouted when she caught up with him. "Home to Great-Aunt Alice!"

Chapter 21

Lybrarians at Work

THE POUCH SEEMED TO burn in Dorrie's hand as she and Marcus dashed toward Great-Aunt Alice's house. They sprinted through the driveway gates that led into the yard and together hammered on the locked back door. It opened and Dorrie screamed as Mr. Biggs emerged, carrying the enormous, drooling lizard that Dorrie had seen him with in Athens.

"Good of you to return. I had just asked my assistant to go look for you."

"Where's Great-Aunt Alice?" whispered Dorrie, backing away with Marcus and raising her sword.

"Aw, isn't that cute, Mr. Biggs," said a voice behind her. "She has a 'weapon.'"

Dorrie and Marcus whirled. A man with long, stringy hair and one ear was leaning on the driveway gate. Even with the bowler hat crammed down on his head, Dorrie recognized him from Athens as well. He held a stout-looking stick in his hand. A chain hung from one end. From the bottom of the chain hung a second black stick. He made the bottom stick swing ever so gently.

"Adorable, Mr. Lamb," said Mr. Biggs mirthlessly.

Dorrie's heart began to thunder. The air felt dangerous, as Mr. Lamb draped his chained sticks over one shoulder.

Mr. Biggs trailed his gloved hand along the lizard's great jaws. "Now. I'd like my book back."

"What book?" challenged Marcus.

The pouch in Dorrie's hand seemed to grow heavy as lead.

"What book?" Mr. Lamb repeated. He began to laugh in an ugly sort of way, showing all his teeth until he abruptly stopped. With blinding speed, he grabbed hold of Marcus and bent his arm behind his back.

"Let him go!" said Dorrie, crouching with her sword pointed in Mr. Lamb's direction.

Grinning, Mr. Lamb bent Marcus's arm so that he gave a shriek of pain.

Dorrie froze.

"I'm not fond of games," said Mr. Biggs, putting the lizard gently down on the ground.

In an instant, he had wrenched Dorrie's sword from her hand and sent her sprawling in the grass.

The pouch bounced away from her. As she lunged for it,

Mr. Biggs kicked a cloud of dirt into her face and scooped it up himself.

"*No*," Dorrie howled, as Mr. Biggs kicked her sword to one side.

He stepped hard on her arm, sending an excruciating pain shooting up it, and hefted the pouch in his hand. After a moment of startled disbelief, his lips shifted into a terrifying arrangement that Dorrie guessed was supposed to be a smile. "Even better."

In the next instant, the broad snout of the library bookmobile exploded through Great-Aunt Alice's driveway gates with a monstrous splintering crash, Mr. Kornberger at the wheel.

Mr. Biggs bobbled the pouch, dropping it, as the vehicle screeched toward them on two wheels. With a low growl, he leaped out of the vehicle's way, and Dorrie, freed from the crushing weight of his foot, lunged for the pouch and rolled out of the way.

When she could look up again, she couldn't see Mr. Biggs, but Mr. Lamb had let go of Marcus and was bearing quickly down on her. Trying to scramble away, Dorrie watched in amazement as, for no apparent reason, Mr. Lamb came to a sudden jerking stop, Looking utterly blank, he toppled to the ground. Dorrie looked back at the bookmobile. Ebba, her face still screwed up in concentration, was leaning from one of its windows, her slingshot in her hands.

"Ebba!" cried Dorrie.

"To me," shouted a familiar voice.

Dorrie scrambled to her feet to see Savi, wearing the eye-popping flowered raincoat, leap out of the bookmobile. She and Marcus streaked to his side. In the driver's seat, Mr. Kornberger was working hard to untangle himself from his seat belt.

Dorrie stared up into Savi's grim, relieved face. "How did you—"

"Two keyhands. One key-mongoose," he answered, drawing his sword. He jerked his head toward Mr. Lamb as he cut down a length of the Barnes clothesline. "Who's that? "Where's Gormly?"

"We left Mr. Gormly in the park. This one works for Mr. Biggs!" Dorrie felt a stab of panic as Savi bound Mr. Lamb's hands behind his back. She looked wildly around the yard, filled with a terrible dread. *Where had he gone?* She ran for the back door. "We've got to find Aunt Alice!"

"She's right here," said Mr. Biggs in his velvety voice as he stepped into the yard through the back door.

Dorrie skidded to a stop. Mr. Biggs had his arm around Great-Aunt Alice as though escorting her into a fancy dinner party, except that her hands were trussed behind her back, and he held a gun near her pale, drawn face.

"Great-Aunt Alice!" Dorrie called, both relieved and horrified.

Marcus looked to Savi, whose eyes narrowed. In the sudden silence, a horrible, wet sort of growling arose from the lizard.

"Almost dinnertime, Darling," said Mr. Biggs. He nodded in Savi's direction. "You put that sword down, and the girl will hand me over that pretty little star she's holding."

Dorrie glanced at Savi. He stood stock still, his eyes flickering, as if making calculations. Heart bucking, she squeezed the pouch tightly, unsure of what to do.

Mr. Biggs gave a luxurious sigh. "I assure you, I have plenty to bargain with." He spun Great-Aunt Alice around. Dorrie gasped. Elder, his wrinkled face a cut and swollen mess, was tied back-to-back with Great-Aunt Alice.

"Elder!" Dorrie cried out, aghast. "Savi, he's a friend!"

"Now," said Mr. Biggs, his voice everyday and conciliatory. "I'm going to guess that you'd prefer that they not die. So for the last time, hand me over that pretty little star." On the grass, the lizard opened her mouth wide and took a few steps toward Savi, tail swishing back and forth like a great, meaty windshield wiper. Strings of yellowish goo stretched between her jaws.

Mr. Biggs moved the gun closer to Great-Aunt Alice. "You have three seconds to hand it over. One, two…" Dorrie's head filled with desperate fear-choked whispers. She looked pleadingly at Savi.

"Give it to him," barked Savi.

Dorrie threw the pouch at Mr. Biggs feet.

"You see, Darling," said Mr. Biggs, picking up the pouch and slipping it into the pocket of his suit jacket, "a friendly request does it every time." He surveyed the bookmobile thoughtfully. "Alas, I need to get away, and my trussed friends will have to come with me. I'm afraid I won't be able to return them." As betrayed rage screamed through Dorrie, Elder suddenly bent forward, lifting Great-Aunt Alice off the ground. She kicked mightily at Mr. Biggs's arm with her good leg. The gun sailed out of his hands and disappeared in the thick ivy that grew along the edge of the yard.

Savi dived at Mr. Biggs, who, shielding himself with Alice and Elder, snatched Dorrie's sword off the ground. Savi leaped around to Mr. Biggs's other side before he could drag Elder and Alice around. Furious, Mr. Biggs shoved them hard so they fell onto the stones of the patio. Savi and Mr. Biggs's blades crossed and clanged as Marcus searched frantically for the pistol in the ivy. Amanda and Ebba—her long, yellow poncho flying—burst from the bookmobile and ran with Dorrie to Elder and Alice. They clawed at the ropes.

"Aunt Alice, you were amazing!" shrieked Dorrie.

"It was Elder's idea," Aunt Alice panted. "He's hurt." A chill tumbled through Dorrie. She crawled around to Elder's side. He looked terrible. For a horrible moment, she thought he was dead.

"Elder!" Dorrie cried, touching the red smear near his shoulder. "Oh no."

A grunt from Mr. Biggs made Dorrie glance up. He thrust viciously at Savi, trying for a killing stroke, which Savi dodged in a blur maneuvering Mr. Biggs across the yard and away from Elder and Alice.

"What should I do, friend?" cried Mr. Kornberger to Savi. He was finally free of his seat belt and holding aloft his stage-combat sword.

"Absolutely nothing," ordered Savi, as he met another of Mr. Biggs's blows.

A slash of Savi's blade opened up Mr. Biggs's suit jacket pocket. As walnuts, broken and whole, tumbled to the ground, a glint of fear mixed with the cold business in his eyes. He managed to grab hold of the pouch before it fell, but Savi flicked his weapon upward and sent Mr. Biggs's blade flying. With a sweep of a leg and a shove, Savi forced Mr. Biggs to the ground, a foot away from where "Darling" snapped and slobbered, filling the air with a putrid cloud of foul breath. Savi pressed the point of his sword against the skin of Mr. Biggs's throat. "*We* need to get away. Throw the pouch to Dorrie."

Mr. Biggs slowly unbent his elbow. Dorrie trembled with relief and held out her hands, but instead of throwing the star, Mr. Biggs grabbed Darling's tail. In a flash, he'd swung the lizard at Savi's face. Savi leaped backward. With the lizard under one arm, Mr. Biggs scrabbled to his feet and ran toward the narrow gap between the bookmobile and the garage, scooping Dorrie's sword up once more.

With a bellow, Savi pursued Mr. Biggs. Unable to squeeze through the gap, Mr. Biggs slid with his back along the garage wall, thrusting first the sword and then the lizard forward to snap and slobber in Savi's direction. Dorrie danced along helplessly behind Savi.

"I'll give you three seconds to hand that pouch over," Savi said, his face furious, "or I'm going to run you and that dragon through, defensive policies be damned. One, two…"

At that moment, Darling decided she'd had enough and clamped his her jaws down hard on Mr. Biggs's arm. With an enraged roar, Mr. Biggs dropped the pouch and staggered backward, frantically trying to wrest his hand from between the lizard's jaws.

Darling, for reasons of her own, suddenly let go, and Mr. Biggs fell through the open door that led into Dorrie's father's workshop. Savi leaped over the lizard and dived in after him. Dorrie heard glass shatter and then the sound of heavy things crashing to the ground. She ran for the pouch but hesitated a few feet away. The lizard stood over it, gnashing its teeth. Dorrie's head snapped toward the garage door as another crash and an eardrum-bursting hissing sound erupted from inside.

Mr. Kornberger shot past her and into the workshop, his blade held high. "You are not alone, Cyrano de Bergerac!"

"No!" shouted Dorrie.

"Dorrie, look out!" yelled Ebba. Dorrie turned back to see the lizard launch itself at her leg. Time seemed to slow as Darling's jaws yawned toward her. It sped up again as the beast jerked in midair and flew off to one side.

Her heart pounding, Dorrie lunged for the pouch and scrambled up to see Amanda hauling on what was left of the Barnes' clothesline. The lizard bucked and jumped, its jaws held fast by a noose. "I've been practicing for a moment like this since I was five years old!" cried Amanda.

A yelp and a streak of French swearing came from the garage, and then silence, except for the hissing. *Mr. Kornberger!* Dorrie charged through the garage door.

Mr. Biggs, breathing hard, had something cold and smile-like on his face, and Mr. Kornberger in a shielding headlock, Dorrie's sword to his throat. Dorrie's father's workshop was in shambles.

"God's fillings," croaked Mr. Kornberger, his face utterly drained of color.

"You idiot!" shouted Savi.

Marcus appeared in the garage door. "I couldn't—" He stared from Mr. Kornberger to Mr. Biggs to Savi, and to the wreckage of the workshop, where one of Mr. Barnes' helium-suit prototypes lay in an explosion of torn pieces. "Uh-oh."

"I'll take my little trinket back, thank you," said Mr. Biggs, "and be off with my new friend here."

Dorrie clutched at the pouch in her hand.

"Give it to me," Savi said to her tightly.

Dorrie stumbled over and put it in Savi's free hand.

"You let him go, and I'll give you your trinket," said Savi.

"I don't think so," said Mr. Biggs. "You give me my trinket, and I'll let go of this cunning warrior."

"It's a stalemate then," shouted Savi over the hissing, which was growing steadily louder. "For if you even begin to harm him, I will be upon you."

Dorrie saw Marcus's eyes catch on the overturned helium tank, from which, she now realized, the hissing sound issued. Dorrie and Marcus locked eyes.

"Savi," Dorrie said slowly. "We should just go."

"Your friend is a bootless, clay-brained muttonhead," spat Savi, "but I don't intend to abandon him!"

"Just outside for a minute," begged Dorrie. "I have, uh, something private to tell you."

"Private?" barked Savi.

Mr. Biggs looked at her suspiciously.

"Trust me," Dorrie said, grabbing hold of Savi. She hauled him backward through the door. Marcus slammed it shut and threw the bolt.

"Don't worry about me," said Mr. Kornberger faintly from inside.

"What are you doing?" shouted Mr. Biggs through the door.

"The valve's broken off a tank of helium gas in there,"

whispered Marcus. "The gas will knock them right out. We just have to make sure we open the door after they're unconscious but before, you know, they die."

"I'll kill him if you don't open that door immediately!" shouted Mr. Biggs, his voice sounding more high-pitched with every word.

"Will he?" whispered Dorrie, alarmed.

"No," scoffed Savi, sounding regretful. "It's his only bargaining chip. Why ever is he talking like that?"

"Helium changes your voice," said Marcus.

"You don't know who you're dealing with!" shouted Mr. Biggs, now sounding like Miranda.

"Help!" squeaked Mr. Kornberger. After a moment of silence, Dorrie heard two thuds.

Chapter 22
Hello, Good-Bye

G REAT-AUNT ALICE, EBBA, AND Amanda had done their best to make Elder comfortable, making a pillow out of an old Windbreaker they found in the bookmobile.

He was beginning to stir when Savi and Marcus returned from dragging Mr. Lamb into the garage and retrieving Mr. Kornberger from inside it. They lowered Mr. Kornberger to the grass, where he flopped backward.

Great-Aunt Alice looked at Savi, from where she knelt beside Elder, her face pink. "You serve Petrarch's Library, I take it."

Savi gave her an appraising look. "I do. And you?"

"It's been my hope," said Great-Aunt Alice.

Dorrie stared disbelieving at her great-aunt's lined face, around which locks of white hair swung, loosened from their customary bun. As Savi knelt beside Elder, Dorrie sought out

Great-Aunt Alice's eyes. They looked at each other for a long moment. For the first time since she'd come to live with her great-aunt, Dorrie felt invited all the way in. Savi picked up Elder's hand to feel for a pulse and then went completely still. Staring at Elder's fingertips, Savi brushed them with his own and looked carefully into Elder's face.

"What is it?" Dorrie demanded, certain he was going to pronounce Elder dead.

Savi cleared his throat, his face pale. "It's Kash," he said, a terrible wonder in his voice. "But old. So old."

Dorrie and Marcus traded amazed glances. Ebba gave a little cry, her hand to her mouth.

"Elder's the missing keyhand?" Marcus said, staring at the face he and Dorrie knew so well.

Savi leaned down closer to Elder's ear. "Kash?" he murmured. "It's Cyrano. It's Savi. Can you hear me?" Savi brushed Kash's cheek tenderly.

"How do you know it's him?" Dorrie asked, taking Elder's other hand protectively.

"I'd know him anywhere," answered Savi, a catch in his throat.

At that moment, Elder's eyes fluttered open. He looked vaguely around, and then his eyes caught on Savi. "I had an apprentice once with a nose even bigger than yours."

"Is that right?" Savi said, a helpless grin breaking out all over his face.

"Elder!" Dorrie cried.

He turned his head to her. "Dorrie B. How did—"

Dorrie felt tears pricking at her eyes. "We found Petrarch's Library. Accidentally."

Elder winced. "We've been checking for weeks. Hoping." He closed his eyes again. Dorrie longed to ask him more questions, but he seemed so tired.

Savi's face darkened. "Kash, the Lybrariad's been looking everywhere for you. Why didn't you get to Thebes? Where are you in Egypt?"

Elder swallowed with what seemed like great effort. "Egypt?" he said, licking his swollen and cracked lips. "That was so long ago. Such a lifetime ago." He seemed to be thinking very hard. "A boy came to me there. He wanted to tell me about a threat to the past from the future that could unravel all the Lybrariad's efforts. He wanted to give me something he called Petrarch's Star. For safekeeping. We made plans to meet again. When I went to the appointed place, others were waiting."

His eyes bored into Savi's. "They kept me in a temple at Kom Ombu for a while. Tried to make me tell them who had come to me. Then they took me into their headquarters." Elder struggled to take a breath. "I thought the boy must be dead or imprisoned himself, but he soon came to my cell, the thing he called Petrarch's Star hidden in a book."

Dorrie glanced meaningfully at Savi, who tore off the pouch

that he'd slung over his neck and threw it to her. He leaned forward and used a small dagger to tear away the bloody cloth around Elder's wound.

Dorrie fumbled with the pouch's knots as Elder rubbed his lips together. "The boy had a key to my cell."

Pain came into Elder's face and he gripped Savi's arm hard. "The people who took me call their headquarters the Stronghold. It's like Petrarch's Library in that it opens into other times, but wholly different. I don't know what holds it together but I saw prisons and barracks. Opulent offices and throne rooms. The people operating it have dreams of controlling the world that rival the Foundation's." Elder clawed harder at Savi's arm. "The Stronghold connects to a hundred wherens in the future, and now they're fighting to move into the past."

Dorrie felt her heart slow and heard Great-Aunt Alice inhale sharply. Dorrie looked to Savi. His dark eyes held Elder's eyes steady in a terrible, bright gaze.

"What happened after the boy freed you?"

Elder's hand slipped from Savi's arm. "He had me drink something he said would allow me to escape the Stronghold. Before we could pass back into Egypt, Stronghold guards came after us. In the fighting, the boy and I were separated. He with the book, and I with the star. I escaped into one wheren—the United States, 1956—and the boy into another. I had no idea what Petrarch's Star actually did until I met Alice."

Dorrie's trembling fingers worked at the pouch string's last tangle.

"My father served as an ambulance driver during World War I," said Alice hurriedly. "He met an injured boy in a field hospital in Germany. At first he thought the boy was delirious, talking about magical libraries and passages to times and great danger for the world. The boy made my father take a book. Its pages had been hollowed out in the shape of a star."

Dorrie upended the pouch and shook it violently. A round, gray stone landed on the grass. Dorrie stared at it in horror.

"That's not the star," said Marcus.

"But we saw Mr. Gormly put it in here," cried Dorrie. She looked at Marcus desperately, as a horrible vision of Mr. Gormly handing the star to an operative from the Stronghold flashed in her mind.

"We saw Mr. Gormly put *something* in the pouch," said Marcus.

Dorrie couldn't bear to look at Savi or Elder. "Mr. Gormly must still have it! He made us think—Oh, Elder, I'm so sorry!"

Elder's eyes closed, and Dorrie's heart went into her mouth.

"He needs a hospital," said Great-Aunt Alice.

Elder pulled at the front of Savi's shirt. He licked his cracked lips. "No hospital."

"But you're very hurt," said Great-Aunt Alice. "You could die."

Elder shook his head weakly. "Too many questions. Get me back to Petrarch's Library. Get me to…Ursula." His head lolled.

"But we can't," whispered Dorrie turning desperate eyes on Savi. "Mr. Gormly said we've locked ourselves out."

Savi paled, as if when he'd chased after them into Passaic, he hadn't given the problem of their return a second thought. He glanced at the bookmobile where Moe sat chittering angrily at them through the windshield. "Unless, of course, that hole happened to finish its cool-down before Moe took Ebba and me through."

They all stared at the mongoose as the sound of sirens reached their ears.

"Bound to be the police," said Great-Aunt Alice. "After a crash like that."

Marcus swallowed hard. "Help us, Obi Won Ke-Moe-bi. You're our only hope."

✳ ✳ ✳

At the Passaic Public Library, Amanda backed the bookmobile up against the rear door of the library. She hurried off to find Mr. Scuggans and keep him out of the way, while Mr. Kornberger took care of Elder, and Savi stood guard over the tightly bound Mr. Biggs and Mr. Lamb. They'd left Great-Aunt Alice behind to make up a story for the police.

Dorrie, Marcus, and Ebba scrambled down out of the bookmobile, Ebba holding tightly to Moe, and ran for the staff room, where they let themselves in with Amanda's key. Locking it behind them, they tore through the mop closet and threw themselves down onto the floor at the edge of the hole. The Roman bath lay far beneath them, glinting and winking. With trembling fingers, Ebba held Moe out over the hole and brought him down slowly toward the hard, invisible barrier.

Dorrie's breath came in hard little pants as Moe wiggled and twisted. Ebba spoke to him softly, and he relaxed, one forefoot scrabbling in midair just at the floor's level, and then as Dorrie stopped breathing altogether, his foot seemed to dig below the level of the invisible barrier. Ebba gave a cry of delight as his head sank out of sight below the jagged edge of the visible floor. She hauled him back up and held him tight against her chest.

"I'll get the others," shouted Marcus, jumping to his feet and disappearing through the mop closet.

Dorrie wanted to sing and shout and leap into the air, but as she stared with joyful relief down into Petrarch's Library, a thoroughly overwhelming thought suddenly took her in its teeth and shook her to the bone.

She startled when Marcus and Savi staggered back through the door carrying the unconscious Elder. They laid him down gently on the floor and ran back to the door to fetch the others.

"Wait!" cried Dorrie, speaking all in a rush. "Now that we know where the Stronghold people were keeping young Kash out in Egypt, the Lybrariad could find that place, couldn't it?" Dorrie's felt like her heart was tearing and swelling all at once. "The Lybrariad could still go to that time and that Kom Ombu place and free him, right?"

Savi looked at her steadily, his eyebrows drawn together. "Yes," he finally agreed, his voice brusque.

"Then Elder, I mean Kash, would have a chance to live his real life," said Dorrie breathlessly. "Not the one the Stronghold people made him live."

Savi breathed deeply, his face a mix of hunger and uneasiness. "There would be consequences."

"Elder won't ever get to Passaic in the twenty-first century," whispered Ebba.

"So we'd never meet him," said Dorrie, trying to sound more brave than miserable.

"And we'd never get to Petrarch's Library," said Marcus.

Dorrie's voice cracked. "You have to get him back."

As soon as they returned to Petrarch's Library, Savi turned Mr. Biggs and Mr. Lamb over to the Lybrariad and disappeared to pull a team together to rescue young Kash from Egypt. Ursula took over care of old Kash, making him as comfortable as she could in the repair and preservation department, while Dorrie, Marcus, and Ebba waited anxiously in the corridor, peeling and feeding Moe the dozen hard-boiled eggs that Sven had read out for the mongoose when he'd heard what Moe had done.

Dorrie and Marcus had ditched the trench coat and parka and pulled on their old Passaic clothes.

Dorrie reached into the pocket of her pirate coat for the caramels that Sven had also given them. She handed one to Ebba. "That was brilliant thinking about Moe being a keyhand."

Ebba smiled faintly. "Lucky that Savi needed to cut through the baths to ring the emergency bell."

Dorrie fussed with one of the buttons on her coat. "Mom's probably wondering what happened to the driveway gates, about now," she said glumly.

Marcus leaned his head back against the wall. "And Dad is definitely going to be curious about his wrecked workshop."

"Well, you won't get in any trouble at least," said Ebba, scratching Moe between the ears. "That whole time stream's about to be obliterated."

Dorrie felt a wave of misery. "Do you think we'll feel it when our history goes different?"

"I don't know," Ebba answered, burying her face in Moe's fur.

They stopped talking and scrambled to their feet as three figures turned into the corridor.

"Savi?" said Dorrie, staring at the one with the biggest nose.

He bowed deeply to her. He and the other man wore pleated white skirts, and the woman a long straight white dress. They all wore sandals, wigs, and heavy eyeliner.

"You sure about the eyeliner?" asked Marcus.

"Great for sun glare," said the other man, whom Dorrie had never met. He bowed to them as well. "Kemnebi. Second keyhand of Middle Kingdom Egypt."

"Excuse us for a moment," said Savi to the others, steering Dorrie a short way down the corridor. "I want to thank you for all your assistance to the Lybrariad and to me, personally. I'm very happy to be getting one friend back but—"

Dorrie felt the tears that had been threatening ever since Elder's rescue finally spill from her eyes. She threw her arms around Savi's waist and hugged him fiercely.

He held his arms out to either side as if unsure what to do with them. "But I'm truly sad to be losing another," he finally said in a hoarse voice, patting her head gently.

"Were you able to speak to Madeleine?" murmured Dorrie.

"Oh that. I made a horrible hash of it," said Savi. "I'll do better next time." He tilted Dorrie's face back away from his middle. "You'll make a fine swords-woman some day."

"For all the good it'll do me in the twenty-first century," sobbed Dorrie, imagining herself in Passaic setting the table, and taking books out of the library, and acting in one of the Academy's staged sword fights and knowing nothing about Petrarch's Library. Reluctantly, she finally released Savi.

After Savi and the others disappeared, Dorrie felt a sick wildness inside. "I wonder if we'll remember anything about any of this."

"How could we?" Marcus said. "We won't have had the experience to remember."

Dorrie's head throbbed at the thought of such things.

"Maybe somewhere deep in your cells you'll know," said Ebba.

"Great," said Marcus dully. "I'm not exactly on regular speaking terms with my mitochondria."

"We'll remember you," Ebba said, her voice soft. "At least you'll be in the *History of Histories* book." She pulled a watch on a chain up out of her blouse, glanced at it quickly, and then began to rummage in her satchel.

"I don't want to be part of the Lybrariad's history!" exploded Marcus, "I want to figure out a way to bust Timotheus out of prison! I showed him those rhythms he got in trouble for."

Dorrie looked hard at her brother. For the first time in weeks, she really noticed the words on Marcus's T-shirt. "Apathy Is Hard Work." The shirt looked too small for him.

Marcus picked up one of Moe's eggs and hurled it down

the corridor. "I want to take a whole year of Casanova's stealth and deception practicum!" He sank into a dejected heap. "So should we just sit here until history changes?"

Ebba pulled a folded bit of paper out of her satchel. "I forgot. This is for you. It's from Master Casanova."

Dorrie unfolded it. "I don't believe him!" She looked up. "He's still going to stage *The War of the Stars* tonight for the conference guests, and he's expecting us 'barring a time-stream disappearance' to still play our parts."

"I think he's big into 'the show must go on,'" said Marcus.

Dorrie read more. "All cast members are expected to meet in the Mission Room at four o'clock to run lines."

"It's four o'clock now," said Ebba. They found bicycles and creaked through the hallways, Dorrie taking in every familiar corridor and room, feasting on them with her eyes, and taking great whiffs of the leathery, papery smells until at last they reached the Mission Room.

Dorrie pushed open the door. A cheery fire still crackled below the fireplace's marble mantelpiece, but now the room was utterly filled with people.

Ebba hugged Dorrie. "Everyone wanted to say good-bye," she said in a choked voice. Dorrie hugged her back tightly. Marcus was pulled into the room by Saul and Mathilde, and propelled through the crowd.

When Ebba finally let go of her, Dorrie turned around

and found herself face-to-face with Millie, who had her hands jammed in her pants pockets.

"I'm sorry things didn't work out," she said. Dorrie thought she looked horribly pleased. Millie hesitated. "And I'm sorry if I was hard on you." She paused and attempted an expression of deep maturity. "I just had to look out for the Lybrariad. Nothing personal."

"…You morons," whispered Marcus in Dorrie's ear as he passed by.

Dorrie faked her own smile at Millie and moved on to say good-bye to Egeria and Phillip, Sven and Kenzo, Callamachus, Izel, Mistress Wu, and Casanova. Even Mistress Lovelace had come to see them before they disappeared, and she didn't say a word about the disintegrated chitons. Apprentices and lybrarians, some whom they'd never met, shook Dorrie and Marcus's hands, and thanked them for their efforts to get back Petrarch's Star.

Efforts, thought Dorrie bitterly.

At last they came to Hypatia. She stood in front of the fire in her rustling, blue silk tunic. Dorrie looked fearfully into her face, unsure of what Hypatia thought of her now.

To Dorrie's relief, Hypatia smiled at her. "I want to thank you for reuniting us with Kash."

Dorrie cleared her throat. "Elder, um, Kash, told us that the boy who helped him escape from the Stronghold gave him something to drink. Something that would let Elder navigate the Stronghold's slips. Elder told us it turned his fingernails black for years." For some reason, it felt unpleasant to Dorrie to have to say the next part, but Hypatia was listening carefully. Dorrie held out her hand so that her thumbnail showed.

"Same as this. I think Miranda, my sister, took a bottle from Mr. Biggs and poured something out of it into my orange juice the day we came here. I was thinking it could have been the same stuff." Dorrie took a deep breath. "Maybe that's why I could…"—she forced herself not to look away from Hypatia— "go back and forth into Athens."

Hypatia looked intently at Dorrie and Marcus. "There is much the Lybrariad does not yet understand about your arrival here, and of course, who is operating within the Stronghold and what their intentions are. It's possible that the star or the substance from Mr. Biggs's bottle forced a way into Petrarch's Library for you. It's also possible that Petrarch's Library opened for you of its own accord."

Please let the Library have opened for me, Dorrie found herself wishing furiously. "What about the star book?" she thought to ask. "Won't it disappear when we do?"

"I have our Irish monk friends copying it at a furious speed right now," said Hypatia. "What's made in the Library stays in the Library, no matter what happens outside of it." She looked around the room at the other lybrarians and apprentices. "We only wish that we could copy you as well."

"Even Francesco?" Marcus said dubiously.

"Even Francesco," repeated Hypatia firmly, "once he hears what's happened." She reached into a soft cotton bag she carried and pulled out two silver circlets, each set with a black stone alive with pricks of light and cloudy white swirls.

"Apprentice armbands," Dorrie murmured.

"If it was in our power," said Hypatia, "we would have offered to take you on as full apprentices, hoping that perhaps one day you would fully embrace our calling and work toward the possibility of becoming keyhands, or at very least"—she glanced at Marcus—"true ninja lybrarians of Passaic."

"Even after losing the *History of Histories* page?" quavered Dorrie, "and not telling you about going to Athens?"

"Sooner would have been better, but you did the right thing eventually," said Phillip, his nose looking oddly red and swollen.

"They're yours," said Hypatia, holding them out. "You've earned them."

Dorrie and Marcus took them carefully from her.

"We won't even remember getting them," said Marcus, his face slack.

"Well, at least in this moment, you know that we value you."

Dorrie thought she knew what Hypatia meant. "I'm sorry we couldn't get the star back."

"We get Kash back," said Hypatia, "and now we know about the star's existence. For that we are deeply grateful to you."

Ursula stuck her head into the room. "Kash is awake. He'd like to see his rescuers."

"Good-bye," sobbed Dorrie, hugging Phillip fiercely again. "Good-bye to all of you." After another round of desperate hugs and handshakes, the room emptied. Hypatia, Callamachus, and Phillip followed Ursula down the hall. Dorrie and Ebba were about to follow them when they heard Marcus call out down the corridor. "Egeria, wait!"

Turning back, Dorrie saw Egeria pause and look at Marcus expectantly, her head cocked to one side. Marcus ran to her and bit his lip nervously. "I just wanted to...once...since we're never going to meet again..."

Dorrie's eyes and mouth flew open as Marcus leaned forward and quickly kissed Egeria full on the lips. Egeria took a step back, looking at Marcus the way Dorrie had seen her mother look at Miranda when her little sister had tried to clamber up on a too-big bicycle.

"I'm definitely going to remember that," Marcus said faintly. He fled past Dorrie and Ebba.

In the repair and preservation department, they clustered around Elder's bed. He stirred. "Ursula," he said slowly, the love of a dear friend in his voice.

"Hello, Kash," Ursula said, her voice shaky.

"It's been a while," Elder said. He looked from Callamachus to Hypatia to Phillip, and touched his gray hair. "For me, at least." Elder squeezed Ursula's hand. "I'm terribly glad to see you all again." He turned his head to the side and caught sight of Dorrie, Marcus, and Ebba. "Well, well," he said, holding out his other arm to them. They approached him shyly. He took Ebba's hand. "I see you're all right with leaving the Library these days." With his other hand he patted Dorrie's arm. "That was some Sword and Pen Festival, wasn't it?" He turned his head so he could see the other side of the room. "Where's Savi?"

Ursula took his hand. "He went to Kom Ombu with a team. To get younger you out."

Elder struggled to sit up, his face deeply troubled. "To get me out? You have to stop him!" he croaked. "Right away." He fell back exhausted, as the keyhands looked at one another in consternation. A wild bumping began in Dorrie's chest, as Elder went on speaking. "I don't want anything about the way I've lived my life to change. It's been a good one. An unexpected one, but a good one. I missed you all so much, and I know I'm not all I was—I forget things, I'm slow and weak—but I saw and did important things. There's so much to tell you."

He looked around the room. "I don't want that life to disappear. And at least now we know wheren to look for the star. If you succeed in getting the younger me back, there's no guarantee that we'll ever come this close to it again. Anything can happen."

There was a stunned moment of silence, and then Hypatia swept to the foot of Elder's bed. "You're certain?"

"Dead certain," Elder said.

"Is there any chance of catching Savi?" Marcus asked, touching his lips as if to make sure they were still there.

Nobody answered.

Chapter 23

Passaic

S TRONG MID-MORNING SUN WOKE Dorrie from the exhausted slumber she had finally succumbed to. She stretched her legs and winced. All yesterday's fighting had made her sore. It had been some Pen and Sword Festival. Dorrie pushed her covers back and scooped up some random clothes from the floor. She wiggled into them.

In the hallway, she nearly collided with her father, who was carrying a toolbox. Miranda held his other hand.

"Dad!" cried Dorrie. "You're back!"

She thought he looked very handsome, even with the scruff on his chin and his faded work clothes. She hugged him tightly and enjoyed feeling small for a moment. Miranda wrapped her own small arms around them both.

"Well, that's a nice good morning—though not very

piratical," said her father. He held her at arm's length. "How was the Pen and Sword Festival?"

Tiffany's jeering face flashed before her. "I survived."

"You must have exhausted yourself. Mom said you and Marcus were asleep before she and Miranda even got home."

Dorrie hesitated, not sure how much to tell him. "We did a lot. Our regular performance and the Melee."

Her father raised his face to the heavens dramatically. "Do you realize that because of your selfish need for sleep, I had to eat a half-gallon of ice cream all by myself?"

Dorrie raked her fingers through her tangled hair. "Is Marcus up yet?"

"Oh, I do love a good joke in the morning. Wake him up, will you, and tell him to come help me out in the workshop. Some days this place seems to fall apart faster than other days."

"Okay," she said, starting for Marcus's room.

Her father headed down the staircase. "And keep an eye on Miranda, would you?"

Dorrie ran back, grabbed Miranda by one plump hand, and hauled her to Marcus's door. She was about to open it when she glanced down at Miranda's ever-present necklace of random objects. Today, her ribbon held three CDs, a hole punch, and a squat, silver bottle. Now that Dorrie looked at it closely, she saw that it was the shape and likeness of a walnut. Dorrie slowly knelt beside Miranda.

"Where'd you get that?" asked Dorrie, pointing to the silver bottle. It had a little screw-on top, with the letter B engraved upon it.

Miranda shrugged. "From that big man's pocket." She shook the bottle. "And you can't have any more medicine 'cause I already gave it all to you."

"You gave it to me?"

Miranda stomped her foot. "I already told you that. I put it all in your juice so you'd get strong for sword-fighting." Miranda began to pick her nose.

Dorrie stared at the little walnut-shaped bottle. "Well, I like it anyway. I'll trade you something for it. Anything in my room you want!"

"It's got to be something *big*," said Miranda.

"Sure, big," said Dorrie. "Let's wake up Marcus first."

Inside Marcus's room, Dorrie let go of Miranda's hand and picked her way across the patches of floor that could be seen beneath the piles of half-dissected appliances, books, and glasses full of molding liquid. Miranda squatted happily in front of a keyboard. Marcus was sprawled diagonally across his bare mattress, the sheets balled up underneath him.

"Marcus," Dorrie hissed. "Marcus!"

She rolled him back and forth. He turned over, smacked his lips a few times, and began to snore. Dorrie ran to the window and released the drawbridge so that it crashed loudly onto the roof of the chicken shed. Marcus rolled over again and slid off the bed entirely.

Dorrie climbed over the bed and peered down at Marcus, who had gone on snoring despite his slide to the floor. "Unbelievable."

Beneath Miranda's fingers, the keyboard suddenly produced a crashing cornucopia of notes. Dorrie covered her ears.

"I'm up, I'm up," Marcus said, getting to his feet with his eyes still closed. He swayed and then collapsed on the bed, nearly crushing Dorrie.

Outside Marcus's window, Dorrie heard her father opening his workshop door, and then a sort of strangled choking sound. "Good grieving gargoyles!" he finally shouted.

"Wait a minute," said Marcus, sitting bolt upright, his eyes wide open.

"Yeah, about time!" cried Dorrie. Together, she and Marcus pushed up their sleeves, grinning. Just below their left shoulders, bands of silver, set with white-flecked black stones, encircled their arms.

MASTER PHILLIPUS AUREOLUS THEOPHRASTUS BOMBASTUS VON HOHENHEIM'S GUIDE TO PETRARCH'S LIBRARY

PEOPLE

Aspasia: Friend to Socrates and partner to Pericles (an Athenian statesman), Aspasia enjoys all the intellectual freedom she wants within Petrarch's Library of course, but she's also found a way to enjoy it out in Ancient Athens. This is no small achievement. In fourth-century BCE Athens, women are not generally educated or given an opportunity to discuss art, theater, writings, or political ideas. Only a class of women known as the "hetairai" are invited to develop their intellectual powers, and then only to better entertain the men who hire them for stimulating companionship.

Basho: A revered Japanese poet who's living out in the seventeenth century. He hates cities and writes a lot of haiku, a kind of poem that can only ever have three lines. The first must have five syllables, the second seven, and the third, five. Here's one about breaking wind by one Barry Beans from out in your time:

> *"When underwater*

JEN SWANN DOWNEY

*It is difficult to hide
Bubbling evidence"*
Try writing one yourself!

Callamachus: When not running Petrarch Library's Reference Services, Callamachus writes rather ground-breaking poetry and brings order to the Alexandria Library's chaos out in the third century BCE. He's very devoted to his pet project: Cataloging the entire contents of the Alexandria Library. Though he's already filled 112 scrolls, the job is nothing compared to what Callamachus has had to catalog in Petrarch's Library!

Casmir Liszinski: A Polish nobleman, currently on the Lybrariad's Mission List. He studied philosophy with the Jesuits, a religious order of the Catholic Church, for eight years and it got him thinking. Out in 1687, he's working on a treatise (a paper that goes into mind-boggling amounts of systematic detail on a subject) titled "The Non-Existence of God." The Catholic Church is powerful in that wheren. History books in later wherens say that a man who owed money to Mr. Liszinski stole the treatise and showed it to Church leaders, who then accused, tried, and executed Mr. Liszinski for not believing in God. Let's hope the Lybrarians can get to him before that happens!

Catherine the Great, Empress and Autocrat of All the Russias: A champion of free expression? Maybe. We'll see. She's out in the Russian Empire in the late 1700s, ruling away. Alexander Radischev, one of her subjects, just wrote a book called *Journey from St. Petersburg to Moscow*, which is quite critical of Russia's rulers. It's going to irritate her and test the strength of her free expression principles. For certain? She has great taste in hats.

Cornelius Loos: As you know, Cornelius Loos, a Catholic priest, spoke and wrote against the witch trials he witnessed out in 1580s Trier. Out in the 1590s in Brussels, Church officials forced him to publicly recant his "errors." On his knees. One official, Martin Del Rios, kept close watch on him after this, having Loos imprisoned several times for "lapsing" into the "wrong" kind of thinking. When Loos died of the plague, Mr. Del Rios apparently felt cheated of the chance to execute him.

Cyrano de Bergerac: I'm positive that Savi would be highly relieved that you now know he is a real person and not just a figment of Mr. Rostand's dramatic imagination. If you want to read more about him, look up a biography by a woman living out in your time named Ishbel Addyman. (No relation to Barry Beans.) She did the best she could (quite well!) making sense out of his life, but since she doesn't know Cyrano serves as a keyhand of the Lybrariad, do take her conclusions with a pinch or two of salt.

Egeria: Besides conducting her work as a Lybrarian, it appears from current history books that Egeria will find it necessary to do quite a bit of traveling out in the fourth century, mostly in the Middle East. She'll visit Mount Sinai, Mesopotamia, Jericho, Jerusalem, and other places. Apparently someone finds some of her field notes in the late 1800s, takes them to be an interesting extended sort of postcard to her sisters and publishes them. They've been read in all kinds of wherens under the title *Itinerarium Egeriae*, or the Travels of Egeria.

Gabriel Naude: Monsieur Naude works, of course, as a keyhand in seventeenth-century Paris but he also works as a librarian for Cardinal Mazarin, who is unaware of Monsieur Naude's other job.

Giacomo Casanova: When not teaching his Stealth and Deception Practicum or torturing the world with his dramatic creations, Casanova is employed by Count Joseph Karl von Waldstein in the Castle of Dux in Bohemia out in the late 1700s. After a lifetime of extreme gambling, business, and romantic exploits across Europe he has his friends and enemies convinced that, flat broke, he has reluctantly settled down to write an autobiography. He describes it to anyone who asks as "the only remedy to keep from going mad or dying of grief." A convincing cover story, don't you agree?

Hypatia: Taught philosophy, mathematics, and astronomy for many years out in ancient Alexandria before deciding to move into Petrarch's Library full-time and take on her current position of Director. I hesitate to say more, or Mr. Martine will surely accuse me, and rightly so, of a lack of polite circumspection.

Katherine Henot: At the moment (spring of 1625), she works as the first Postmaster in Germany, running the post office in the town of Cologne. Count Leonhard II von Taxis is part of the Imperial Court, and he wants a centralized Post Office. Katherine thinks that's a bad idea and has said so. Believe me, there's a very good reason she's on the Lybrariad's Mission List.

N'Sync: According to Marcus, N'Sync qualifies as a "boy band" of the "unlistenable" variety common out in your era. If you simply must have more information about them, he advises something called a "Google search."

Petrarch: Francesco Petrarco to his fellow Italians. Out in his fourteenth century, he was known for his poetry, his discovery of lost manuscripts by ancient writers, his love of travel, and the letters he wrote to centuries-dead "imaginary" friends like the Roman statesman Cicero. (Only, as you've probably guessed, Cicero and Petrarch did speak on more than one occasion at the Library.) Historians out in the later wherens consider Petrarch the father of "Humanism"—a system of values and beliefs that people are basically good and that problems can be solved using reason instead of religion. If they only knew the half of it.

Phillippus Aureolus Theophrastus Bombastus von Hohenheim: Also known as Paracelsus. When I'm not doing my small part for Petrarch's Library or snacking, I do spend some time out in the first half of the sixteenth century making discoveries in medicine, toxicology, and chemistry; also lots of friends, and perhaps an enemy or two.

Sima Quin: Out in second century BCE China, Sima Quin has finished a monumental history of his country, called Record of the Grand Historian. He was born into a family of astrologers, and will eventually hold the title of Court Astrologer. But perhaps he didn't read the stars correctly. As of now the history books say he pays dearly for speaking well of someone that Emperor Wu had blamed for a military defeat. I'm sure the Lybrariad will put him on the Mission List soon.

Simon Morin: Currently on the Lybrariad's Mission List. In his wheren of Paris 1663, poor Mr. Morin suffers from a delusion that he is 1: a good cook and 2: Jesus Christ. This should hardly be a problem for anyone but himself, except that he has a frenemy who just talked a high-ranking priest into taking Mr. Morin prisoner for his "crime."

Strabo: Out in the first century BCE Strabo (philosopher, historian, and geographer) has been exploring Egypt, Ethiopia, Tuscany, and Corinth. Eventually, if history holds, he'll settle in Rome. Sadly, one of his major works (forty-seven volumes!) has gone entirely missing. Out in your time, only a tiny piece of "Historical Sketches," written on a scrap of papyrus can be found. You'd have to go to the University of Milan (Italy) to see it. Marcus advises asking your parents if they have any frequent flyer miles you could use.

Su Shi: I'm glad to report that this late-eleventh-century Chinese poet, painter, and statesman is no longer on the Lybrariad's Mission List. If you look him up, you'll see that his current fate—banishment—while still not just, is far less horrible than his old fate (trust me!). And many of his writings have survived!

Timotheus of Miletus: History books in later wherens don't have anything to say about the musician named Timotheus who Marcus met while visiting Athens 399 BCE, but curiously they do mention a musician named Timotheus of Miletus who lives a couple of generations later. Actually, they mention him in connection with the development of a "new music" based on unusual rhythms, ones that especially irritated the philosopher Aristotle. You don't suppose the latter-day Timotheus could have had a grandfather who met Marcus, do you?

Vitruvius: Another Roman. Loves designing buildings and has definite ideas about how to best do it. Out in the first century BCE, he's busy writing (in Latin and Greek, naturally) "The Ten Books on Architecture." It will soon say that buildings must be solid (*firmitas*), useful (*utilitas*), and beautiful (*venustas*). Oh, and you know that image that Leonardo da Vinci likes to draw out in the fifteenth century—the man standing with his legs and arms outstretched within a circle and a square? It's famous in all the later wherens. Da Vinci called the figure his Vitruvian man because Vitruvius believed that beauty lay in natural proportion, and that the human body, inscribable in both a circle and a square, showed how perfectly elegant its proportions. All that said, I'm afraid I have it on very good authority that Vitruvius didn't have much of a sense of humor and made a dull dining companion.

PLACES

Library of Celsus: If your name is Gaius Julius Aquila, and your father is named Tiberius Julius Celsus Polemaeanus, then you just have to build a library in your dad's honor. Or at least organize other people to build it. I don't think Gaius dragged much stone around himself. The library was finished in 135 CE, and filled with 12,000 scrolls. Tiberius loved to read. He was buried (once suitably dead) in a sarcophagus below the library's floor. Unfortunately, out in the third century, most of the Library of Celsus fell down in an earthquake, but out in the twentieth century, its facade has been rebuilt! They put a few bits in the wrong places but on the whole did a pretty good job.

Passaic Public Library: Out in the twenty-first century, the Passaic Public Library stands on Gregory Avenue in Passaic, New Jersey.

Porte de Nesle: Out in Cyrano's wheren, the Porte de Nesle is a passage through the thick stone wall built to surround Paris during the middle ages. It stands beside the Tour de Nesle on the left bank of the river Seine.

The Serapeum: A library built in Alexandria out in the third century BCE. This very grand temple was dedicated to Serapis, a sort-of patchwork god invented to help Greeks and Egyptians get along when the Greeks took up residence in Egypt. In later times, it houses a library, and then I'm afraid it does eventually come to Petrarch's Library as a ghost library.

Villa de Papyri: Pool, bronze sculptures spitting water, terraces, gardens! The views from this residence built on the side of a volcanic mountain called Vesuvius were *spectacular*! Until the day the lava decided to get out and see a bit of first-century Herculaneum. The mountain is still smoking out in that wheren and the residence has more or less disappeared. However, out in the eighteenth century, one Karl Weber has tunneled into the cooled lava and found the house's library with its 1,785 charred papyrus scrolls. Out in your time, because of the invention of multispectral imaging, people are reading the scrolls! I'd explain the technique to you, because I completely thoroughly perfectly understand it, but I must get on with this list.

Books, Songs, Long Rambling Speeches, and Assorted Other Expressive Works

"Declaration of the Rights of Women and the Female Citizen": Document. You know that French Revolution that happened out in the late 1700s, not long after the American Revolution? When the crowd in charge published their "Declaration of the Rights of Man and of the Citizen" they weren't kidding. Women were not granted equal rights. Playwright and activist Olympe de Gouges tried to point this out in her own Declaration.

A Vindication of the Rights of Women: Book. Meanwhile out in England, Mary Wollstonecraft, hearing about events in

France, is writing A Vindication, laying out the reasons she feels women should have access to education, among other things.

"Areopagitica; A speech of Mr. John Milton for the Liberty of Unlicenc'd Printing, to the Parlament of England": Document. Mr. Milton has yet to give this as a speech, though as you might have figured out, he does love to talk. He just published it out in the wheren of England 1644, after Parliament passed a law requiring writers to have their books and pamphlets approved by the government before they can be published. Did I mention that a civil religious war is raging out there? So far, no one in Milton's wheren seems to be listening to him, but out in other wherens, his arguments are influencing John Stuart Mill, John Locke, and the framers of the United States Constitution.

Cyrano de Bergerac: Dramatic Play. Not Savi's favorite, but the crowds went *wild* for this play when it premiered in France out in 1897. Edmond Rostand wrote the entire play in rhyming couplets. Here's an English translation of one of the fictional Cyrano's lines: "My nose is Gargantuan! You little Pig-snout, you tiny Monkey-Nostrils, you virtually invisible Pekinese-Puss, don't you realize that a nose like mine is both scepter and orb, a monument to my superiority?" A valiant group of actors is probably performing the play right now somewhere out in your time.

Kidnapped: Book. Stolen inheritances! Kidnappings! Desert Islands! Robert Louis Stevenson wrote this adventure tale out in the 1880s, but based it on real events like the "Appin Murder" and the political upheavals going on in Scotland in the mid-1700s. I do love those kinds of books...

Socrates and Athenian Society in His Day: Book. A. D. Godley wrote it and got it published in London out in 1896. But most people out in your time (and by most I mean hardly any) know A. D. Godley for his funny poems. (My favorite is "Megalopsychiad.")

Martine's Handbook of Etiquette and Guide to True Politeness: Book. It seems bad manners drive Mr. Arthur Martine up the proverbial wall and halfway across the ceiling. Out in 1866, he just published this handbook. It's packed with helpful if rather stern commands such as: "You will sip your soup as quietly as possible from the side of the spoon, and you, of course, will not commit the vulgarity of blowing on it, or trying to cool it, after it is in your mouth, by drawing in an unusual quantity of air, for by so doing you would be sure to annoy, if you did not turn the stomach of the lady or gentleman next to you."

"Plaisir d'Amour" or "The Song Sung Terribly in Chapter Four": Please don't tell the Archivist I referred to it in that way. Written out in 1784 France by Jean-Paul-Egide Martini, the song takes as its subject the pleasure and stabbing pains of love. Though Martini wrote the music for the song, the words came from a poem written by another French guy named Jean-Pierre Claris de Florian. Chew up a cracker and then try to pronounce that. I dare you.

***The Princess Bride: S. Morgenstern's Classic Tale of True Love and High Adventure*:** Book. Abridged by William Goldman into the "good parts version." Dorrie pressed the tale into my hands, saying "it's the best book ever." I suspect hyperbole, but it's now on my nightstand.

Sears and Roebuck & Company catalog: Sent out in mass mailings in 1895 United States, these catalogs are big—532 pages big! People living far away from stores can flip through its pages and order wood-burning stoves, coffee grinders, and teapots. A family eking out a living on an Appalachian mountain probably doesn't have much cash available to place an order, but when hung on a nail in the outhouse, the catalog makes a terrific toilet-paper supply.

***Star Wars*:** A motion picture. I understand that in your wheren you can "download" them to a device that you can fit in your pocket.

***The Three Musketeers*:** Book. By Alexandre Dumas. "All for one, and one for all." Dumas lives out in nineteenth-century France. He based his novel on a memoir (a fancy name for an autobiography or biography) that he took out of the Marseille public library and apparently never returned. He spends a lot of his free time fencing for the fun of it.

"True and False Magic": Document. Out in your time, history books say that the manuscript of Cornelius Loos' "True and False Magic" disappeared in 1593 and wasn't seen again for three hundred years until discovered out in 1886 by one George Lincoln Burr in the Jesuit Library of Trier. This is troubling to the Lybrariad. After all, Udo succeeded in getting the manuscript to Savi, didn't he?

Expletives, Inventions, and Other Uncategorized Marvels

Gayetty's Medicated Papers: Just recently put on the market in the U.S. in 1857 by one Joseph C. "enough with the corn-cobs" Gayetty, these flat aloe-saturated squares make wiping a revolutionary breeze for Americans. Toilet paper. It's what the Chinese Emperors have been using since the 1300s (only available to them in two-by-three-foot rectangles).

"God's Dentures": Well, this is a real swear phrase for Mr. Kornberger. In his own special way, he is trying to swear like a person living out in sixteenth-century England with Queen Elizabeth and Shakespeare. But out there you'd be more likely to hear a woman yell "God's Teeth!" after doing something like accidentally slamming her hand in a door.

Method Acting: Out in the 1930, in NYC, actors working with the Group Theatre are exploring the ideas of Constantin Stanislavsky, who himself is out in 1910 Russia pursuing the holy grail of "theatrical truth." Soon actors and teachers will start developing the "Method" techniques for delivering realistic performances on stage and in films. Some Method actors try to think and feel and dress and talk like their characters even when not performing. Out in your time, *Cracked* magazine has called method acting: "The art of torturing yourself to prove you're an artist."

Mongolian Gerbils: Animals. Recently, Ebba informed me that out in 1954 Mongolia, Dr. Victor Schwentker is busy capturing forty-four pairs of the creatures. Apparently, in another fifteen years, great hordes of American children are going to be begging for them as pets, and building tubal paradises for them to dwell within out of a newly invented material called "plastic." Too fetchingly cute for even me to eat.

Punch and Judy: Particularly disturbing puppet characters. Versions of them haunt many wherens.

Ragtime: Ragtime is the name of a style of music being played out in the late 1800s and early 1900s, especially in the U.S. The "ragged time" of the music makes it very bouncy and dance-able. It may surprise you to know that Mistress Lovelace is a serious fan. It is rumored she has a photograph of Scott Joplin, a huge writer and performer of ragtime music, hung on her bedchamber wall.

Rollerskates with five-inch-high bicycle-style wheels: Out in early 1900s England, businessmen like to skate between their homes and offices on them. They have no braking mechanism. There have been accidents.

Spotted Deadnettle: As Egeria would be the first to emphasize, this plant, unlike many other nettle family plants, does not sting. The plant is hardy and edible, and rampant in many wherens. No wonder Egeria spends so much time on it in her Foraging class.

Water Clocks: At least as old as writing itself, water clocks are used out in many of the early centuries connected to Petrarch's Library. People in China, India, Babylon, Egypt, Greece, southern Europe, Byzantium, and Syria are all making use of various types of water clocks. No electricity or complicated gearworks needed!

Acknowledgments

Y OU DON'T UNDERSTAND WHY acknowledgment pages run so long until you write a book and quickly realize that the single name on the book's cover is a version of Mother Ginger's skirt, voluminous and hiding the talents and generosity of a legion of friends, family, and other collaborators, plus a set of stilts.

The first reason I got to begin writing this book at all is because I have a gallant and courageous adventurer for a life partner. His name is Matt Rohdie, and he regularly says things like, "Sure I'll quit my full-time job and invent and run an organic donut-making company that will keep us in toilet paper and bread and electricity, but also give me the flexibility I'll need in order to take care of the kids twenty hours a week, so you can have time to write because I know you can do this."

The reason I got to finish this book is because of the largesse and beautifully critical eyes of old and new friends who each in his or her own particular way, at different stages, patiently taught me how to write this book. They made it better than I could ever have possibly done on my own. Thank you Heather Warren, Jim Naurekas, Johanna Lindholm, Matt Rohdie, Stephen M. Downey, Rebecca Downey, Christina Downey, Anna Ford, Bethany Myers, Rebecca Barnhouse, Mary Esselman, Erika Raskin, John Gibson, Jenny and Audrey Ragsdale, my editor, Aubrey Poole, who offered me a place at the Sourcebooks Jabberwocky table with gracious enthusiasm, and my agent Susan Hawk, who took a flyer on me and my fixer-upper of a manuscript, and has been a source of support, knowledge, good humor and professional vim and vigor ever since. True creative friends!

The reason this book looks as lovely as it does is entirely due to the patient and painstaking work of Jillian Bergsma, Susan Barnett, Diane Dannenfeldt, and the hardworking Sourcebooks design and production team.

The reason I didn't lose my mind while finishing the book is because of the loving cheerleading and often gut-splitting diversion provided by my friends and writing cottage–mates Kate Bennis, Denise Stewart, Patty Culbertson, Lisa Wood, and Whitney Morrill, and my virtual partner in snack-shacking and writing crime—Bethany Myers.

The reason my beloved children Finn, Lil, and Georgia

survived the endeavor (wait—let me count them. Okay, all there) is because they are 1. Very patient and resourceful; 2. Good at dressing their own wounds; 3. Lucky nieces and nephew of John Potter, Brynne Potter, Nell Downey, Christina Downey, and Jim Downey, who all stepped in and offered entertainment and food when writing deadlines loomed.

The reason I wanted to write this book in the first place is because there are heroes in the world. People like Oscar Romero, Giordano Bruno, Sophie Scholl, and Bayard Rustin. Thanks to all those who gather their courage and speak. And thanks to all the librarians of the world who help us hear their voices.

ABOUT THE AUTHOR

J EN SWANN DOWNEY LIVES (with her family) in a clut-
tered house in Charlottesville, Virginia. This is her first
work of fiction since age nine when she penned a play about a
nearsighted St. Nick who kept leaving very strange but interesting presents for children, including a live alligator and a set
of false teeth.

Her professional aspirations and adventures have included
circus dog trainer, lawyer, actor, electrician, populist econo-
mist, investigative journalist, midwife, lampshade maker, and
donut mogul, but believes she has finally figured out what
she wants to do with the rest of her grownup life. Write more
books for children! Over the last five years, she has achieved a
state of near-fantastic nearsightedness.